THE BROWN FAMILY

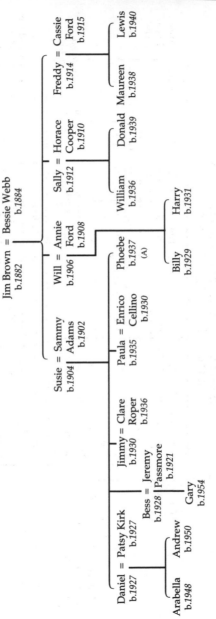

2

UPS AND DOWNS

UPS AND DOWNS

Mary Jane Staples

BANTAM PRESS

LONDON · TORONTO · SYDNEY · AUCKLAND · JOHANNESBURG

TRANSWORLD PUBLISHERS
61–63 Uxbridge Road, London W5 5SA
a division of The Random House Group Ltd

RANDOM HOUSE AUSTRALIA (PTY) LTD
20 Alfred Street, Milsons Point, Sydney,
New South Wales 2061, Australia

RANDOM HOUSE NEW ZEALAND LTD
18 Poland Road, Glenfield, Auckland 10, New Zealand

RANDOM HOUSE SOUTH AFRICA (PTY) LTD
Endulini, 5a Jubilee Road, Parktown 2193, South Africa

Published 2005 by Bantam Press
a division of Transworld Publishers

A catalogue record for this book is available from the British Library.
ISBN 0593 053974

Typeset in New Baskerville by
Kestrel Data, Exeter, Devon.

Printed and bound in Great Britain by
Clays Ltd, St Ives plc.

1 3 5 7 9 10 8 6 4 2

Papers used by Transworld Publishers are natural, recyclable
products made from wood grown in sustainable forests.
The manufacturing processes conform to the environmental
regulations of the country of origin.

UPS AND DOWNS

THE ADAMS FAMILY

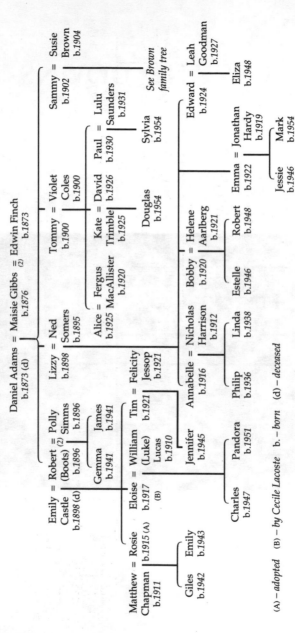

Daniel Adams = Maisie Gibbs = Edwin Finch
b.1873 (d)   (2) b.1876   b.1873

(A) – adopted   (B) – by Cecile Lacoste   b. – born   (d) – deceased

Chapter One

December, 1956.

Mrs Patsy Adams, American wife of Daniel, elder son of Sammy and Susie Adams, was upset, and to such an extent that she was storming around her house in Kestrel Avenue, close by Denmark Hill in south-east London.

She and Daniel had had their first real quarrel, all over their son, six-year-old Andrew. The boy hadn't wanted to go to school that morning, saying he didn't feel well. Daniel said he'd tried that before. Patsy said no, if he didn't feel well he should stay home. Daniel said there was nothing wrong with the lad except liking his own way, and he packed him off to school with his sister, eight-year-old Arabella. Then he told Patsy she was spoiling the boy. That did it. They quarrelled, and were still throwing wounding words at each other when Daniel left for his work at the Adams offices in Camberwell Green.

Patsy fumed. High-spirited and as mettle-some as any modern American woman of twenty-nine, she threw things about. Cushions from the lounge furniture went sailing through the air to pummel the walls. She couldn't believe that Daniel, her fun guy, could have been ratty enough to accuse her of spoiling their son. Her temper wasn't improved by knowing she did give in to the boy sometimes, but after all, he was only six.

The advance of the morning didn't cure her of her upset and resentment. At eleven o'clock she came down from tidying up the bedrooms. Reaching the open door of the kitchen, she stiffened. There was a face at the window, a grubby bearded face under an old floppy hat. The face of a tramp. He didn't see her, his eyes were travelling around the kitchen. He moved, he disappeared, and she heard the slight sound of the back door handle being turned.

Patsy was in too much of a temper to be frightened, and when she heard the sound of the back door opening, she rushed, picked up a saucepan, rushed again and came face to face with the intruder. He was clad in a tatty old overcoat, and she caught the smell of unwashed clothes and body. He stared at the sudden apparition of a flushed, seething housewife with a saucepan in her hand.

Patsy struck, and the saucepan bounced on his floppy hat. His head rang muffledly from the metallic blow. Patsy struck again. The tramp staggered, flung up his mittened hands to ward off another hurtful whack, turned and ran out through the open back door. Patsy chased after him in the cold of the damp morning. Around the side of the house he went, down the drive and out through the gate, Patsy on his heels and close enough to hit him again. He gasped and pelted down the avenue as fast as his legs could carry him, his head suffering. Patsy, breathing hard, pulled up and waited until he disappeared, along with his bruised and aching head. She felt a bit better then.

At which moment a small white van appeared, bearing the sign BEADLES THE FLORISTS. It pulled up outside the house, and the driver, a woman in white overalls, stepped down. She was carrying a wrapped bouquet of huge bronze chrysanthemums. She met Patsy at the gate.

'Mrs Adams?'

'Yes?'

'Our pleasure, Mrs Adams.' Smiling, the woman handed the bouquet to Patsy, who gathered it to her, along with the saucepan.

'You're sure these are for me?' she asked, flush receding.

'Quite sure, Mrs Adams,' said the woman,

checking the house number. 'Good morning.' She returned to her van, while Patsy carried the bouquet and the saucepan into the house by way of the still-open back door. She dropped the saucepan into the sink, where it rang with the satisfaction of a job well done. Then she looked for a card. She found one. It bore just a few words.

'I still love you. Daniel.'

At which Patsy, of course, sat down and cried.

Five minutes later, Daniel took a private phone call in his office.

'Daniel?'

'Patsy?'

'Don't ever make me so miserable again.'

'Hearing you, Patsy, but haven't you received my gesture of apology, some flowers?'

'Yes, and they made me cry. Daniel, I'm so sorry we quarrelled like that. Don't let it happen again.'

'You held your own, you know.'

'It was awful. Let's be forgiving. The flowers are lovely.'

'So are you, Patsy.'

'We'll talk to Andrew this evening.'

'Good idea.'

'Daniel, thank you.'

'See you, Patsy.'

'See you, Daniel.'

They talked to Andrew that evening and discovered what the real trouble was. He didn't get on with one of the teachers.

So the following morning, Patsy went to the school herself, spoke to the teacher in question, pointed out that Andrew was only six and persuaded her to be more tolerant of his little bouts of childish obstinacy. He did have such moments. Patsy had her own way of getting on the right side of people, including harassed teachers, and as a result Andrew received kinder words in class, and made no more fuss about going to school.

Patsy's arrangement of the chrysanthemums glowed in its vase.

The year had seen more than the occasional tiffs among lovers. It had seen, for instance, the ever-growing popularity of Elvis Presley, a former truck driver from America's deep South. Now undisputed king of rock 'n' roll, he had a voice like melting velvet. It was a voice that sent American teenage girls dotty, stopped the traffic and actually overtook the crooning tones of Frank Sinatra in the charts, and induced rapture in vast numbers of young females in the British Isles. Further, at live American concerts his rhythmic body language brought

13

him extra renown as 'Elvis the Pelvis'. That really got to susceptible girls. Some fainted and keeled over. Others had fits of bliss. In Britain, young girls like Emily Chapman, thirteen-year-old daughter of Rosie and Matthew Chapman, worshipped Elvis from afar, and sent their parents potty by playing his records over and over again.

Generally, however, the United Kingdom's young stars, such as Tommy Steele and Terry Dene, had created their own following of teenagers, leading them into undreamed-of realms of jive and swing. It looked as if young people in the West were beginning to enjoy a world of their own.

It was a pity, accordingly, to note that in Eastern Europe things were uncomfortably different. Indeed, in Hungary an uprising by the people against the oppressive rule of Communism had been crushed by Soviet tanks. But then, the Kremlin discouraged musical self-expression, full stop, and if an Elvis Presley or a Tommy Steele had emerged in Moscow or Budapest, either would have disappeared overnight as a corrupter of Communist culture.

Chapter Two

Two months ago, in October, France, Britain and Israel had all declared war on Egypt. Its President, Colonel Nasser, had taken over the Suez Canal, thus claiming control of this vitally important waterway, which suited France and Britain not at all.

However, the war proved only a half-hearted attempt to seize it back. For a start, President Eisenhower wasn't in favour. He considered his wartime allies well out of order. Further, no great enthusiasm for the conflict was shown by the people of France and Britain.

A few bombs were dropped, a few ground sorties took place, but it was plucky Egypt that grabbed the headlines. And the opposition of America, now the world's supreme power, quickly induced the French and British governments to withdraw their forces. Britain's Prime Minister, Sir Anthony Eden, found himself decidedly unpopular. He was a nice enough bloke, with high principles, and he dressed impeccably. But he was no Churchill, and he resigned without a fight in January 1957, whereupon he was replaced as Prime Minister by Harold Macmillan.

This somewhat upset a certain Lady Maisie Finch of Red Post Hill, south-east London. Born a cockney in Walworth in 1876, she had travelled through life from a hard-up beginning and years of striving widowhood to become the wife of a man of distinction, Edwin Finch. His services to the Crown had earned him a knighthood several years ago, and that made Mrs Maisie Finch no less than Lady Finch, much to her embarrassment at the time. She had learned to live with it, but was always telling someone or other in her family that it wasn't what she was born for. It was different with people like Lady Eden, she said, she was born a lady.

'And why a nice gentleman like her husband had to resign, I'm sure I don't know,' she said, when his name came up over breakfast one morning.

'Unfortunately, Maisie, even the nicest people occasionally make a mistake,' said her husband, Sir Edwin, slim and silver-haired at eighty-three. Actually, he was too slim for her liking. Sometimes alarm bells rang on his account, although their doctor assured her Sir

Edwin was as fit as a man ten years younger. However, Maisie, still known to her sons and daughter as Chinese Lady, a nickname that went back to her days in Walworth, did worry about him. She herself expected to go on for ever, almost, and she wanted Edwin to be with her. She listened as he went on to say that Sir Anthony Eden's mistake in going to war with Egypt had been a rather foolish one.

'Oh, that,' said Chinese Lady, 'I don't call that much of a mistake. We didn't get any air raids or sirens, nor soldiers coming home all bandaged up, like that first war. I can still remember wounded men with crutches and only one leg.'

Sir Edwin smiled. Her memory was taking her back, as it often did, to the Great War of 1914–18, the Kaiser's war, when casualties of a single day's battle ran into many thousands. And one could indeed see crippled soldiers in hospital blues taking the air in the grounds of military convalescent homes.

'Well, Maisie,' he said, 'despite the mistake of trying to win back control of the Suez Canal, our casualties were so light they were hardly noticeable. And the family has the consolation of knowing that Phoebe's fiancé, Philip, will soon be returning home, or so I imagine.'

He was referring to Phoebe, adopted daughter

of Sammy and Susie Adams, and Philip Harrison, one of Chinese Lady's great-grandsons. Philip, a pilot officer in the RAF, had been out in the Middle East with his squadron since the days leading up to the abortive war with Egypt.

'Well,' said Chinese Lady, 'I just don't know that Philip ought to be flying one of those war aeroplanes, especially when he's so young and such a long way from home with no-one to keep an eye on him.'

Sir Edwin coughed, then said, 'Maisie, I must point out he's nearly twenty-one.'

'Yes, didn't I just mention he's too young?' said Chinese Lady, and this time Sir Edwin let it go. One couldn't always find the right answer to some of his wife's inimitable observations.

In their solid old Victorian terraced house in Bow, East London, Jimmy Adams, younger son of Sammy and Susie Adams, was listening to his wife, Clare. They'd been married three years, and were still lovey-dovey. Clare was twenty-one and bubbly, Jimmy twenty-six and elastic. That is, he could give and take, and, like his dad, stretch his principles a bit if obstinacy didn't pay. He worked for his dad as personnel manager at the family firm's factory in the East End, which meant looking after the interests of

18

over two hundred employees for the mutual benefit of both the workers and the firm. Jimmy, along with his elder brother, Daniel, had inherited a fair slice of Sammy's business acumen. All three knew that watching the interests of the workers induced them to accept the fact that bosses liked to make a profit. Such a policy helped to keep yearly balance sheets looking pretty.

'So what do you think?' asked Clare finally.

'Let's see now,' mused Jimmy, 'what was it you were talking about?'

'You can ask that?' said Clare. Her dark hair, touched with auburn, and her dark eyes, framed by thick lashes, were very much in the approved mould of an Adams wife. 'If you can, then you haven't been listening.'

'Was it something about a family?' suggested Jimmy.

'Well, it would be nice to start one of our own,' said Clare. They had spent three years enjoying married life and each other, having agreed in the first place that that was what they'd like to do before becoming parents.

'Now I know what you were talking about,' said Jimmy, 'yes, I get you now.'

'You'll get something else in a minute,' said Clare, 'a poke in the eye.'

'Never mind knocking me about, let's be

serious,' said Jimmy. 'Let's start proceedings now by having an early night.'

'That's not being serious, that's being a comic,' said Clare. 'In any case, it's only eight o'clock and I want to watch Jimmy Edwards in *Whack-O!*'

'Good idea,' said Jimmy, 'let's have a laugh before we do get serious.' The weekly television show in question was a laugh all the way, Jimmy Edwards being a natural comedian capable of sly winks and saucy innuendoes.

So they watched the programme of mirth and jollity, then they had a cup of tea and a ham sandwich each, then they tidied up and went to bed.

There they engaged in the serious matter of procreation, except that seriousness floated away up the bedroom chimney and they had fun together. Well, it wasn't just a one-off event. It repeated itself. Clare had a healthy body, Jimmy a vigorous one, and well did the twain meet. There was an interval, of course, during which Jimmy went downstairs and brought up three bananas, two for himself and one for Clare, which they scoffed happily. They both believed in the efficacy of bananas as an energizing fruit. Even so, not long after, Jimmy quit the field on the grounds that he'd run out of engine power.

'Never mind,' he said, 'let's eat a large break-fast tomorrow and do it again.'

'Crikey, tomorrow after Sunday breakfast?' breathed Clare.

'Tomorrow night,' said Jimmy. 'It's definitely a serious business, starting a family and making sure of it.'

'What a man,' murmured Clare, and sank into sleep.

They had bacon, eggs and tomatoes for breakfast. Oh, and a banana each to start with. Imported fruit had become plentiful after many years of austerity.

Chapter Three

March, 1957.

Phoebe, daughter of Sammy and Susie Adams, received a letter from her fiancé, Philip Harrison.

'Dear Phoebe,

'I'm still missing you. The squadron's still stuck here, and here is somewhere in the Middle East.' His squadron had taken up that station some months ago in the expectation of action in the war against Egypt. Although that had fizzled out, the squadron remained under orders in the event of an emergency, since another conflict, a real one, was violently disturbing the peace. Egypt and Syria were at war with Israel in an attempt to smash that independent young nation. 'Lord knows what we're doing here, not very much, believe me, and I could be doing a lot more if I were home and swinging it with you.'

I know what I mean by swinging it, thought

Phoebe, but what does he mean? They're a wild lot, these fighter pilots. Still, I wouldn't want my one to be a tame wallflower.

'In one of your recent letters, you said you enjoyed a lively Christmas with your family. There are some WAAF personnel here who might have helped to make our Christmas a bit lively too, but they're all very correct and you can't get that type to wear paper hats or step under the mistletoe unless they're a bit tiddly, which our lot weren't.

'Life here in winter sunshine is all right up to a point, but at the moment I'd rather be making snowballs with you back home and chucking them at saucy kids or our dads, seeing yours and mine are both sporty. There's one bloke here, Chippy, whose dad is a university professor and so absent-minded he sometimes forgets he's got a wife and two sons. Last time Chippy saw him he asked if they'd met before. Imagine your dad asking that of you. Anyway, so long for the present, keep looking fabulous and let's hope I'll be home by June. Lots of love and kisses. Long live Elvis and his pelvis. Philip.'

Phoebe wrote back at once, telling him he'd better be home by June or else, because the third Saturday in that month was their appointed wedding day. (Liking 'appointed', she underlined it and used it again.) Appointed wedding days were supposed to be sacred, she said, and not even the RAF should be allowed to mess them about. And as for your trying to get WAAFs tiddly so you can drag them under the mistletoe, you've got a nerve even mentioning it to your forthcoming wife. (She crossed out 'forthcoming' and substituted 'future'.) If I showed your letter to my dad, she went on, he'd think twice about allowing me to marry you, so just watch it, my lad.

'Still,' she wrote, 'I just have to put my trust in you as an officer and gentleman. When I told Mum the other day about me marrying an officer and gentleman, she said I couldn't marry him as well, it would be bigamy. Just make do with Philip, she said, he's quite nice and we all like him. You'd never think my mother only had an elementary education, because she's really smart in lots of ways, especially when putting Dad in his place. Dad's a born loser when it comes to getting the better of Mum but he keeps trying because he doesn't know it, and even if he did he wouldn't believe it.

'Oh, that reminds me,' she continued, 'Dad says to tell you to remember who's supposed to wear the trousers in marriage. What's he mean by that? Do you know? I think I do, ha ha.'

Phoebe ended by asking her officer and

gentleman to come home soon as it was a bit dreary without him, and they were missing all the latest excitements of rock 'n' roll concerts, and new bands that were all inspired by Bill Haley and his Comets.

'With love from your one and only Phoebe.'

When Philip received this epistle, Phoebe's own gem, he laughed over it, read it three times and then put it with other prize billets-doux she'd written.

Mrs Rosie Chapman and her husband Matthew had sold their farm and were now living with their children, Giles and Emily, in a lovely family house on Red Post Hill, close to Grandma and Grandpa Finch. It also put them closer to more of the Adams clan, for most lived in that area of south-east London. Family ties with that part of London went back to the days when Chinese Lady's sons and daughter were successively in their cradles. Matthew soon found that Sunday teas with various of his Adams relatives happened quite frequently. Not that he minded, not a bit, for he was a family man himself, and was all in favour of old-fashioned customs, like Sunday tea in a parlour. Regrettably, young Emily confided to her new schoolfriends that Sunday teas with relatives were boring. Now if Tommy Steele or Terry

Dene were invited, she said, she'd feel she was living. Some hopes, said her new schoolfriends. A girl can always dream, said Emily, already on close terms with precociousness. But then, so were other young girls in an era when teenagers were beginning to instinctively oppose the idea that children should be seen and not heard.

Rosie, on giving up chicken farming, had joined the family firm on a part-time basis, as assistant to her adoptive father, known simply as Boots, and to Mrs Rachel Goodman in the offices at Camberwell Green. They soon found her invaluable. Rosie had graduated with honours from university years ago, and was accordingly no slouch in the matter of intelligence.

Her uncle Sammy, founder of the whole outfit, called her in one day. She entered his office in a smartly styled dress of royal blue, her hairdo a golden crown. Well, thought Sammy, here's a wife who's the mother of teenage kids, and what do I see? Female managerial material, which Chinese Lady might think wasn't what God ordered. Chinese Lady didn't believe in female managers, only female wives and mothers, as per the Lord's wise design.

'You wish to see me, sir?' said Rosie.

Sammy grinned.

'How did I get to be sir?' he asked.

'Well, you're my chief,' said Rosie. 'You're everyone's chief.'

'The first time I get to be your dad's chief,' said Sammy, 'will be the day when the man in the moon takes a donkey ride to Southend. Have you ever been to Southend, Rosie?'

'And had a plate of cockles and mussels?' said Rosie. 'So far, no.'

'Well, if Tim and Daniel, on behalf of our property company, can bring off purchase of a shop there, we'll be opening up a Southend dress emporium,' said Sammy. Tim, Boots's son, and Daniel, his own son, were joint managers of the property company, and running it well.

'A dress shop in Southend, the holiday favourite of London's workers?' said Rosie.

'Where they spend their money like they were rolling in it,' said Sammy.

'But only during the holiday season,' said Rosie.

'Clever girl,' said Sammy.

'So you mean a shop that opens only during the summer months,' said Rosie.

'It's a prospect' said Sammy, 'and you can always get shop assistants just for the holiday season in Southend. So one day later on, I'll take you and Rachel there, and you'll see for yourself the kind of summer wear we'll be stocking. Popular designs at popular prices.'

'I'll enjoy a day trip to Southend,' said Rosie.

'I'll throw in a fish and chips lunch,' said Sammy. 'Now, about our shop down below.' The offices were above his original shop. 'It's all right up to a point, but not a great money-spinner these days on account of the build-up of heavy competition and being on the wrong side of the Green's post-war development. Take a pew, Rosie.'

'Thank you, Uncle Sammy,' said Rosie, seating herself, 'how kind.'

'Don't mention it,' said Sammy, and went on to refer to the fact that the firm had applied more than once for change of usage as far as the shop was concerned. So far, the council's response had been negative. But the office staff had expanded considerably.

'Waistlines are a problem?' said Rosie, tongue in cheek.

'Numbers,' said Sammy, and pointed out that they needed to turn the shop and its storeroom into something that accorded with modern staff requirements. 'There's nearly thirty of us, Rosie, and you might have been told by your dear old dad that we're thinking of a staff canteen.'

'My dear old dad, bless him, has told me that, yes,' said Rosie, 'but what can I do about it?'

'Well, seeing you and Rachel have got what me and your dad haven't, female sex appeal,' said Sammy, 'we thought we'd follow up our last application to the council by getting you and Rachel to corner the planning committee chairman in his office, and pin him to the wall. His name is Cox, he's new to the job and has said he's willing to listen to a detailed outline of the firm's new application.'

'Sammy, how charming of you to mention our sex appeal,' smiled Rosie, 'but pinning a council officer to his wall is out of order.'

'Well, you know what I mean,' said Sammy. 'Arrange an appointment with the bloke, take yourselves along and spin the kind of stuff he won't be able to say no to. No gent could fail to appreciate a heartbreaking fairy story from two female charmers like you and Rachel. Ask after his family and his old mother, something like that.'

'Exactly who suggested this?' asked Rosie.

'Your dear old dad,' said Sammy.

'My dear old dad deserves a poke in the eye,' said Rosie, 'but I'm game, if Rachel is.'

'She is,' said Sammy. 'I'd like to point out, by the way, that the storeroom alone would give us enough space for a canteen.'

'Shall we call it a workers' cafeteria?' suggested Rosie. 'The council might favour that.'

'Good point, Rosie, it's a Labour-controlled outfit,' said Sammy.

Rosie said it might also favour the possibility that change of usage to a canteen and extra office space might mean an increase in the rates. Could the firm cope with that? Sammy said Rosie's mental equipment was working right under his nose. The firm could cope easily enough with a rates increase, and selfsame increase might make Mr Cox lick his lips.

'I'm tickled, Rosie, to know you've got your full share of mental facilities.'

'Faculties?' said Rosie.

'Same thing,' said Sammy.

'Your compliments, Sammy, are welcome,' said Rosie, and looked at her watch. The time was coming up to three, her leaving moment. She was always home before Giles and Emily came in from school. 'I must go now.'

'Regards to Matt,' said Sammy. Her husband, Matthew, was busy developing a site in Peckham for the repair of cars and vans, as well as for the sale of petrol. He had bought the site from the firm's property company at a very reasonable price. Well, he was one of the family, and Sammy was against excess profit at the expense of any member of the clan. In fact, when Matt was open for business, Sammy fondly expected the family as a whole to give him their custom in respect of any car repairs.

Charity, in Sammy's opinion, began at home.

Sometime later, Rosie had cause to fall out with daughter Emily. Like Giles, her brother, the girl usually arrived home from school by not later than four thirty. Today it was nearly five fifteen before she turned up. Rosie, fretting and worrying, had phoned the school to find out if Emily had been kept behind for some reason or another. She was assured this was not the case, that Emily left when classes ended. So when the girl belatedly appeared, Rosie wanted to know why she was so late. Emily said she'd been at the house of a schoolfriend, Marion Mortimer. Marion, she said, had invited her in to listen to some new records. There was nothing wrong with that, was there?

'Why didn't you phone me to let me know where you were?' Rosie was cross.

'I couldn't,' said Emily, 'their phone wasn't working. I had a laugh about it, I said to Marion it was because her dad hadn't paid the bill. Anyway, it wasn't as if—'

'I wasn't laughing here,' said Rosie, 'I was worryng about where you were, and what might have happened to you. Didn't you think about that?'

'Mum, of course I thought about it,' said Emily, 'I would have rung you if the phone hadn't been out of order, wouldn't I? Anyway,

31

Marion's home is only in the next street, so I was as good as only next door. You didn't need to worry.'

'Don't be so silly,' said Rosie. 'I'm not telepathic, I had no way of knowing where you were. You're not under any circumstances to do this kind of thing again – Emily, are you listening?'

'Yes, Mum,' said Emily. 'Is Giles having tea and cake? I'd like some too, I wasn't offered anything at Marion's.'

'How would you like bread and water?' asked Rosie.

'Oh, all right, I'm sorry about not letting you know,' said Emily, 'so is there some tea in the pot?'

Rosie shook her head, not to indicate the teapot was empty, but to suggest talking seriously to her daughter was like pouring water on a duck's back.

It didn't affect the inevitable outcome. The duck sat down to a cup of tea and a slice of cake a minute later.

Chapter Four

It was a week later when Mr Gerald Cox, chairman of the council's planning committee, received two representatives from Adams Enterprises Ltd in his office. A man of pleasing looks and amiable disposition, he was also highly principled and unlikely to crumple under any two-pronged attack, except by elephants. Nevertheless, he blinked a little when the representatives turned out to be two ladies, one a handsome, full-bodied woman of lush brunette looks, the other an entirely lovely blonde. It has to be said, however, that neither looked expensively attired, for although the day was wintry, both had chosen not to wear furs, just plain and simple coats. Boots had suggested that a Labour council official would hardly look kindly on two ladies whose apparel implied they were rolling in lolly, and might accordingly be part and parcel of a business profiteering at the expense of downtrodden workers.

The time was nine fifteen, and Rachel and Rosie had come directly from their respective homes.

'Hello, am I expecting ladies?' Mr Cox, recovering from his initial shock, asked the question of the elderly clerk who had shown them in.

'Yes, Mr Cox. From Adams Enterprises. And by appointment.'

'I didn't know I was going to mee—' Too late. The clerk was already gone. 'Well, good morning, ladies. Might I have the pleasure of knowing exactly why you're here?'

'It's to do with our application for a change of usage for the shop,' said Rachel. 'You've been kind enough to let us know you'd be willing to listen to a detailed outline of exactly what we have in mind.'

'Is that so?' Mr Cox looked amiable but doubtful. 'I think there's some mistake. I don't discuss planning committee matters on a personal level. However, do sit down while I call my clerk.' He raised his voice. 'Mr Grimling?'

The door, ajar, opened up and the elderly clerk reappeared.

'Mr Cox?' he said.

'Mr Grimling, who arranged this appointment?'

'There was a phone enquiry, which I took,

and which, on reference to you, resulted in an arrangement to see two representatives from Adams Enterprises.'

'Ah, yes, now I remember.' Mr Cox smiled at the ladies. 'But was it necessary?'

'At the time, it was a matter of courtesy,' said the efficient Mr Grimling. The dialogue was taking place over the heads of Rachel and Rosie.

'Oh, yes, Adams Enterprises, of course,' said Mr Cox. 'So sorry to be vague, ladies, but the pressure of work, with a continuing stream of applications arriving every week – well, yes, I'm sure you understand you should be dealing with Mr Grimling.'

'Do we assume that no decision has yet been made in respect of our long-standing application?' said Rachel.

Mr Cox fingered an eyebrow.

'I recall something relevant,' he said. 'Isn't there a letter somewhere, Mr Grimling?'

'There will be when it's been typed,' said Mr Grimling.

'Good, perhaps you'll get it typed now and then hand it to these ladies,' said Mr Cox. 'Good morning, Miss Um – good morning, Miss Er – thank you for calling. Do excuse me now.' He ushered them out into the care of Mr Grimling.

Neither Rachel nor Rosie knew quite what to

say, not when the moment was almost comical. However, Rachel, coming to, addressed the clerk.

'What's in this letter, Mr Grimling?'

'Oh, merely the committee's decision on your application,' said Mr Grimling, thereby implying the decision was all one to him, whatever it was. 'Of course, I'm not allowed to divulge the contents here and now, it's against the rules. As to your appointment with Mr Cox, I think he forgot to cancel it once the decision had been made. So sorry, but he's such a busy man. Perhaps you'd like to wait in reception while I get the letter typed? I shan't be long.'

When Rachel and Rosie left twenty minutes later, Rachel was carrying the letter, but had no idea what was in it. Nor had Rosie. Mr Grimling had emphasized the rules wouldn't allow him to speak on a personal level, any more than Mr Cox could. Which Rosie thought a lot of well-cooked rhubarb.

'Curiosity is killing me,' she said, 'so if it's all right with you, Rachel, I suggest we have morning coffee now, and over it we'll unseal the envelope and see for ourselves what dark secrets lie within.'

'My life, what an excellent idea,' said Rachel, 'and after all, we don't have to go along with council rules. Also, we're on closer terms with

Mr S. Adams, Managing Director, than anyone on the planning committee.'

Rosie said it was against her better judgement to carry the letter back to Sammy without knowing what was in it. To do so would reduce her and Rachel to the status of mere messenger boys.

'No go,' she said.

'No go,' agreed Rachel, and they took themselves off to a Lyons teashop. There, while they waited for their coffee, Rachel was able to carefully lift the flap of the envelope by rolling a silver pencil under it. Newly sealed, it came free without spoliation. Rosie said if Rachel ever resigned from Adams Enterprises, she could get a job with MI5. Rachel said she wasn't cut out to be a Mata Hari, especially if it meant the risk of being shot at dawn by a KGB firing squad.

The coffee arrived just as she drew the letter from the envelope. She devoured its contents, then passed it to Rosie. Rosie read it, looked up, returned Rachel's smile and put the letter back in its envelope. She carefully resealed it. Then she had a murmured heart-to-heart with Rachel. They agreed that Boots and Sammy were a couple of crafty old darlings who had sent them into the lions' den to do what, for once, they hadn't been able to do themselves, win a face-to-face discussion with council officials. They had tried more than once, without success, and Boots, unused to such failure, bore scars. So did Sammy.

'So sending us was a last desperate throw of the dice?' said Rosie.

'My life, what a throw,' said Rachel, 'it was a hope that your sex appeal would do the trick.'

'Mine?' said Rosie modestly.

'Yours, my dear, is far younger than mine,' murmured Rachel. She was fifty-four, Rosie forty-two. 'Mine, in fact, is only a figment of someone's imagination.'

Rosie smiled. There weren't many members of the family who didn't know that Sammy had always had a soft spot for Rachel, although it had never led him into any acts of major indiscretion, the kind that would have badly interfered with his marriage.

'Well, someone's figment needn't be considered way off the mark, Rachel.'

'I should be hopeful of catching the eye of an eighty-year-old millionaire?' said Rachel, laughing softly. 'I can live without one, thank you. I now propose we let Sammy and Boots have this letter, and allow them to infer we were responsible for the decision being made in the firm's favour.'

'Not half,' said Rosie, 'why not? And by inference, as you suggest. No porkies.'

'Perish the thought,' said Rachel.

'We deserve some credit,' said Rosie.

'How much?' asked Rachel. 'I mean, what did we actually do?'

'We caught Mr Cox off guard,' said Rosie, 'which was as good as pinning him to the wall. Which was recommended by Sammy as a starter.'

'One has to admire his way of making himself understood,' said Rachel.

They finished their coffee, and left the tea-shop to make their way to the firm's offices at Camberwell Green.

'Well?' said Sammy on the arrival in his office of his long-established personal assistant, Rachel, and his niece, Rosie.

Rachel said yes, they had kept their appoint-ment with Mr Cox of the planning committee. Rosie said he had proved a likeable gentleman. Rachel said they seemed to have caught him at a vague moment, but he really had been very charming.

'Very,' said Rosie.

'I'll say this much,' observed Sammy, 'charming council gents are a bit rare, but as I'm up to my ears at the moment, I don't have too much time to listen to Mr Cox's man appeal. So could you just give me the nuts and bolts?'

'It took us a little time,' said Rosie ambigu-
ously.

'Putting our case?' said Sammy.

'My life, Sammy, you must know one can't
rush council officials,' said Rachel. 'They're all
subject to rules and regulations.'

'Do I know that?' said Sammy. 'You can bet
your life insurance I do. The point is, who
won?'

'Neither Mr Cox nor his assistant gave us the
answer on the spot,' said Rosie, 'but they did
hand us a letter.'

'Do I like the sound of that?' asked Sammy.

'Here it is,' said Rachel. She extracted the
letter from her handbag and placed it on
Sammy's desk. He eyed it suspiciously.

'Be of good cheer, Uncle Sammy,' said Rosie.
'Mr Cox's assistant was nicely helpful at the last
moment, getting the letter typed on the spot,
and we happen to know that a change of usage
has been granted. I think you'll find the letter
says so.'

'Eh?' said Sammy.

'Yes, permission granted, Sammy,' said
Rachel.

Sammy opened the letter, read it, then rang
through to Boots and asked him to come in.
Boots entered seconds later.

'So you're back,' he said to the ladies.

'And before your very eyes,' said Rosie, taking off Arthur Askey, the short-legged comedian of radio and television.

'And with highly welcome news,' said Sammy, looking proud of the part he had played in persuading the ladies to go get the chairman of the planning committee, while he himself stayed back at the ranch.

'How high is highly?' asked Boots, regarding Rosie with the affection of a father never able to fault his adopted daughter.

'Change of usage granted,' said Sammy, 'so how about that for a piece of expert negotiation by Rachel and Rosie?'

'I'm impressed,' said Boots, 'considerably.' Rachel and Rosie smiled sweetly but modestly. He smiled himself. There was more to these two charmers than met the eye on some occasions. 'Well done. Incidentally, how was it done?'

'Oh, in about twenty minutes or so,' said Rosie, staying with ambiguity. 'Mr Cox lent a very receptive ear, especially to Rachel.'

'Oh, just as much to Rosie,' said Rachel.

'I'm delighted,' said Boots, not in the least taken in, but quite happy, under the circumstances, to go along with whatever details the ladies came up with. 'And I'm doubly impressed.'

'Oh, no problem, ducky, so don't mention it,' said Rosie.

'Any conditions?' asked Boots.

'I believe the committee wants to see and approve our architects' plans covering the conversion,' said Rachel. 'I think it's all in the letter.'

'There's a letter?' said Boots.

Sammy waved it about like the flag of St George.

'It's here, Boots,' he said. 'Rachel and Rosie charmed old Cox and his committee. What a pair of turtle doves.'

'Coo-ee,' cooed Rosie.

It was one up to the ladies.

Maureen Brown, eighteen-year-old daughter of Cassie and Freddy Brown of Walworth, was living on cloud nine these days. With the help of Amos Anderson, photographer of Camberwell Green, she had become London's girl next door in the eyes of the readers of popular dailies and men's magazines. Generally, her poses were representative of a shy young lady 'accidentally' showing her good-looking, nylon-clad legs. Such shots promoted the girl-next-door image, and since this was the age when some periodicals were venturing into the realms of saucy sex appeal, especially if it looked accidental, Amos was not short of editors willing to buy. He paid Maureen twenty-five per cent of all fees received, which had prompted her into giving up her job as a copy typist to aim for the heights as a top glamour model and cover girl. She was hoping that Amos would come up any moment with a really super assignment for her.

Amos, affable but shrewd, knew his stuff and the wisdom of having started Maureen off as a girl-next-door type. Copy typists were nobodies. Shy but leggy girls were much in demand. Copy typists were paid a few quid a week. Photogenic girls doing pin-up poses could earn two guineas an hour when sitting for a photographer.

At this moment, in his studio, Amos was after a new angle. Well, new as far as Maureen was concerned. London's girl next door was wearing a defining yellow sweater and a blue flared skirt over a snowy petticoat. And she was riding a bike against a painted rural backdrop, creating an impression of how to bring sex appeal into the countryside. In blue nylons, her round knees sparkled and shone.

'Is this all right, Amos?' she asked.

'It's OK, better than all right,' said Amos, fortyish and cheerful, and always able to achieve rapport with his sitters, whether kids, newly-weds or grandmothers. Or cockney girls wanting to be pin-ups. There were always some. Most, however, lacked personality. Personality of the right kind was something that imbued a photograph with a bit of magic. Maureen had that kind.

'I think it's ever such a good idea, getting me on a bike in a skirt,' she said, feet obediently working the pedals.

'You're in a skirt, not the bike,' said Amos, eyes concentrating on his subject.

'Pardon?' said Maureen.

'No worries,' said Amos.

'Is my outfit nice?' asked Maureen.

'Just right for a bike ride in the country,' said Amos. 'Sailors like legs, soldiers like sweaters, and airmen like flying high, isn't that so? And they all like oomph. Don't they?'

'My oomph?' said Maureen. She was riding the bike with her hands on her hips so that her back was straight, her sweater tightly pouting.

'Both of them,' said Amos, clicking away from various angles.

'Amos, you cheeky thing,' said Maureen, but with a giggle.

'So sorry,' said Amos, his professional ethics always governing his attitude to pin-up sitters, which meant not to be foolish by being familiar. He was one of Camberwell's busy Jewish people.

Like Rachel Goodman, however, he was of the unorthodox kind, which enabled him to work on a Saturday without offending himself. 'Ah, that's good, Maureen, very good – we love it, riding a bike, don't we?' The pressed plunger of his Rolleiflex camera created an instant and brief flood of light that bounced off the ceiling and captured the appeal of London's girl next door.

'Yes, and look, no hands,' said Maureen. They were still clasping her hips. Her feet were pedalling, knees going up and down, her frilly white petticoat shyly peeping, legs, nylons and bosom to the fore.

'No hands on the bars is good, isn't it?' smiled Amos, curly hair dark and springy. 'It gives you an air of careless rapture, keeps your back straight and your – er – chest out.'

'Crikey,' said Maureen, legs taking a rest, 'I don't want to look like one of those female sergeant majors that's in the WAAFs.'

'You won't, and you can take my word for it, not half,' said Amos. 'We shall see you again in one of the dailies and in men's magazines as the girl next door on a bike, won't we? You bet.'

Maureen resumed posing, her back straight, her skirt and white frills riding up, her dazzling sweater outlining her figure.

Talk about oomph.

Not that Chinese Lady would have approved. Bosoms should be proud but not forward, that was her fixed belief.

Maureen, however, had never heard Chinese Lady expressing herself on the subject of bosoms. Come to that, nor had even the closest members of her family. The subject was sacred, and accordingly not for discussion. The nearest she had come to airing her opinion was when, one day some years ago, she and Boots had passed a thin woman with hardly any bosom to speak of.

'Poor woman,' Chinese Lady had said.

Boots didn't ask what she meant. He knew.

Chapter Five

Late March.

Phoebe was in an excited state, having been the thrilled recipient of a letter from Philip to say that his squadron would soon be back at their home station. Would Phoebe put the kettle on and wear something eyecatching as he'd seen all the Arabian burnouses he ever wanted to, thanks very much. He's daft but sweet, thought Phoebe, happiness surging.

'Mum, Dad, Philip's coming home,' she said, exhibiting the letter over the breakfast table. 'Isn't that great? He'll be knocking on our door soon.'

'Lovely,' said Susie.

'Where's his plane landing?' asked Sammy. 'On our front lawn?'

'What a thought,' said Phoebe. 'Mum, we can definitely order my wedding dress for June now.' She had held back on that, thinking superstitiously that if the gown was in her wardrobe before

June, the bridegroom would fail to be home at the right time.

'So we can,' said Susie, 'and the bridesmaids' dresses too.'

'Let's see,' said Sammy, 'how many bridesmaids will there be?'

'Four,' said Phoebe. 'Cousins Linda, Jennifer, Gemma and Emily.'

'That's a platoon,' said Sammy, enjoying a welcome Saturday morning breakfast of eggs and bacon, which could be eaten at leisure. 'So who's forking out?'

'You are, Sammy love,' said Susie, 'as well as for a new outfit for me.'

'Don't say things like that out loud,' said Sammy, 'or my wallet will faint.'

'Tell your wallet that forking out is the privilege of the bride's father,' said Susie.

'Well, seeing it's going to make our Phoebe happy,' said Sammy, 'I'll try to make it a pleasure as well.'

'Good old Pa,' said Phoebe, a girl presently in love with life.

Naturally, she spent most of the morning composing a rapturous reply to Philip's letter.

On a Sunday afternoon later that month Chinese Lady was at her kitchen sink, washing up the dinner dishes. Sir Edwin was doing the drying, the tea towel flapping about. The day was cold, and they were both looking forward to two hours beside the fire in their living room before visitors arrived for tea. Sir Edwin, glancing at Chinese Lady's rubber-gloved hands dipping plates in and out of the hot water, frothy with suds, wondered how many thousands of times she had done this particular chore.

'Maisie,' he said, 'I know you've turned down the suggestion before, but I'm now going to insist that we take on a housemaid at least for weekdays. It's time, my dear, that you did have a daily help, and I hope you won't say no.'

Chinese Lady, who had long cherished being independent of any kind of daily help, was touched. Accordingly, her response was a happy surprise to her husband.

'Well, Edwin, perhaps it would be nice to have some work taken off my hands,' she said.

'So you'll let me advertise for a daily?' said Sir Edwin.

'It's very kind and thoughtful of you, Edwin.' She was thinking of him as much as herself. He had always helped her with some chores, such as the washing-up, and she felt he ought not to have to worry about it any more on weekdays. As for Sundays, well, it would always be nice to have the house to themselves on the Sabbath.

'Of course, neither of us is very old, but we're not as young as we were.' Which was a gentle piece of wishful thinking now that they were both in their eighties. 'We'll see if advertising will bring someone nice and respectable to our door.'

'I'll do something about that tomorrow,' said Sir Edwin, delighted at her willingness. He knew she would come to appreciate a daily help. True, she was far from frail, but age was slowing her down just a little, and their home was far too large for her to continue the housework unassisted. 'Meanwhile, who are we expecting to tea today?'

He knew something else, that Sundays for Maisie were never quite what they should be unless someone came to tea. And she was still a good cook, still able to produce a fine oven-baked cake or a medley of fruit buns and jam tarts.

'Oh, yes, Lizzy and Ned,' she said. Daughter Lizzy and son-in-law Ned were frequent visitors to Sunday tea. She and Lizzy enjoyed a good gossip, while Ned and Sir Edwin talked about world affairs, anathema to Chinese Lady. To her, world affairs only ever meant some politicians somewhere were making life difficult for some people elsewhere. That man Hitler had made life difficult for just about everybody everywhere. 'Boots and Polly are coming too, and they're bringing Lizzy and Ned in Boots's car.' That was a reference to the fact that Ned, because of his acute heart condition, no longer drove. And Lizzy wasn't keen on taking his place. She'd had two lessons, and two were enough to convince her she'd never be able to make a car do what it ought. She was convinced it was much more likely to run away with her.

'Are Boots and Polly bringing the twins?' asked Sir Edwin hopefully. He enjoyed the company of the youngsters.

'Not this time,' said Chinese Lady, 'they're going to a friend's tea party today.'

'Oh, well, some other time,' said Sir Edwin, always philosophical about ups and down, little or not so little.

Boots and Polly were at the home of Lizzy and Ned at three forty. Lizzy opened the door to Boots and received an affectionate, brotherly kiss.

'Ready, Lizzy?'

'Yes, we're ready, Boots, I'll just get Ned away from his Sunday paper,' said Lizzy, and crossed the hall to the living room, where Ned sat in front of the fire with his Sunday read. The paper was on the floor, however, and he looked as if he'd nodded off. His head was forward. Lizzy touched his shoulder. 'Wake up, love, Boots and Polly are here.' There was no answer, no stirring. 'Ned, come on.' She lightly shook his shoulder. No response, none at all, except that his head lolled. Sudden alarm took hold of her. She stooped and lifted his chin. His eyes were open, and lifeless. Her heart seemed to stop. 'Ned, oh, my dear, no!'

But she knew he was gone, she knew it. His faulty valve had at last given up. All the years, all of them since their marriage in 1916, all gone now, and life would never be the same for her. Such a good man, such a caring husband and father. Gone during the few seconds she had taken to answer Boots's knock. Was it right for a man to be snatched so quickly from life and family? Was it a kindness that he had probably suffered only a fleeting moment of pain? Her heart froze at her sudden loss.

'Lizzy?' Boots was at the open door of the living room, hat in his hand, his eyes expressive of concern, for his sister's face was stricken.

She swallowed and spoke, huskily.

'He's gone, Boots, Ned's gone.'

Boots moved swiftly to stand beside her. He leaned, put a hand under Ned's chin and lifted the lolling head. He looked at the waxen face and the sightless eyes, and there he saw the death of his oldest friend who, years ago, at the age of only seventeen, had met and fallen in love with Lizzy, then a mere fourteen.

'Jesus Christ.' Boots was stunned. He and Lizzy looked at each other, Lizzy white and tragic.

'Boots, are we . . . are we sure?'

'Your GP, it's Dr Mason?'

'Yes.'

'Stay here, Lizzy, while I phone him.'

Using the phone in the hall, Boots rang the doctor. Although not on duty, he said he would come at once. Boots thanked him, put the phone down and stood in silence, wondering how to do the impossible, console his sister.

A shadow fell across the open front door.

'Boots, why the delay?' It was Polly.

Boots crossed the hall, drew her in and closed the door.

'Polly,' he said, 'I think Ned's heart has just given out.'

'What?' Polly's fur-clad body quivered, then stiffened. 'Boots, no.'

Very quietly, Boots said, 'I think we've just lost one of our own, one of the old brigade.'

That was it, one of the old brigade, one of the men who had served in the war of the trenches. In that war, Ned had lost a leg, Boots had been blinded, and Polly had spent four long years driving an ambulance. The three of them were old comrades.

Polly was as stunned as Boots. No-one in the family had ever quarrelled with Ned, or about Ned, a peace-loving man if ever there was one.

'Boots, are you telling me it's just happened?'

Boots, thinking of Lizzy, sighed.

'It seems, Polly, that he went in between Lizzy answering the door to me and going to tell him you and I were here.'

'Oh, my God, poor Lizzy,' breathed Polly. 'Where is she?'

'In the living room with Ned. Go and talk to her, Polly. I've phoned Dr Mason and he's on his way. I'll wait at the door for him.'

Polly took a deep breath, then went into the living room. Dr Mason arrived in his car only a minute later. Boots was at the front gate when the doctor alighted, bag in his hand, his expression full of concern. Lizzy and Ned were his friends as well as his patients.

'Mr Adams?' he said. He knew Boots.

'Glad to see you, doctor,' said Boots, 'but shattered by what I'm sure has just happened.'

'Let me see.'

Lizzy, Polly and Boots were all present as Dr Mason carried out the necessary examination, unbuttoning Ned's jacket, waistcoat and shirt to test his heart. He took time to reach a conclusion, sighing as he freed the stethoscope from Ned's lifeless body.

'Doctor?' whispered Lizzy.

'Mrs Somers . . . my dear lady . . . I'm terribly sorry.'

'He's really gone?' said Lizzy, catching her breath.

'I'm afraid so. Heart failure. I can issue a certificate to that effect.'

Lizzy slumped into an armchair and covered her face with her hands. A sob racked her. Boots crossed to the cabinet. He knew where Ned kept his brandy, a fine old cognac. Ned had been a connoisseur of wines and spirits, having ended up a long career in the trade as a director of the company for which he had worked since 1912.

Glancing at Dr Mason and showing him the relevant bottle, Boots received a nod of approval. He poured a little of the cognac into a glass and took it to Lizzy. She lifted her head, showed wet and cloudy eyes, and took the glass.

'You need it, Lizzy,' said Boots.

'May I have a little?' asked Polly, voice strained.

'Shall we all have one?' suggested Boots. 'As a farewell toast to Ned?'

Lizzy might have considered that entirely out of order, but she didn't. She understood it as an antidote to collective shock, and as a human gesture. So did Dr Mason.

'I think I'd like to join you,' he said. 'I think I'm as shattered as all of you. Just give me a moment, Mr Adams, while I phone for an ambulance.'

There were no words over the cognac. Each made a silent farewell to Ned after Dr Mason had finished his phone call. The spirit mitigated the shock felt by Boots and Polly, and put a little colour back into Lizzy's cheeks, although it didn't take the stark grief from her brown eyes.

Chinese Lady was beginning to worry about what could have happened to her expected guests, and Sir Edwin was just about to enquire by phone, when the front door knocker sounded. Answering the summons, Sir Edwin found Boots on the doorstep, and he knew at once from his expression that something was very wrong.

'Boots?'

'I need to talk to you,' said Boots.

'Come in, Boots, come in,' said his step-father.

Chinese Lady stayed in shock all day at the news of Ned's death. She regarded every related person as her own, from her sons and daughter all the way down to her great-grandchildren. For some she had a special affection, and Ned had been one of those. He had given Lizzy all she had ever wanted, a house with a bathroom and a garden, he himself as a husband, and, in time, children. Together, they had built a family home, and Ned had never failed as a husband and father. Nor had he ever looked at anyone else from the time he first met Lizzy. And he'd been an army officer when he married her in 1916, she of humble background but always clean, respectable and remarkably pretty.

It was cruel to have him depart this life when he was only sixty-one. To Chinese Lady, and others of her kind, that was far too young for any nice man to die. Her day of grief for Lizzy was bearable only because of the comforting presence of Edwin, although he himself was as shocked as she was. He had been the family's lodger in Walworth during Lizzy's growing years, and had come to feel a deep affection for her. Indeed, it was this affection for Lizzy, and a special regard for the family as a whole, that influenced him so much in his eventual decision to break with the aggressive militarism of his native Germany. It was a decision he had never regretted.

Now, with Chinese Lady, he grieved for Lizzy.

By the end of the day the various Adams families knew they had lost Ned. They included those who lived well away from south-east London. Down on their Kentish farm, Bess and her American husband, Jeremy Passmore, had been informed. So had Alice and her Scottish husband, Fergus MacAllister, at their home in Bristol, and so had David and Kate Adams at their Westerham dairy farm.

Ned's daughters, Annabelle and Emma, and his sons, Bobby and Edward, were shaken to their core. All had known a caring and understanding father, one who had never laid down the law. Bobby and Edward took charge of the funeral arrangements in concert with Shakespeare and Sons, undertakers of Camberwell Green. Boots asked if he could help.

'Yes,' said Bobby, 'be chief escort to my mother, while Edward and I look after our wives.' His own wife, Helene, had wept copious tears at the death of a man who, with Lizzy, had been so kind and welcoming on her arrival from German-occupied France in 1940.

'Polly and I will both take care of Lizzy,' said Boots.

Chapter Six

The funeral took place at the Denmark Hill church on Friday, five days after Ned's death. The undertakers had never known so many floral tributes, so many cards of remembrance, although the coffin was crowned with just one solitary and colourful wreath, that from Lizzy herself. However, the graveyard reception area was carpeted with every kind of floral arrangement.

The day was kind, for it was mild and clear. All members of the Adams families were there, except for Philip, still abroad. Also present were many friends, as well as old colleagues of the wine trade. The service was simple but moving, the hymns chosen by Lizzy. 'Now the Day Is Over', and 'O, Valiant Heart'. That was how she would always remember Ned, valiant all through his existence, as a striving young man, as a soldier of the trenches, as an old soldier with an artificial leg, and as a husband and father who worked to give his family all he could, no matter what.

Arm in arm with Boots, she said her final goodbye to her husband at the graveside, spilling tears along with a handful of earth. The tears she could not help, much though she strove to control her emotions.

Beside her, Polly dropped something else on the coffin in addition to a handful of earth. It was a wreath of red poppies, secured through the good offices of the British Legion's local branch. There was a card with the wreath, bearing the words 'To Ned. Never forgotten, old comrade. Love from Polly and Boots'. The poppies had been Polly's idea, the words her own.

Brittle though she still was sometimes, Polly could not deny herself such a gesture. Rosie, watching from close by, loved her for it.

Lizzy's own wreath, of flame-coloured lilies, Ned's favourite flowers, bore its card. Its message was typical of her kind, the kind who always believed in God and the hereafter.

'Goodbye, darling Ned, we'll meet again one day. All my love, Eliza'.

He had always called her by her baptismal name.

The funeral breakfast was at Lizzy's home, and put together by her daughters, Annabelle and Emma, with help from her daughters-in-law, Helene and Leah.

The house was full of mourning black, and echoing to voices that having been fairly hushed all through the funeral, now began to let words flow freely, if soberly. Older members converged until they formed a group consisting of Boots, Polly, Tommy, Vi, Sammy, Susie and Rachel.

'I'm so sad,' said Rachel, 'such a kind and civilized man, wasn't he? My poor Leah is heartbroken at losing so good a father-in-law.'

'We've lost one of us,' said Sammy. 'You realize that, Boots? One of us.'

'I realize it, Sammy,' said Boots, who, along with Polly, had known it from the shattering moment of truth five days ago.

'It's still a shock to me, I tell you,' said Tommy. 'I mean, he wasn't old, not much more than any of us. It'll take Lizzy ages to get over it.'

'Tommy love, don't make me feel worse than I already am,' said Vi.

'Have any of us any idea of what Lizzy is going to do?' asked Susie.

'You mean will she go and live with Bobby and Helene?' said Vi.

'Annabelle says she can't live on her own, especially not for the first few months,' said Susie.

'Annabelle's a nice girl,' said Sammy, 'but I don't know if she's right about her mum.'

'What do you think, Boots?' asked Tommy.

A faint smile touched Polly's face. It would always come down to that in a crisis. It would always come down to asking for Boots's opinion and letting that govern the collective decision, if a decision was necessary.

Boots said, 'If some of you will join me, I think I'll opt for a stiff drink.' Away he went, then stopped, turned and said, 'Tommy, I think we all know Lizzy will never leave this house, not until her own time comes and she's carried out feet first.' And he made for the table on which bottles and glasses had been laid out.

'He's right all right,' said Sammy, 'but I wish on a day like this he hadn't mentioned feet first. Come on, let's have a drink, we all need one.'

They all gravitated in the right direction, all, that is, except Polly. She waited, staying apart for the moment from the general throng. She felt, as she had on the death of her father, that with Ned's going, the country had lost one more of its old and distinguished warriors of Flanders fields. She needed something to lighten her sadness, and she wondered exactly what Lizzy needed, aside from a miraculous resurrection of Ned.

'Polly?' Boots was back, with a Scotch for himself and a gin and tonic for her.

'Thank you, darling,' she said quietly.

'You're welcome,' said Boots.

'To Ned?' she said.

'To Ned,' he said, and they touched glasses before drinking. It was one final gesture.

'Where are the twins?' asked Polly.

'In the parlour, with their grandparents, talking with Lizzy,' said Boots.

'The young and the old, consoling Lizzy together?' said Polly. 'I like that. Let's join them.'

Rosie and Matt came up, and all four entered the parlour, where they found not only Gemma and James, but also Rosie's own two, Emily and Giles, along with Tim and Felicity's daughter, Jennifer. Also present were Phoebe, Chinese Lady and Sir Edwin. Everyone had something appropriately touching to say to Lizzy. The family regarded funerals with ingrained, old-fashioned respect, inherited, as so much else was, from the behavioural patterns of the matriarch, Chinese Lady.

The house was crammed with relatives, friends and close neighbours, and as usual at any large gathering, everyone in the family seemed to be talking to everyone else. Someone had to knock twice on the front door before it was answered. Sammy did the necessary. On the step stood a young and lanky RAF officer, recognized immediately as Philip, son of Annabelle and Nick, and presently due to keep an important appointment with Phoebe.

'Hello, Uncle Sammy.' Philip spoke soberly.

'Hello yourself, Philip,' said Sammy. 'You're home, then, and you know, do you?'

Philip, stepping in, said his squadron was back a day earlier than expected, and that a neighbour had told him why no-one was at home.

'I can't tell you how sorry I am, Uncle Sammy. Grandpa Ned was a fine man, and I expect the whole family's cut up. I thought I'd come round and see Grandma Lizzy, and everyone else.'

'I think Phoebe would like to talk to you first,' said Sammy. 'Stay put for a tick and I'll let her know you're here.'

Philip stayed in the hall, conscious that the sound of many voices was a subdued but constant flow. From the parlour, a girl in a black costume emerged, her hat a little grey pillbox. But the black and grey were offset by the glow on her face. She swooped.

'Philip!' She was unable to deny gladness, the kind that sat involuntarily on sorrow. 'Oh, it's good to see you.'

Philip took her into his arms, and with her face buried in his shoulder, the happiness of reunion struggled with the sadness she felt for Aunt Lizzy. That turned her eyes wet.

'Go ahead, Phoebe, I understand,' said Philip.

'Oh, it's so sad, Philip . . . Aunt Lizzy's being so brave . . . but we all know she's grieving . . . we all are.' Phoebe spoke in muffled spasms.

'So am I, Phoebe, now that I know,' said Philip. 'How's my mother taking it?'

The question was very relevant, since his mother was Grandma Lizzy's elder daughter.

'She's badly shaken.' Phoebe thought of her Aunt Annabelle's tears at the graveside. 'Well, you know how much she and Emma loved their dad. Philip, look, shall I fetch her and your dad so they can talk to you here?'

Annabelle and her husband Nick appeared then, along with Philip's sister Linda. Sammy had told them of Philip's arrival. Annabelle, so like her mother in her brunette looks, was growing a little plump at forty. Nick, forty-four, still looked fit and healthy. Linda at eighteen was over the years of being thin, and had developed belatedly but happily. She was a sweet-natured girl, and ready to meet a kind young man, who didn't have to be the equivalent of Prince Charming. Simply, someone quite nice would do, even if most modern girls, when dreaming, were apt to conjure up images of Elvis Presley.

Linda and Phoebe, together with Annabelle and Nick, formed a talkative quartet around Philip, and mourning was put aside for the moment. Bronzed from his time in the Middle East, the young pilot officer looked vital and alive, and far removed from the dead and the dying of this world. He was, to Phoebe, her definite idea of the man she most wanted to spend the rest of her life with.

Talking came easily enough. They spoke, of course, of Grandpa Ned's sudden death and of how difficult it was going to be for Grandma Lizzy to cope without him. But they also spoke of the excitement of the forthcoming wedding, and at some length, until Philip said he really ought to go and pay his respects to his grandma. Lizzy received him with a brave hug, a kiss of welcome, and delight at knowing he was home again.

Philip wanted her to know that if she ever needed the kind of help that he could give, he'd be only too pleased to give it. Lizzy assured him that her sons and daughters intended to keep an eye on her, and that this probably meant there'd be a lot of unnecessary fussing. She was quite all right, she said, even if the occasion was a sad one. Naturally, she was missing Ned and would do so for a long time to come, but no-one was to worry, she'd see the day through. Philip gave way then to other relatives who wanted to pay their respects to his endearing grandma.

The day was a strain for her. There were all Ned's friends as well as so many relatives pressing around her in their wish to do what they could to console her. However, Lizzy had reserves of strength and spirit that would indeed help her to see the day through.

For Phoebe, things were a little better, while Jimmy, Sammy's younger son, and his wife Clare thought it tactful to say nothing of the fact that, on this day of mourning for a relative gone, a new life was on its way. Clare had just been informed she was pregnant. That news was for the family's ears on a happier day.

Vi's mother, known to the families these days as old Aunt Victoria, wasn't present. Almost seventy-nine, she was in failing health and keeping mainly to the room she occupied in Vi and Tommy's house. Staying away from the funeral, however, did not mean Ned's death hadn't upset her. In her eyes, Ned had always had the makings of a gentleman, and Aunt Victoria favoured that kind. Which meant she turned her nose up a bit at cockneys, while going out of her way to look admiringly at Boots, who, although born in cockney Walworth, was in her opinion a gentleman by nature.

On the return home of Vi and Tommy from the funeral, she wanted to know all about everything, particularly what the funeral service had been like. Had it paid proper respect to Ned, who'd always been so well behaved and respectable? Vi assured her it had, and described the burial itself for her mother's interest. The old lady nodded in approval.

'Well, if he had to go, poor man,' she said, 'he went quick and without suffering. I'm glad his funeral was fitting, like he deserved. Did you give my condolences to Lizzy?'

'We did,' said Tommy, 'and she sent you her thanks and good wishes.'

'I hope her family won't leave her to herself tonight,' said Aunt Victoria.

'In that respect,' said Tommy, 'Bobby will make the right decisions. He's the one with most up here.' Tommy tapped his forehead. 'Annabelle, well, being the eldest, she'll have her say, you bet, like she always does, but Bobby's the one that'll work things out for Lizzy's best interests tonight, tomorrow and the future.'

'Tommy, you just made a nice speech,' said Vi.

'Could someone make me a hot chocolate for my bedtime?' asked old Aunt Victoria.

As it happened, Bobby and Helene stayed with Lizzy all day and overnight. On Saturday they were rejoined by Annabelle and Nick, Emma and Jonathan, and Edward and Leah. Annabelle, first in seniority, opened the discussion by insisting that this family conference about her mother's future was necessary, which meant they were to decide where she was to live and with whom. In that respect, she said, Nick and herself had first claim.

Helene may have been only a daughter-in-law and not a daughter, but she spoke her piece immediately.

'Naturally, Annabelle, if Mama is to live with any of us, it will be with Bobby and me.'

'Why naturally?' asked Edward, at thirty-two not disposed to see himself disadvantaged as the younger son.

'It is not a question you need to ask,' said Helene, a firm-bodied and firm-minded French-woman who had become as much an Adams as any of the in-laws. She meant that Edward, as the younger son, did indeed have to give way to Bobby in the event that a choice was necessary. Further, as far as it concerned Annabelle, Bobby was wiser and more sensible than his elder sister.

'Jonathan and I can always find room for Mum,' said Emma.

'True,' said Jonathan, Sussex-born. 'Emma and me, we be ready and willing now and any time.'

Bobby said nothing. He knew that if the question was going to be resolved, then his mother would resolve it herself.

In fact, before any of her well-meaning family could persuade the others to believe she was a helpless old lady, Lizzy cut the conference short. She had no intention of going to live with any of them, she said, and had every intention of staying where she was until her time was up, thus echoing the comment made yesterday by Boots. She knew what was in their father's will, she said, something for all of them and the remainder to herself, including the house.

'With my—' She stilled a momentary quiver of her lips. 'With my widow's pension and what your dad is leaving me, I shan't be in want.'

'Full marks to Dad's foresight,' said Bobby quietly.

Annabelle fidgeted, then said she honestly didn't like the idea of her mum living alone.

'Well, Annabelle lovey,' said Lizzy, pale but in control for the most part, 'I'm sure you're all concerned, and I won't say it won't be a bit hard for a while, but I'll manage. You've all got your own lives, busy lives, what with your children and everything, and that's a good state to be in. You're all young too, and don't need any help from me, bless me, no. I'll be all right here in my own home.' What she meant, of course, was that living anywhere else would be like leaving Ned. She was sure his spirit was still around, and she could take comfort from that. 'You don't have to worry about me, any of you.'

Full marks to you too, Mum, thought Bobby. She was being entirely sensible, in his book. But Annabelle, as the eldest, spoke up again, saying she still didn't like the idea of their mum being alone. Lizzy said she wouldn't really be alone, that their dad would always be present in spirit, and in any case, she'd be busy around the house. There'd always be something to do, and chores to catch up with. She wouldn't, she insisted, do any sitting around and moping. Emma came up with the declaration that, like Grandma Finch, their mum had always been independent, and accordingly wouldn't want to rely on others until she was in a wheelchair. Then she'd really need help and someone close by.

'My life,' said Leah, 'should we speak of wheelchairs?' Twenty-nine, she was a dark-eyed brunette with looks that her husband Edward thought were like those of Elizabeth Taylor, the film star, and only the very critical would have said he was biased.

71

'I was just making a point,' said Emma.

'You could have been more tactful,' said Annabelle.

'No, I know what Emma meant,' said Lizzy, 'and of course, I'm not going to be backward in asking for help with the garden.'

'Mama, Bobby and I will do that,' said Helene. She and Bobby had regularly helped Ned with his garden. 'Nothing could keep us away.'

'Any time you and Bobby can't make it,' said Emma, 'I'll send Jonathan along.'

'Kind of you, Emma,' said Jonathan, with the lightest of smiles. He was mightily fond of his Emma, not thirty-five but still with a great sense of fun. Her sister Annabelle was nice enough, but had developed a streak of bossiness.

'No-one gardens quite like Jonathan,' said Emma, 'and my kitchen floor proves it.'

That produced a light moment. Everyone knew Jonathan could not break himself of the habit of coming in from the garden still wearing his gumboots.

'Well, in my time,' said Lizzy, 'I did have cause to tell Ned off a few times about that kind of thing.' She ended with a catch in her voice, but at once brought herself back under control. 'I'll be after Jonathan with my broom if he walks into my kitchen in his gumboots,' she said.

'Now we'll all have a nice cup of morning coffee.'

And that was that. Nothing was going to make Lizzy live anywhere except in the home she had shared with Ned for forty years.

That night, in their bedroom, Polly watched from the bed as Boots came in from the bathroom. He was, as usual, wearing only his pyjama trousers. He always went through his last ablutions of the day in that way. It did not diminish him, for he still had a fine, firm body. One might have said he went through life almost casually for the most part, thus avoiding the strains and stresses that afflicted other men.

As he slipped into his pyjama jacket, Polly said, 'Are you over it a little now?'

'Over the funeral?' Boots mused. 'I've wondered what Ned thought of it. I've a recollection that he once mentioned he favoured cremation.'

'If he ever mentioned it to Lizzy,' said Polly, 'I'm sure she'd have talked him out of the idea.'

Boots leaned over the bed and looked down into her eyes, glimmering in the glow of the bedside lamp.

'I agree, Polly. What kind of goodbye is there for a tin container of ashes?'

Polly's arms reached and encircled his neck.

'Do me a favour, old sport,' she murmured.

'Such as?'

'Stop the clock.'

Boots smiled.

'For you and me?' he said.

'Yes, for you and me,' sighed Polly, as if she and Boots alone were destined to grow old and feeble.

Boots smiled again and lightly kissed her.

Out went the lamp and he slipped into bed beside her. She turned and they snuggled up, much as if Ned's passing had brought them to a new awareness of how much they meant to each other.

Chapter Seven

June arrived and with it a lessening of Lizzy's grief. She kept herself busy and there were always some members of the family rallying round in support.

The summer days were alternately bright and not so bright. However, it was lovely on the fifth day of the month when Sammy Adams called on his old friend, Eli Greenberg, at his Camberwell yard, a place stacked with second-hand furniture under a new roof. Sammy knew what the new roof meant. Business was profitable, something he and Mr Greenberg had both favoured all their lives.

'You there, Eli old cock?'

Mr Greenberg at once appeared at the door of his office. His office was an old green shed. He himself at seventy-seven was a prime example of how not to let age turn a man decrepit. His frame was still sturdy, and if his hair and beard were flecked with white, they were still bushy, and his face showed no deep wrinkles. His round rusty black hat never left his head in favour of a trilby except on his Sabbath, and, as a courteous gesture to his Gentile homeland, on Sundays.

Seeing Sammy, he beamed. If he loved any family more than his own, it was the Adams clan.

'Vhy, Sammy, vhat a pleasure, ain't it?' He had given that greeting many times to Sammy during their long years of doing business together.

'Same here, Eli,' said Sammy, a figure of wholesome masculinity in his light summer suit of fine grey worsted, hat in his hand, his dark brown hair well brushed. At fifty-five, he was as mentally energetic as ever, blue eyes quick and electric. Women were beginning to eye him invitingly. Some women, that is. Widows and the lonely, and minxes who favoured mature men. There were frequent undercurrents at the Camberwell offices, all to do with the man appeal not only of Sammy, but of Boots as well. Both, despite maturity of age, were still personable enough to cause a bosom to flutter, or even to heave a bit. It all passed Boots and Sammy by. In any case, neither had ever fallen for a heaving bosom outside of marriage. Along with brother Tommy, they'd been brought up by Chinese Lady to behave in strictly proper fashion, which meant hands off what didn't legally belong to them.

'What brings you to my yard, Sammy?' asked Mr Greenberg, still beaming.

'Your pony and cart,' said Sammy.

'Vhich I don't keep here, Sammy, but in a stable down New Camberwell Road, ain't it?'

'Which is convenient,' said Sammy, 'seeing there's a family wedding taking place next Saturday fortnight.'

'Sammy, you giving me advance notice that you vant me to do the usual honours?' Mr Greenberg's beam glowed.

'Family custom, Eli old mate,' said Sammy. It went back a long way, the custom of Mr Greenberg driving an Adams bride to the church in his pony and cart. In fact, it went back to 1916, when Lizzy married Ned. 'Phoebe's going to make a happy bloke of Philip. The ceremony's taking place at twelve at the Denmark Hill church. Can we rely on you, Eli, to be at my front door by quarter to twelve?'

'Sammy, von't it be vun more pleasure, and ain't I honoured?' said Mr Greenberg effusively. 'Young Phoebe, is it? Vell, there von't be a prettier bride, and I'll vear a suit and a top hat, von't I?'

'Be my guest,' said Sammy. 'And about expenses—'

'There von't be any expenses, Sammy, not a penny. Vould I charge for the privilege after all these years? No, no, Sammy, not a penny.'

'Much obliged, Eli, and consider yourself and your missus invited to the reception,' said Sammy.

'I'm touched, Sammy, touched,' said Mr Greenberg and blew his nose on his large red handkerchief, one of several as old as his rusty hat. He was always comfortable with the old and familiar.

'Mutual,' said Sammy. 'Have to push off now, I'm up to my ears back at the office.'

'Vhen veren't you, Sammy, eh?'

'Well, it won't do to let the overheads suffer on account of not being where I should be,' said Sammy. 'So long, Eli.' He shook hands with his old friend and left. He did have work to do, work involving reorganization of the offices. The shop and the rest of the ground floor were being pulled apart and knocked about for the purpose of providing extra office space and a staff canteen. The two shop assistants had been transferred to other branches of the Adams retail business. Now Sammy had to consider employing a cook and a serving assistant. Lunches would be provided at a nominal cost of one shilling and sixpence, tea and coffee free, cakes or biscuits a few pence.

Together, Sammy and Rachel had worked out that prices would cover cost of ingredients, after which the firm would stand the outlay, including wages for cook and assistant. If that dented profits a bit, well, as Rachel pointed out, some sacrifice could be made without causing any real pain, and the goodwill between employer and employees would increase twofold. Sammy said he supposed twofold meant twice as much. Rachel said yes. So Sammy said she was right, that there'd be no real pain.

He had a word with her when he got back from seeing Mr Greenberg.

'Rachel, I've been thinking. What I know about cooking and making up a menu is nobody's guess. At home, I just eat what Susie serves up, and as I haven't been disappointed yet, I've got faith in what women know about menus. So as soon as the canteen is beginning to take shape, I'll leave you to interview applicants for cook and assistant.'

'Very well, Sammy, and thank you for the compliment,' said Rachel. 'By the way, do you realize one of our lady bookkeepers has a bit of a crush on you?'

'No, I don't know,' said Sammy, 'so don't tell me. It'll make me nervous. I once had a funny female assistant who kept brushing up against my suit. Fortunately, she migrated somewhere. To the Isle of Cats and Dogs, or some place like that. Which makes me ask you, Rachel old friend, what's up with some females?'

'Men like you and Boots, Sammy.'

'Well,' observed Sammy, 'I can understand about Boots, him being educated and a wartime general—'

'Colonel, Sammy.'

'Same thing to a dotty female. But he's getting on a bit, so if anyone in these here business offices does have a crush on him, tell him to wear his Crimean war medals and to talk to her like a grandfather. Incidentally, what's all that hammering down below?'

'It's the building contractors, Sammy, doing the conversion job.'

'Someone tell 'em to mind my head.'

Rachel was smiling on her way back to her office. Sammy, the love, couldn't cope with feminine adulation. It simply embarrassesd him. Boots treated it like a head cold. Head colds had a short life and a definite finishing date.

The lady bookkeeper in question, the one who fancied Sammy, was actually a married woman of thirty-three, Mrs Lily Chambers. She and her husband had no children, and as he was only a postman, with only a postman's wages, being free to earn a wage herself meant they had been able to afford the small luxuries that would otherwise have been denied them, as well as paying off the mortgage on their little house in Bavent Road, near Coldharbour Lane. Her own small luxuries were new clothes bought at sale times. A blond woman of round countenance and rounded figure, her machine-knitted jumpers paid their tribute to her figure, and her lipstick gave a touch of 'kiss-me-quick' to her looks. A bit of a flirt, she nevertheless had a serious side, and it was this that had pointed her at bookkeeping during her last year at school. She liked the look of books devoted to the entry of numerals that related to the excitement of pounds, shillings and pence.

She had been working for Adams Enterprises for just over a year, having left her previous employment with a firm of heating engineers after responding to an advertisement in the *South London Press*. The subsequent interview told her she would earn twelve shillings and sixpence more with Adams Enterprises. She enjoyed the job from the start, because there was a kind of up-and-coming atmosphere present, even if the senior bookkeeper was a bit of an old goat. After all, she wasn't actually working for him, but for the bosses, the two

Adams brothers. And one of them, Mr Sammy, was a man after her own heart. He too loved to see a book that recorded entries of pounds, shillings and pence, especially if it was obvious that the figures relating to income were keeping a healthy lead over those relating to expenditure. A man like Mr Sammy could take that in at a glance. It was always a pleasure to have him occasionally inspect the books she kept concerning the income and expenditure figures of the firm's retail shops. Numerals invigorated him, just as they invigorated her. What an interesting man he was, to be sure. He often made her wish he would take as much notice of her figure as some of those entered in her books.

One evening at home, when her husband Joe was down at the local pub, playing for the darts team, she was entertaining her sister. She took the opportunity to make a confession.

'Listen, Ivy, I've got something to say to you. I think I'm probably going to have an affair.'

'You're what?' said Ivy, a single woman of thirty-five who worked at Woolworth's in Peckham High Street, and lived in a flat over a shop. 'You're what?'

'I think I'm probably going to have an affair,' repeated Lily.

'Either you're out of your mind or I'm not

hearing straight,' said Ivy, almost put off the cup of tea and slice of cake Lily had set before her. 'Did you actually say you're going to have an affair?'

'Probably,' said Lily.

Ivy came to a little and took in a mouthful of cake.

'Of course, you're not serious,' she said.

'Well, I am, actually,' said Lily, 'I've got a fancy for a very sexy man.'

'Oh, no, not another one,' sighed Ivy. 'You're always getting fancies for some bloke or other, you silly moo. Might I remind you that even on your wedding day you had a fancy for Archie Cope, Joe's best man?'

'Oh, that wasn't serious,' said Lily.

'Nor were any of the others,' said Ivy, drinking hot tea to fortify herself for argument. Lily had always had a roving eye for a good-looking pair of trousers, but it had never amounted to much more than some flirtatious winks and coy gestures. If, during her married years, any bloke she made up to started to respond in earnest, she as good as ran a mile. She had never been serious, although sometimes Joe reckoned he had good reason to come close to smacking her bottom. Joe was easy-going, up to a point. He wasn't going to like the fact that for the first time Lily was actually talking about having an affair. 'Come on, this one's not really a serious fancy, is he?'

'He's special,' said Lily.

'So have all the others been,' said Ivy, 'but nothing's ever happened, lucky for you. Isn't it about time you stopped behaving like a soppy schoolgirl having crushes?'

'I'm not having a crush now,' said Lily, 'I'm having this feeling about starting an affair. I don't get much out of Joe these days, not now we've been married for fourteen years.'

'You don't have to let him down by going in for adultery, do you?' said Ivy.

Lily said she'd be obliged if her sister didn't use nasty words like that. She wouldn't be surprised, she said, if Joe was living it up with some woman on the evenings when he was supposed to be playing darts. Some husbands do that sort of thing, she said. Ivy said she didn't think Joe was that kind of husband, and that Lily on the whole was fortunate to be his wife. She reminded Lily that she herself had been robbed by the war of the chance to marry her fiancé of the time, because he was killed in the desert fighting. The poor man was driving a tank, and all he did was to pop his head out for just a tick to get a bit of air, and in that time it was blown off, which was horrible for him and tragic bad luck for her.

'Yes, I remember that,' said Lily, 'and we all sorrowed for you and his family, but it's got nothing to do with me and me present fancy.'

'Yes, it has,' said Ivy, 'because it should tell you you're lucky and that you ought to be grateful. Who is this bloke you're soppy about?'

'I'm not telling you,' said Lily. 'If I do, you'll tell Joe and Joe will go round to see my fancy and do something silly.'

'Something silly? A bit violent more like,' said Ivy, 'and who'd blame him? I ask meself who would and I answer I wouldn't, for a start.'

'I don't want any trouble,' said Lily, 'just a chance to enjoy a bit of romance.'

'A bit of adultery, you mean,' said Ivy.

'Didn't I ask you not to use nasty words like that?' said Lily rather querulously. 'Look, I wanted to talk to someone about me feelings, and I thought me own sister would be the right one.'

'Well, I am the right one,' said Ivy, 'because I'm telling you you're talking like a daft parrot. Anyway, I don't believe you really are serious, I think it's just another of your silly crushes that only last a fortnight.'

'I'm in love,' pronounced Lily.

'Oh, me aching foot,' said Ivy, 'you'll make me suffer heart failure in a minute.'

'Course you won't,' said Lily, 'you're not the kind.'

'I can only stand so much of all this bunkum,' said Ivy.

'Listen,' said Lily, 'don't you realize I've met a man I really admire?'

'All I realize is that you're off your silly head,' said Ivy. 'That was a nice piece of cake, by the way. Is there any more?'

'There you are, help yourself,' said Lily, and lifted the deep lid of the china dish to disclose what was left of a home-baked madeira cake.

'Oh, ta,' said Ivy, and cut herself a slice. She also helped herself to another cup of tea. Discussion and argument fuelled one's appetite for cups of tea and home-baked cake. 'Lily, you wouldn't really do Joe down, would you?'

'I couldn't answer for what me passion might make me do,' confessed Lily, which nearly made Ivy choke on cake. 'It comes on very urgent sometimes, especially when he's close to me.'

'Don't say any more,' begged Ivy, 'I'm having a fit. If you could only hear yourself, you'd have one too.'

'One what?' asked Lily, mentally calculating the answer to three pounds, twelve shillings and sixpence multiplied by fifty-three. Fifty-three was the number of weeks she'd been working for Adams Enterprises.

'One what? A fit, of course,' said Ivy.

'Bless me, who'd have believed it?' murmured Lily, having reached the sum of a hundred and ninety-two pounds, two shillings and sixpence as an answer. Some people did crossword puzzles. She did mental arithmetic. 'All that much?'

'Now what you talking about?' asked Ivy.

'I think I've said enough.' Lily was firm about that. 'You'll have to leave me to decide my own fate.'

Ivy said that whatever that might be, watch out for what Joe might do if he finds out.

Chapter Eight

Chinese Lady was living a new kind of existence, due to the fact that Sir Edwin had managed to hire someone very willing and efficient to help her with the housework, a forty-two-year-old widow, Mrs Harriet Plumstead. With her two daughters off her hands, and living in a small flat in Herne Hill, Mrs Plumstead was only too pleased to do a daily job from nine to two thirty, including Saturdays, at two shillings an hour, which amounted to three pounds and six shillings a week. This was pretty good money for a char, and entirely due to Sir Edwin's recognition of a deserving cause. He had instinctively felt the lady would be deserving. Those earnings, added to her widow's pension, would, she said, help her to live like a queen.

A bony, strong-looking woman, Mrs Plumstead was of the perpetually cheerful kind. Not at all awed at working for what she told her daughters were a lord and lady, she addressed Chinese Lady in cockney fashion as 'ducks' or 'dearie' or 'mum'. Chinese Lady found this a mite more acceptable than something like 'Your Ladyship'. As she informed Sir Edwin, she had never been born a ladyship, just one of the people. Sir Edwin assured her they were both of the people.

Conversations between Mrs Plumstead and Chinese Lady were generally of the following kind.

'I've done the bedroom, dearie, I'll start downstairs now, if it pleases you.'

'Yes, do that, Mrs Plumstead.'

'Oh, like I've said, you don't have to be formal. Call me Harriet, like me friends do. How's yer hubby this morning? What a nice gent he is, to be sure. Me own old man, Johnny, he was nice too, and it was 'ardly fair him being taken when he was still young.' Mr Plumstead had been a bus driver for years until pneumonia took him off at the age of forty-four, which Mrs Plumstead considered unfair indeed, considering some men with no manners and no graces were still getting on people's nerves at sixty.

Mrs Plumstead liked work, liked being busy. She washed up the breakfast things when she arrived, then began the housework, made coffee at ten thirty, did more housework, and cooked lunch for one o'clock. Chinese Lady insisted she had her own share of the meal, and she did, enjoying it in the kitchen. After that, she washed up, tidied up, made sure that nothing that should have been done was left undone, and then departed. Incidentally, on Tuesdays she ironed what was necessary from the Monday washing. Chinese Lady was particularly grateful for that, since ironing had begun to give her a backache.

The paragon was paid daily by Sir Edwin, which pleased her no end. It meant, she confided, that she always had a bit of money in her purse, which she hadn't had before.

To Chinese Lady, the important factor was that the hired help relieved her of the major part of her domestic chores, which gave Sir Edwin a deal of satisfaction on her behalf, and pleased her more than she would admit. At the same time, however, she declared she didn't want her hands to get idle. Sir Edwin encouraged her to take up knitting again, and in a busy way, so she was now turning out woollies for her great-grandchildren, of which there were more than a few. Sir Edwin, hearing her humming old-fashioned songs, felt convinced that hiring a competent daily help was the best thing he had done for his wife in years.

Mrs Plumstead addressed him as 'Sir' in acknowledgement of his distinguished look and his good manners, not his title. She considered him a genuine gent, both in appearance and graciousness.

'Sir, I've done your study right through this morning. My, all them books you leave about, I've tidied them up again.'

Sir Edwin refrained from telling her he didn't want them tidied up. He felt she'd insist, anyway. She was a great believer in tidiness. It caused him to consult Chinese Lady at times.

'Maisie, have you seen my morning paper?'

'Oh, it's been tidied up, Edwin.'

'And where has it been tidied up?'

'In the rack for papers and magazines, Edwin, and it's nicely folded.'

One could accept an excess of zeal from such a worthy asset, but all the same, Sir Edwin made what he thought was a relevant point.

'I beg you, Maisie, to assure our invaluable help that should the thought occur to her, there's no need to iron my *Telegraph*.'

'Edwin, what a silly idea, no-one irons a newspaper.'

'Some butlers do, I believe, and I've a feeling that one day, Mrs Plumstead might begin to iron mine.'

So, at an opportune moment, Chinese Lady spoke to her hired help. It was when the agreeable lady was 'tidying up' Edwin's newspaper.

'Mrs Plumstead, you're not thinking of ironing that, are you?'

'Beg pardon, mum?' said Mrs Plumstead.

'My husband says there's no need to.'

'To iron his newspaper?' Mrs Plumstead looked bemused for a moment. Then, 'Oh, d'you mean he'd like me to? I never heard of any gent before that wanted his newspaper ironed, but if that's what your hubby would like, I'd be pleasured to oblige.'

'Oh, I only meant that if you were thinking of doing so, you needn't worry.'

'Well, I won't, dearie, I won't put an iron to any bit of your hubby's newspaper.'

'I'll tell him that.'

'Tell him it's a promise, mum.'

Chinese Lady told Sir Edwin. The telling so diverted him that he laughed out loud, so Chinese Lady, of course, wanted to know what was funny about it.

'I confess, Maisie, that I never thought you'd take me literally,' said Sir Edwin.

'What's that mean?' asked Chinese Lady. 'I just thought you wanted me to make sure Mrs Plumstead didn't run a hot iron over your paper.'

'Well, that was very nice of you, Maisie, and I'm greatly obliged for your intercession.'

'I don't know what intercession means,' said Chinese Lady, 'I just know you won't have to worry about your paper being ironed.'

'Thank you, Maisie. What a good woman you are.'

On a day during the second week in June, Rachel took on the responsibility of interviewing two applicants for the job of canteen cook.

The ground-floor conversion was progressing well, and the question of hiring a cook and assistant for the canteen needed to be attended to. The first applicant for cook was a large, rosy-faced lady whose blouse buttons were straining at the leash. She was expansive of mood as well as figure, beaming happily as she detailed her credentials. She was a married lady of fifty, but used to doing a weekly job. A job such as was being offered, a canteen cook, was just up her street, seeing the kind of experience she'd had.

'What experience is that?' asked Rachel, looking like the firm's most comely executive.

'Why, the kind that you want, I'm sure,' beamed the lady. 'Didn't I spend years doing the customers proud in the Walworth Road fish and chip shop?'

'You mean your experience was in the frying of fish and chips?' said Rachel.

'Wasn't I doing that for a good seven years and never getting one complaint?' The applicant beamed again in happy self-satisfaction.

'I'm not sure we have lunches of fried fish and chips in mind,' said Rachel. 'I think we favour a choicer menu.' She referred to her notes. 'I see that when you phoned for an interview, you did say you had wide experience as a cook.'

'Yes, that's right, madam, I did say that, and I said right, because before I did me seven years at the fish and chip shop, I worked ten years at the pie and mash shop in the East Street market, where the menu was very choice. Customers could have just pie and mash, or pie, mash and baked beans, or pie, mash and green peas.' The large lady beamed yet again. 'Then there was me hot gravy, which customers got very fond of.'

Rachel, with an effort, kept her face straight.

'So your experience as a cook has been mainly confined to hot pies and mashed potatoes, and fried fish and chips?' she said.

The happy, self-confident applicant said not to forget all the cooking she'd done for her husband as well, and right through thirty years of marriage, and never once had her old man suffered a stomach ache on account of what she served up daily, although during the war when he did a lot of ARP duties and needed a bit of good food, her cooking at home was affected by rationing. Her old man liked a hot stew, for instance, especially in winter, but you couldn't get the proper ingredients while the war was on. Of course, now and again she was able to take home some pie and mash for both of them.

'With a jug of me gravy as well,' she added. 'Of course, I warmed it all up in the oven when I got home. That's if there wasn't no air raid on. If there was, we had to wait till it was over.'

'Frightful days and nights,' said Rachel.

'Yes, wasn't they?' said the expansive lady. 'When would you like me to start the job? I'm not working at the moment, so any time will suit me, and what would be the hours?'

As tactfully as she could Rachel explained that she had other applicants to interview, and that she wouldn't come to a decision until she'd seen them all.

'Then we'll write to you,' she said.

'Oh, all right, but you haven't said what the hours would be.'

'We're thinking of from ten in the morning until four thirty in the afternoon, since the provision of afternoon tea will come into the reckoning,' said Rachel. 'The lunch hour will be from twelve thirty to one thirty, the tea break from three thirty to three forty-five.'

'Well, all that'll suit me fine,' said the large lady, and departed still beaming. With her going, Rachel detected that something went with her. The faint aroma of fried fish and chips.

The second applicant was much more encouraging, being a young woman who had excelled in domestic science at school, particularly in all that appertained to the skills of a chef. Just married, she needed a part-time job, she said, and preferred a local one rather than having to travel up and down to somewhere in town. As a newly married woman, she wanted to make sure she had time to cope with the housework, as well as with the preparation of the evening meal.

Rachel, at this early point, recognized the picture of the happy and eager young newly-wed who, after spelling out her qualifications, sensibly asked what were the hours of work, and what was the pay. Rachel quoted the hours, and said the pay would be four pounds, ten shillings a week. The young woman, Mrs Mary Tindall, expressed sastisfaction with that, and the interview continued. Rachel pointed out that all staff would use the canteen, and that included directors and managers. Mary Tindall, with a smile, said she would welcome the challenge of preparing menus to tempt the high as well as the low.

'I think you might suit us very well,' said Rachel, 'but I must be frank. Do you and your husband propose to start a family?'

What had Sammy said? Try not to take on any married female whose husband might be thinking of putting her in the club. We don't want her leaving just when she's well into the job. Someone about forty would be best.

Young Mrs Tindall was nowhere about forty, or even thirty. Accordingly, Rachel had to ask the necessary question.

Mary Tindall answered promptly.

'Well, I'm only twenty, and my husband's only twenty-two, and we both come of large families, which means we've both got all the relatives we need right now. We're not going to start our own family for at least two years. That's so we can enjoy Saturday night dances, rock and roll concerts, and be active members of the Elvis Presley fan club.'

'Mrs Tindall,' said Rachel, 'I'll speak to our managing director, and if he accepts my recommendation, that will mean the job is yours. I'll write you accordingly, and let you know the starting date. Will that do for now?'

Mary Tindall said thanks very much, and that

she hoped to hear she really had got the job. When she had left, Rachel popped into Sammy's office and let him know how she had got on with both applicants. Sammy fell about when told of the large, expansive woman who thought fried fish and chips or pie and mash alone should form the canteen menu. He liked the sound of Mrs Mary Tindall, however, and when assured by Rachel that the young lady and her husband were far more interested in Elvis Presley than babies, he expressed himself willing for her to be taken on.

'But might I ask incidental who this bloke Elvis Presley is? I sometimes get a feeling he's the Invisible Man following me about.'

'He's the world's top pop star,' said Rachel, 'and you could well call him the Invincible Man as much as the Invisible. My daughter Leah informs me he's unbeatable, and has left even Frank Sinatra far behind. My life, Sammy, Leah is thirty this year, and here she is with the same taste for pop music as teenagers.'

'Not to worry, it won't last,' said Sammy. 'It'll be on the way out in a year of so, and we'll get Bing Crosby back as the number one crooner.'

'Sammy,' said Rachel, 'should I argue with that? I should. Crooners in another year or so will be as dead as the dodo.'

'Pity,' said Sammy. 'Anyway, back to work, so ask Mrs Whatsername to let me see the February and March bank statements for our Clapham and Brixton shops, will you?'

'I think you mean Mrs Chambers,' said Rachel, hiding a smile. Mrs Chambers was the woman who had a thing about Sammy. Sammy, the dear man, had no idea his favours were coveted by the lady.

Chapter Nine

When told she was wanted by Mr Sammy, and why, Lily showed a slight flush. It signified an undercurrent of pleasure, sweet excitement and an erratic pulse. Carrying the required statements, she went down to Sammy's office.

'Come in,' called Sammy in response to her knock, and in Lily went, round face tinted with light, attractive make-up. Her ivory, pearl-buttoned blouse and long brown skirt seemed, as far as style went, halfway between a 1920 fashion and the New Look era. Neverthless, the outfit suited her.

'Oh, good afternoon, Mr Sammy,' she said, trying not to gush, 'I've brought the Brixton and Clapham bank statements that Mrs Goodman told me you wanted to see.'

'Yes, I do want to see the entries for February and March,' said Sammy. Although every Adams shop now had its own bank account, all statements were sent to the head office. Lily placed the relevant documents on Sammy's desk, in front of him. A little sighing breath escaped her. Mr Sammy Adams, what a man. He had gorgeous blue eyes full of life and energy. He made younger men look really dull. As he took hold of the top statement, she leaned over the desk, and her sighing breath turned into a murmur.

'Mr Sammy?'

'Yes?' Sammy was already into figures and not, therefore, looking into her dewy eyes.

'Would you—'

His desk phone rang. He picked it up.

'Hello?'

'Mr Tommy from the factory wants to talk to you, Mr Sammy,' said the switchboard operator. 'I'll put him through.'

'Right,' said Sammy, unaware that love and hope were hovering. 'Hello, Tommy, what's up?'

'Who's fed up, you mean,' said Tommy, general manager of the factory, 'and if you want to ask I'll tell you it's me. I've got the union on my back again. Like I've mentioned before, I never was in favour of having the workforce unionated.'

'Unionated?' said Sammy, with Lily gazing down at the top of his head and admiring the healthy look of his dark brown hair. 'Is that an operation or something to do with a prostate?'

'Unionated or unionized,' said Tommy, 'what's the difference? It all amounts to the union thinking it's their factory, not ours. I've just had the shop stewards in my office asking for a seven and a half per cent pay rise across the board.'

'Eh?' Sammy couldn't believe his ears. Seven and a half per cent across the board? For two hundred workers? 'Eh?' he said again.

'I think you heard,' said Tommy,

Sammy had heard all right, and was as good as speechless for the moment. Lily, still leaning, drew a breath and prepared to put a question to him while the brief silence lasted.

'Would you like to go to bed with me, Mr Sammy?'

Well, that was what was on the tip of her tongue, but at the precise point when she was about to release it, Sammy came to. He looked up from the phone into the soulful eyes of the lady bookkeeper and said, 'Never mind now, leave these statements with me and I'll let you have them back later.' Then he spoke to Tommy again. 'Listen, did you rate the shop stewards as serious? I mean, is it possible they were trying it on?'

'Oh, they were trying it on all right,' said Tommy, 'and doing it seriously.'

'Well, sod that,' said Sammy, 'they're taking

their orders from Barney Burridge, of course.'
Barney Burridge was the local union big
shot, and an old bowler-hatted opponent of the
Adams brothers. 'He's having a barmy day-
dream if he thinks the garment-manufacturing
industry will wear that kind of pay rise for the
workers.'

Tommy said that that was exactly what he
had told the shop stewards, and he went on at
length about their thick heads and aggravating
arguments. During this discourse Lily departed
from Sammy's office to make her way back
to the bookkeeping department on the second
floor. She climbed the stairs with a sigh, but not
without telling herself that when Mr Sammy
was ready to hand back the bank statements,
she would have a second opportunity to let him
know they could find bliss together. She had a
vague image of Sammy driving her out into the
countryside one day, say as far as Reigate,
where they would make love in some romantic
spot golden with buttercups, and get back to the
office by teatime.

Sammy, totally ignorant of what lay in wait
for him, interrupted Tommy.

'Listen, Tommy old cock, talk to the shop
stewards and tell 'em to tell Barney Burridge to
go fry his bedsocks. Let 'em know that other
factory owners won't wear the demand, and

that I'm objecting personally. Meanwhile, I'll have a word with Boots.'

'Do that, Sammy,' said Tommy, and hung up.

Sammy took himself into Boots's office. His elder brother was in the process of handing to Rosie correspondence she could attend to first thing tomorrow, and thus save him some work he could do without.

'I need to talk to you, Boots,' said Sammy.

'I'm just going, Uncle Sammy,' said Rosie, and Sammy thought what a treat she was to the eye. She always had been, right from her years as a girl, and still was, even though she'd passed forty. Come to that, Susie was still a bit of a looker, even at fifty-two. As for Polly, she was a corblimey miracle at sixty. The family could be proud of its females and their looks. Nobody could have said any of them were like the six-foot circus woman with a beard.

'Don't let me rush you, Rosie.'

'No, I really am just going, it's nearly three o'clock,' smiled Rosie, and left the brothers to each other. Sammy lost no time in acquainting Boots with the garment union's demand for a seven and a half per cent rise across the board. Barney Burridge and his brother bowler hats were trying it on, he said.

Boots gave the matter some thought before

responding. Then he said, 'Sammy, any rise from five to seven and a half per cent has to mean more than one thing for our workforce, never mind what it might mean at other factories.'

'I know it means an injurious leap in overheads for us,' said Sammy, 'and it means cherries on an iced cake for the workforce.'

'Not quite,' said Boots. 'It'll mean they can't even have the cake. That is, in order to offset the cost of increased wages, we'll have to cancel their twice-yearly bonuses and double wage packet at Christmas.'

Sammy smacked his forehead.

'Now why didn't I think of that?' he said. 'Blind O'Reilly, where else could any factory workers get an earnings deal as good as we give 'em? Two bonuses a year, and a Christmas box every December?'

'Sammy,' said Boots, 'tell Tommy to tell Barney Burridge that irrespective of other factories, the case for our workers is that they're being greedy. Not good union publicity, that Sammy, not good at all. Further, get Tommy to point out that the Government's not going to like any rise that increases the price of export goods. The garments industry exports in quantity.'

'One day,' said Sammy, 'I'll get Susie to

congratulate me in public for having an educated brother. Believe me, Boots, I often wish I'd been educated meself.'

'Oh, you're educated, Sammy,' smiled Boots, 'and to a degree that has seen off many a pain in the elbow like Barney Burridge.'

When Tommy heard from Sammy that Boots had come up with a blinder, he asked what it was, and Sammy told him.

'Blimey, I'm getting old,' he said. 'I should have thought about the bonuses when the shop stewards were trying to fry my brains. I'll lay ten to one that none of our workers will want to give up what they get extra twice a year and Christmas as well.'

'And I'll lay the same odds that none of the other factory owners will wear any demands for any kind of a rise right across the board,' said Sammy. 'Skilled workers will always want more than the unskilled, and that includes percentages.'

'I'll talk to the shop stewards, and they can talk to Burridge,' said Tommy.

'Good idea,' said Sammy, 'let them have the privilege of spoiling Burridge's afternoon cuppa.'

'Don't let's laugh yet,' said Tommy soberly. 'The special case for our workers won't stop the big noises like Burridge from calling the workers out. That'll mean ours along with everybody else's. Also, I've just thought. Burridge will tell the shop stewards to stand their ground over the bonuses, and the union won't care a burnt banger about what the Government thinks.'

He was right, because when Barney Burridge heard from the shop stewards that the workers at the Adams factory were against pressing for a rise, and that the Government wouldn't like any rise to increase export prices, he simply said the workers would do as their union instructed them and the Government could cry its eyes out from now until Christmas as far as the TUC was concerned. It was every union's job to win fair do's for its members, so go tell Tommy Adams that.

Tommy, receiving the message, saw trouble ahead. These days, he said, the unions frighten the Government more than the Government frightens the unions. If the crunch came, he didn't think the factory's workforce would disobey an order from the union to down tools and walk out. No worker wanted to be labelled a blackleg, not unless he could take the next boat to Australia and join a gold rush.

Boots, when advised of Burridge's reactions, suggested they should all sit on the problem, and let the union argue the case with the big industrialists of the garments trade. The federation will fight any demand for a rise, he predicted, certainly anything over two and a half per cent. The Government will have to oppose the granting of any rise that affects exports, and they'll hope for public backing.

'Of course,' he added, 'the public would support the Government stance if they thought the union was being influenced by its Communist elements. If the press got hold of a rumour that that was the case, they'd head-line it. Since our factory workers mostly live in Bethnal Green or thereabouts, some probably rub shoulders with the local red revolutionaries. What does this country dislike most, Sammy?'

'Red revolutionaries,' said Sammy, which gave Boots the cue to remind him that Chinese Lady and her like still felt Bolsheviks were bewhiskered bomb-throwers who could give children nightmares. 'I think you're hoping that someone in Bethnal Green will slip a rumour to the local paper,' said Sammy.

'That would be a start,' said Boots.

'Good thinking,' said Sammy.

Lily had no chance to talk to Sammy again that afternoon, for when the working day ended he was still busy on matters other than the bank statements. She would have to wait until tomorrow. Not that she felt disappointed or thwarted. She wasn't the type to be in a hurry. In fact, time fostered anticipation. You could think up all kinds of things for when the happening came, like, in this instance, would Sammy Adams turn out to be as exciting as he looked? She could imagine him being firm and masterful, because that was how he was as a boss. If they did make love in a country field, she hoped being firm and masterful wouldn't get in the way of him taking his shoes and socks off. She admitted she was a bit fussy about that sort of thing.

Once, in the early days of her marriage to Joe, they had made love in a nice quiet spot near Abbey Wood, but Joe had spoiled it a bit by keeping his boots on. Afterwards, when she was remonstrating with him, he said he didn't see how a bloke at that stage of the proceedings could be expected to even unlace his boots, let alone take them off. The trouble with Joe was that he could be a bit common at times. Also, he wasn't exciting, and nor did he bother with romance any more. Darts, they were his real love. He could spend hours fussing over his sets, while he hardly fussed over her at all.

Anyway, tomorrow at the office, when Mr Sammy gave her back the bank statements, she'd definitely ask him if he'd like to make love to her. He might easily be rapturous about the offer, since she supposed his wife, being middle-aged, as he was himself, didn't encourage him to do much else in bed except sleep.

At home that evening, Joe asked her if she had something on her mind. At first she said no, then corrected herself and said well, yes, she did. Could he get a new lid for the dustbin because the present one was so cracked it let smells escape in their back yard, and their neighbours might complain any moment. Joe said she shouldn't let a dustbin lid play on her mind, and not to worry, he'd get a new one from the hardware shop tomorrow. Lily thought well, imagine if tomorrow turns out to mean a dustbin lid for Joe and a romance for me, what a day.

'When's your next darts match?' she asked.

'Tomorrow night,' said Joe, and she thought there, that's it, out most nights at the pub and leaving me all alone Joe just doesn't deserve me. He'd be just as happy with a parrot as with me.

At home with Susie, Sammy was asked by his one and only better half if there really was a danger of a strike at the factory.

'Unfortunately,' said Sammy, 'the answer's in the altogether.'

'Does that mean yes?' asked Susie, who was waiting for the radio music programme to come across with one more rendering of Harry Belafonte's international hit, 'Island in the Sun'.

'Afraid so,' said Sammy. 'We can fight a local dispute whenever Barney Burridge gets a bit stroppy, and we've done that more than once. But as an individual factory we can't fight a national dispute, apart from putting in our pennyworth of protest. What I don't like is the prospect of a long shutdown. That could cost us pound notes and customers. Losing pound notes is hurtful, Susie. Losing customers is worse.'

'Oh, dear,' said Susie. 'Never mind, love, the firm will still have earnings from our shops and our property company.'

'I don't like saying so,' said Sammy, 'but there won't be too many earnings from the shops. Most of what they sell is supplied by the factory.'

'Oh, well,' said Susie philosophically, 'no strike lasts for ever, so I don't suppose we'll actually finish up on the dole.'

'We might come close to having to sell the piano,' said Sammy.

'Sammy, we haven't had a piano for years,' said Susie.

'That's done it,' said Sammy, 'we're worse off than I thought.'

Susie didn't comment on that. She was listening to Harry Belafonte.

Elsewhere, in the house on Red Post Hill, in fact, Chinese Lady was listening to the same music programme while busily knitting. And Sir Edwin was taking in a special report in his newspaper concerning the European Common Market, set up in March by France, West Germany, Holland, Belgium, Italy and Luxembourg. It was an exponent of free trade and harmonization of industry and agriculture. Elements within the British Conservative party thought it might be a good idea for Britain to join. Sir Edwin thought the Market might prove very advantageous to its members, but he wasn't sure if France and West Germany hadn't fashioned the whole thing for their greater good. Time, he thought, would tell. In any event, it was a very interesting development.

While open-minded about it, he was sure Chinese Lady would totally disapprove of any move into Europe by Britain. In his wife's views, Europe was full of foreigners, and Germany was the birthplace of Kaiser Wilhelm and Adolf Hitler. It was no good telling her that Hitler had actually been born in Austria. Chinese Lady had long ago placed him alongside Kaiser Wilhelm as a German warmonger who ought never to have been born, or to have been drowned as soon as he first saw the light of day. His silly moustache, she once said, ought to have told the doctor he was going to be a nuisance to everyone.

Sir Edwin pointed out that at birth Hitler would have had no moustache. Chinese Lady said she was convinced that at birth he had his moustache and all his wicked intentions as well. She said it was like when the Devil was born and God's angels saw that he already had horns. That was why he was cast out. And look what happened, he'd been a wicked nuisance ever since. Lord knows what would happen if the Devil and Hitler were both alive together. Blow the world up, I should think, she said.

One could not dispute with Chinese Lady on this particular subject. One accepted it was one of her favourite hobby horses, and that she rode it frequently and at length.

Chapter Ten

'Right, here we are, Deirdre,' said Sammy at twenty past ten the following morning.

'It's Lily, Mr Sammy,' said the lovelorn lady from the bookkeeping department. 'Deirdre's one of the invoice clerks.'

'So she is,' said Sammy. 'Silly me. Got a lot on my mind, that's the trouble. Anyway, you can have these bank statements back for your files now. I've seen all I want to.'

Mrs Lily Chambers leaned over his desk and reached for the statements. Sammy looked up into her eyes, and she looked down into his. His were blue and very clear, hers were hazel and kind of misty again. She drew a needful breath. She was quite confident about her looks and her sex appeal, but all the same, asking Mr Sammy if he'd like to romance with her in a field of cowslips or whatever, well, it wasn't the easiest thing in the world.

'Mr Sammy—'

'You all right, Lily?' said Sammy. 'Only you look a bit fuzzy.'

'Oh, I'm all right in meself,' said Lily, 'it's me emotions that are getting the better of me.' She sighed, leaned further over and whispered, 'Mr Sammy, if I asked you if you'd like to—'

A knock on Sammy's office door interrupted her, and in came one of the general office girls. She was carrying Sammy's morning coffee and biscuit. Oh, blow, thought Lily, I didn't think about it being as bothersome as this to get Mr Sammy to myself for a few minutes. But I might have remembered how busy these offices always are, especially where Mr Adams and Mr Sammy are concerned. By Mr Adams, she meant Boots. As the eldest of the three brothers, that was how he was addressed.

'Coffee, Mr Sammy,' cooed the girl, glancing at Lily as she placed the refreshments on the desk. Lily smiled kind of vaguely.

'Thanks, Jane, just the job,' said Sammy. He looked up at Lily.

'There we are, then, take the statements and go and enjoy your own coffee.'

'Oh, right,' said Lily, and was accompanied out by the general office girl. I'm being persecuted in a way, she thought. Well, that's what it feels like. But I won't let it stand in my way, I've got to let Mr Sammy know I'm in love with

115

him. I wonder if he'd feel flattered? After all, he's middle-aged, so he might feel flattered at having a young woman in love with him. I'm hardly much over thirty. Well, thirty-three is still young compared to middle age. Not that Mr Sammy looks middle-aged. More like just how a real man should look. Joe doesn't look much except in his best suit, and then not a lot.

I wonder if Mr Sammy will want to meet me regular outside the office, say in a hotel—

'Wake up, Lily, you'll fall over in a minute.'

The sound of a colleague's voice brought her out of her dreams. She realized she was back in the bookkeepers' office and was simply standing there, in front of her desk, the bank statements in her hand.

'Oh, silly me,' she said, 'I was thinking about going to see that film, *Bridge on the River Kwai*. They say it's ever so good.'

The senior bookkeeper reminded her she could think about that in her own time, not the firm's, so would she kindly get on with her work. What an old goat, thought Lily, he'd never understand any woman's emotions.

At the end of the day, Lily made her way down to the first floor. Passing Mr Sammy's office, she stopped, turned back and knocked on his door.

'Come in.'

Lily opened the door and put her head in. Mr Sammy was alone at his desk.

'Oh, I just wanted to say goodnight, Mr Sammy,' she said.

Sammy was poring over a report on the present position of the property company, a report prepared by the company's joint managing directors; namely, his elder son Daniel, and Boots's son Tim. If the garments factory was under threat of a possible strike, well, the progress of the property company at least made for a happy moment.

Looking up to see who it was at his door, he said, 'Yes, goodnight, Lily.'

Lily drew one of her emotional breaths, stepped in, closed the door and advanced with the swiftness of a bird in flight. Arriving at Sammy's desk, she leaned over it and whispered.

'Mr Sammy?'

Sammy came to.

'Lily?'

'Yes, it's me,' breathed Lily, looking down once more into his clear blue eyes. 'I want to ask you something.'

'Something?' said Sammy, ready to leave as soon as he had finished his reading of the report.

'Yes, something very intimate,' whispered Lily, feeling a bit giddy and a bit breathless.

'Come again?' said Sammy, startled.

'Would you like to come and see where I live?'

'Eh?'

'Mr Sammy—'

The door opened and Mrs Rachel Goodman, invaluable asset to the firm, called, 'Goodnight, Sammy – oh, and goodnight, Lily.'

'Wait a tick,' said Sammy, a trifle hoarse.

'I'm in no hurry,' said Rachel, stepping in and holding the door open for Lily.

Lily, thwarted once more, had no option but to step out, doing so with a slightly bitter glance at Rachel. She went down the stairs to the ground floor and out into the street, thinking there had to be a way of locking herself in with Mr Sammy. There had to be some way of preventing any interruptions.

In his office, Sammy spoke to Rachel.

'I think I'll have to talk to Lily sometime.'

'Oh?' said Rachel. 'Sammy, are you looking a little bothered?'

Sammy said he'd just had a narrow escape from a fainting fit, brought about by Mrs Lily Chambers asking him something very intimate. She needed help, he said, and he might have needed some himself if Rachel hadn't appeared at the right moment.

'Why, what happened?' asked Rachel.

118

Sammy said he hardly knew how to explain. Rachel urged him to try.

'You won't believe it,' said Sammy, still off balance, 'and I don't know I believe it meself.'

'Try me,' said Rachel.

Sammy, mentally wandering about in the land of the unbelievable, said Lily had asked him if he'd like to come and see where she lived, and he knew what that meant. He was just about to have the aforementioned fainting fit, he said, when Rachel came to his rescue by appearing at his door. Talk about a lifeboat for a drowning man.

'Might I enquire why you're laughing, Rachel?' he asked.

'I should be crying?' said Rachel. 'Poor Sammy. I told you the lady fancied you.'

'Well, someone had better tell her it's out of order, especially in working hours,' said Sammy. 'She's a married female, ain't she?'

'True, Sammy, she is.'

'Then someone's going to have to tell her to fancy her old man, which is legal and proper,' said Sammy. 'I don't want her to give me another fainting fit.'

'I think everyone here would leave you to do the talking, Sammy,' said Rachel.

'It's just occurred to me that it ought to be woman to woman,' said Sammy.

'Oh, I think man to woman in this case,' said Rachel, quite sure she preferred to stand aside, and that Lily Chambers would accept a talking-to from no-one except Sammy himself.

'Well, I suppose it's got to be me,' said Sammy, 'although I don't know I'm cut out for telling a married female bookkeeper to stick to her ledgers and forget about adultery.'

'You'll find a way, Sammy,' said Rachel, smiling. It had its funny side. Sammy in the sights of a fanciful female was not so much an energetic and fearless business boss as a confused man looking for a way out.

'Be firm, be fatherly.'

'That's something else I don't want to be,' said Sammy.

'And what's that?' asked Rachel.

'Her daddy,' said Sammy. 'Incidentally, Susie's against illegal goings-on.'

'I know,' said Rachel, who, during the course of many long years, had never attempted in the slightest way to come between the twain, even though she had always preferred Sammy to any other man. 'But my life, Lily Chambers isn't? There's a surprise for the innocent. Yes, talk to her, Sammy.'

'I'll have to,' said Sammy, figuratively wiping the sweat from his brow.

★   ★   ★

'You wanted to see me, Mr Sammy?' said Lily the following morning, Friday. She was at the open door of his office, having received a summons.

'Yes, come in, Lily,' said Sammy, bracing himself. Lily entered in a spirit of hope. She'd had a worrying time at home last night. Well, perhaps not worrying. More like puzzling. Getting to be alone with Mr Sammy, even if only for a few minutes, did seem a bit of a puzzle. Joe had asked her again if she'd got something on her mind, which she had, but which she couldn't tell him. And he didn't give her time to, anyway, because he was off to his Thursday darts match almost as soon as he'd asked the question. This morning, however, the summons to come down and see Mr Sammy had raised her hopes. 'Close the door,' he said.

Lily closed the door and Sammy found himself alone with this female bookkeeper who apparently fancied him. Didn't she know he was a happily married man looking forward to the wedding of his youngest daughter? They were a funny lot, women. They didn't coincide with men, so a bloke could never be certain what any of them were thinking. He'd asked Boots once what could be done about the way some women carried on. Boots had said find a magician who can rearrange them.

'Mr Sammy?' said Lily hopefully, her mind on what she had said to him last evening.

'Oh, yes, it's you, Lily,' said Sammy, who was trying to convince himself she hadn't said anything except goodnight. 'Sit down.' Lily seated herself. She looked very nice in a light grey suit and a white shirt-blouse. 'Now,' said Sammy.

'Yes, Mr Sammy?' said Lily, who couldn't think that an hour in the buttercups with him could actually be counted as sinful. Her gaze was soulful.

'How are you finding your job these days?' asked Sammy, doing his best to avoid falling into this barmy female's starry eyes. Long ago, he'd fallen into Susie's optics, and had never been the same since.

Lily, hoping for something more than questions about her job, said she was enjoying her work as much now as when she first started. She liked bookkeeping, she said, much more than typing or operating a switchboard or just being a general office clerk.

'I hope, Mr Sammy, you haven't found me wanting, like,' she said. 'I mean, I hope no-one's had cause to complain about me work.'

'No, no-one,' said Sammy. 'It just occurred

to me that you might be finding it a bit nerve-racking.'

'D'you mean is the work getting on me nerves?' said Lily. 'No, nothing's getting on me nerves except my husband's darts. He's darts mad. But it's not that that's affecting me emotions, it's something else and it's sort of taking me over.' She plunged on. 'It's what made me speak very intimately to you last evening, I just couldn't help meself, and if—'

'I'm trying to forget that.' Sammy's interruption was hasty. 'In fact, I'm trying to tell myself it never happened.'

'Oh, it happened, Mr Sammy—'

'Frankly, it's all a blur to me.'

'Mr Sammy, you fancy me a bit, don't you?'

'Listen, Lily, my favourite female woman is still my wife.'

'Well, I honour you for that, but it needn't mean you can't enjoy a bit of romance with me now and again.'

'It means exactly that.'

'Mr Sammy, don't you want to make love to me?'

'Eh? In my office in working time?' Sammy was totally confused.

'Lor', no, not in here, Mr Sammy, more like in a country hotel or somewhere nice and quiet.'

Sammy nearly fell off his chair. It took a little time to gather himself and talk turkey to her. He told her then that she was halfway round the bend, that she had a husband, he had a wife and that if she didn't get back to her work by the time he counted ten, he'd call in a doctor and have her examined. He also told her it was against the rules to think illegal things in office hours, and that she'd be better off if she took up darts with her old man.

Lily tried the protest of a woman who'd only had their mutual interests at heart. It didn't work. Sammy left her with no option but to return to her desk. She did so unhappily, but after ten minutes or so was convincing herself he was probably already feeling he'd been unkind to her, and also a bit barmy to have turned her down.

Opening up ledgers, she thought again of love in a meadow, and she didn't worry that she was thinking about it in office hours. She was ever the optimist, and often the airy-fairy. As for Sammy, he let Rachel know that he'd talked to Lily and told her to be like her old man and go in for darts. Rachel, of course, thought that very amusing.

On Monday, the daily papers carried reports of a threatened strike in the garments industry.

124

The union concerned spoke of underpaid workers, and of the necessity of obtaining a reasonable wage rise for both skilled and un- skilled operatives. What was reasonable? Not less than seven and a half per cent. Seeing that in black and white almost spoiled breakfast not only for Sammy, but Tommy as well.

The reports included comments from repre- sentatives of the employers' federation, mainly to the effect that a seven and a half per cent rise across the board was not only far from being reasonable, it was non-negotiable. The union, accordingly, must think again. Sammy con- curred, while at the same time sweating, along with Tommy, over what a strike would do to the firm and its retail shops.

On Tuesday, the press reported that the employers' federation had countered union threats with a threat of their own, that of closing down their factories indefinitely. Sammy thought about offering up a prayer, but common sense told him the Almighty would hardly concern Himself with an East End garments factory when there were earthquakes happening in the wider world. Later in the day came reports that the employers had made an offer, a rise of two and a half per cent. If that was not accepted, then the federation would order the shutdown of all factories. The union at once declared their workers had been insulted, and demanded not less than five per cent. Failure to agree would compel the union to order all workers out. Sammy and Tommy spoke to Boots, and Boots said they only had one option. What was that? Wait for the next move, said Boots.

On Wednesday, when Sammy was beginning to feel ill, and Tommy's loyal factory workers were reluctantly preparing to down tools, the employers' federation upped their offer to three per cent. The union leaders discussed this at lunchtime over a glass of beer and a pork pie. By four thirty that afternoon, a compromise figure of three and a half per cent across the board had been agreed. This cured Sammy's feverish brow, since he knew the firm could absorb the cost of that increase without making the balance sheet look unhappy. On his way home from the office, he bought a bottle of champagne. Over supper, he, Susie and Phoebe celebrated the outcome of the negotiations. Phoebe said that what she liked about champagne was that it made you feel expensively squiffy. Susie said that what she liked about it was that it didn't make her feel squiffy at all, just happy. And Sammy said that what he liked about it was the reason for buying it.

Yes, what with the outcome of the strike negotiations and the fact that Lily Chambers had accepted a fatherly talking-to, Sammy considered the reason for buying the bubbly was as good as it could be.

He little knew Lily was lying in wait, as it were.

Chapter Eleven

On the third Saturday in June, the day was bright and clear, with not a cloud in sight. Miss Phoebe Adams, in shimmering white, with a delicate veil and a headdress of imitation orange blossom, arrived at the Denmark Hill church well on time. That is, only five minutes late, which was pretty good going considering how long it had taken her mum and her bridesmaids to get her ready to their and her own total satisfaction. It had been worth every minute. Pretty, dark-haired Phoebe, twenty, looked positively the bride of the year. Well, that was what Sammy thought. And so did Susie.

She arrived in state, Sammy beside her in Mr Greenberg's polished-up cart, pulled by a pony also polished up. Sammy wore a morning suit and a grey topper. Mr Greenberg wore his Sunday suit and a black topper. The pony wore some gleaming brass.

Sammy, descending, helped the bride to

alight, in a rustle of silk and lace. Silver-stockinged ankles peeped above silvery slippers. Phoebe considered that every young lady should look perfect from head to foot on one day in her life, her wedding day.

'Proud of you, pet, proud of you,' smiled Sammy.

'I love you, Daddy, you've been so good to me,' whispered his emotional adopted daughter. She knew the whole tragic history of how she came to belong to Sammy and Susie. The murder of her parents by a madman had left her, a small child, alone and bereft, and subsequently found by Sammy in a Walworth street near the Elephant and Castle. If the story, once it was made known to her, had haunted her, never had she failed in her love for her adoptive parents. Her life was paralleled by that of Rosie, who had been adopted by Boots and his first wife, Emily.

Phoebe straightened the flowing skirt of her gown while Mr Greenberg, having put a nosebag on his pony, did the right thing by preceding bride and father into the church, where he joined Mrs Greenberg. Then, on Sammy's arm, Phoebe advanced to be met by the smiling vicar, with the pink-clad brides-maids standing to one side, all enchanted at Phoebe's arrival in full array.

Inside the church, the organist heralded the entrance of the bride, and the congregation came to its feet. Heads turned. Following the vicar, Phoebe and Sammy slowly walked forward, the bridesmaids behind them, amid murmurs of delight at the colourful appearance of the ritual procession.

Since most of the assembled people were related to both the bride and the groom, there were equal numbers on either side of the aisle. By the chancel steps stood the groom and the best man. Philip was in his RAF uniform, his best man being cousin Jimmy. He watched the advance of his bride with a warm glow in his eyes.

'Jimmy, is that my Phoebe?' he whispered.

'Can't hear a word you're saying,' murmured Jimmy. The organ music was at its mightiest.

Arriving at the chancel steps, Sammy relinquished his daughter to Philip and stepped back. From under her veil, Phoebe regarded her bridegroom. A smile glimmered. Philip returned it.

'Phoebe, you angel,' he whispered.

The vicar took charge then, and the service began. Various members of the Adams families dreamed their dreams of their own times at an altar.

Chinese Lady and Sir Edwin sat on the left

with Susie, Chinese Lady thinking there was simply no end to weddings and births in her extensive family. She knew, as everyone did now, that Jimmy and Clare were going to be parents in October. And before her very eyes, here was young Philip being married to Phoebe. She glanced at her husband, and was pleased to note he was quite alert, following the service with a little smile on his face, as if he was remembering all the other family weddings he and she had attended. He was happy about the fact that she had found a real blessing in Mrs Plumstead. He had said an invaluable maid of all work was her due. Well, not in all her born years had she ever thought anything like that would be her due, especially as she'd been a maid of all work herself in her single days. Dear goodness, how strange life was, and how good the Lord had been to her since her striving days in Walworth following the death of her first husband, Daniel, on the North-West Frontier. If her reflections then took her back into the past, her subconscious kept her in tune with the marriage service.

On the right of the aisle sat Philip's parents, Annabelle and Nick Harrison, with Philip's grandmother Lizzy. Annabelle looked a little misty-eyed. She was remembering her own wedding, more than twenty years ago. She touched her husband's hand. Nick glanced. She smiled. He pressed her fingers. She might be getting a little bossy, but she was still his Annabelle.

Lizzy, of course, was thinking emotionally of her wartime wedding to Ned at St John's Church, Walworth, in 1916. She thought of her ride to the church in Mr Greenberg's pony and cart, and then the ride with Ned to the reception at the old family house in Walworth. It was long, long ago, but today it seemed like only yesterday. Today, Ned was with her in spirit, she was sure. Well, he was most days.

Tommy and Vi sat with Vi's mum, old Aunt Victoria. The aged lady had managed to attend, the warm weather and the special aspect of the occasion drawing her out of doors and into the church. She was mumbling softly to herself, as if repeating the words of the service. Or she might have been inaudibly taking Philip to task for being far too young to shoulder the responsibilities of marriage. Old Aunt Victoria could still spill a grumble or two, mellowed though she was.

Polly and Boots sat with James, Tim and Felicity. Felicity had blurred views of the spectacle, alternating with brief spells of clarity.

Which she rated as miraculous.

It meant that her blinded eyes really were

132

being cured by a long-term process of natural healing. At least, that was what she and Tim believed, and what her specialist encouraged them to believe. She was living in a world that, after many years of being blank to her, had been gradually opening up over a period of a year and more. At this particular moment, Phoebe was a blur of misty white. Seconds later she emerged from cloudiness to become clear and shimmering. The bridesmaids, including Felicity's own darling daughter Jennifer, came through in similar fashion, a blurred conglomerate of pink one moment, and four clear figures of enchantment the next.

Life's punishing hand was easing its grip, positively so.

'How are things looking, Puss?' whispered Tim.

'Lovely.'

The service ended.

'I now pronounce you man and wife.' So said the benign vicar.

Phoebe lifted her veil, showed her happy face to Philip, and received her first kiss as his wife.

There, one more wedding, said Chinese Lady to herself, and who's next, I wonder?

Well, there were several who, by reason of their age, wouldn't be long before they were courting. (Chinese Lady took no notice of the fact that the word 'courting' was now regarded as outmoded as the bustle.) The twins, Gemma and James, and Rosie's two, Giles and Emily, were all in their teens. Lord, she thought, I just hope that some of this fast modern living that I see on television doesn't rub off on any of our young people. I'm sure it isn't what the Lord ordered. I heard Boots say only a little while ago that these days some young people don't recognize the Lord, only Elvis Presley, but he didn't say who Elvis Presley was. I must remember to ask him, though I don't suppose I'll get a sensible answer.

The reception was held in the church hall, the wedding breakfast the responsibility of caterers, the place packed with relatives and friends. Cindy Stevens, fifteen-year-old daughter of Harry and Anneliese Stevens, friends of Polly and Boots, collared James and treated him to an exposition on how she was managing her social life and how she was getting on at her Camberwell grammar school. James, fifteen himself and looking progressively more like his father as he grew up, said he didn't really want to discuss education as he was living with it most days and liked to get away from it at weekends and family weddings.

'Still,' he said kindly, 'you look nice in your

new frock, and I daresay Bruce and Clive will like it.' Bruce and Clive were a regular part of Cindy's social life in Camberwell. Even at only fifteen, she liked more than one string to her bow. In addition, she liked boys who didn't mind being ordered about. In this respect, James played his own tune.

'I'm dressed special for the wedding,' she said. Her lemon-coloured creation was delightfully pretty. 'You sure you like it?'

'Great,' said James.

'D'you want to kiss me, then?' asked Cindy.

'Not just now,' said James. 'I'm eating bits and pieces at the moment.' The wedding breakfast was buffet style, and James, like most people present, had a plate of food in his hand.

'Later, then, when I leave,' said Cindy. 'Oh, I'm going dancing with friends this evening at Brixton. D'you want to come with us?'

'I'll ask my parents,' said James.

'Crikey, you don't actually have to ask them, do you?' said Cindy. 'Don't you just say you're going?'

'No, I ask,' said James, 'that's the way it is in my family. I suppose I could have fought it when it first started, but I didn't, and so I'll have to stick to the rules till I'm older. It's force of habit.'

'Well, your parents are awfully nice, so that

makes up a bit for those rules,' said Cindy, who for years as a very young girl had virtually ordered the life of her widower dad, Harry. He was now married to Anneliese, a German woman, so Cindy had passed her responsibilities to her stepmother, which left her free to enjoy the exciting social life of a modern teenager. 'Oh, there's Giles,' she said, 'I must say hello to him.' And away she went to give James's cousin Giles the benefit of her company and a close-up view of her frock.

'Wow,' said Giles, fifteen and pretty cool, 'is that you, Cindy?'

'None other,' said Cindy. She was coming to see Giles as a bit special, and Giles sometimes thought about having her as a regular girlfriend. But his mother thought regular girlfriends were the privilege of boys of seventeen or more, and his dad said no point in committing yourself at fifteen, sonny, it'll give you a headache. Well, it was all something to think about in a couple of years or so.

'Cindy, you're looking great,' he said.

'Come on, let's eat together,' said Cindy, and they made their way to the buffet and to an afternoon of lively companionship.

Meanwhile, the bride and groom were going the rounds and giving everyone a chance to wish them well. That took time, because every friend and relative had plenty to say. Certainly, plenty to say was endemic with most Adamses, and friends were always encouraged to speak their piece. Eventually, however, the speeches were made and the toasts drunk amid laughter and revelry. Subsequently, while the afternoon was still young, the happy couple were showered with confetti as they were driven away by Mr Greenberg to Phoebe's home. There they would change and Sammy would drive them to the station on the first leg of their journey to their honeymoon destination at Salcombe in Devon.

'Good luck, Phoebe!'

'Good luck, Philip! Happy landing!'

'Yup, watch your undercarriage!'

That brought shrieks of laughter, which somewhat puzzled Chinese Lady. She enquired of Boots what Tommy meant by shouting at Philip to watch his undercarriage. Boots thought about an answer, then said that Philip was an airman and that every plane had an undercarriage, including his own, that it held the wheels and that Tommy was merely reminding Philip not to let them fall off. All of which was as good as double Dutch to Chinese Lady, but typical of her only oldest son's habit of confusing her more than answering her.

Down Denmark Hill the newly-weds travelled,

Mr Greenberg keeping his equipage at a slow walk for the benefit of delighted passers-by and people watching from their windows. The pace also gave the young couple time to enjoy the moment, to which Mr Greenberg thought them entitled.

'Vell, vhat a happy vedding, eh, Mr and Mrs?' he chuckled.

'Lovely,' said Phoebe, eyes bright, and face a little flushed.

'Wizard,' said Philip in RAF lingo. 'Who caught your bouquet? I didn't notice.'

'Jennifer,' said Phoebe.

'Not a bad piece of fielding for a girl only twelve,' said Philip.

True, young Jennifer did have the bouquet. It was resting in her arms as she and the other bridesmaids, colourful in the sunshine, watched the pony and cart on its journey down the hill. She was giggling over her armful.

'See, you're next,' said Gemma, fifteen, and much like Polly, her mother, because of the piquant look of her features.

'Well, I don't suppose it'll be next week exactly,' said Jennifer.

'Or next year even,' said Emily, two months short of fourteen, but with all the self-assurance of an older girl. Her hair, like that of Rosie, her mother, was the colour of golden corn.

'Well, I'm not in a hurry,' said Jennifer, and waved as the pony and cart progressed further down the hill. Then she glanced at Linda. Linda, she knew, would be nineteen next month. 'Go on, Linda, you have this,' she said, and pressed the bouquet into her arms.

'I don't think it counts unless you catch it,' smiled Linda, noted for her undemanding nature. Grandmother Lizzy thought her a sweet girl.

With some guests ready to move from the pavement back into the hall, a young man in a cream-coloured sports shirt and blue slacks approached at a smart pace. He slowed, however, when he saw Linda and the bridal bouquet. He stopped to smile at her.

'A wedding?' he said. He looked to be in his mid-twenties, with a widow's peak to his black hair.

Startled by his directness, Linda turned faintly pink.

'Beg pardon?' she said.

'Have I bumped into a wedding and the bride herself?' asked the young man blithely.

'Me?' Linda went pinker. Jennifer, Gemma and Emily giggled.

'That's your bridal bouquet?' said the young man, looking at it.

Linda made a recovery.

'The bride's in white,' she said, 'and you've just missed her.'

'I get it now,' said the young man, not a bit bashful as he took note that all four girls were clad in delicate pink. 'You're the bridesmaids.'

'Brilliant,' said Emily.

'And you caught the bride's bouquet,' said the young man, addressing Linda again. 'That means you're going to be next. Who's the lucky chap?'

'And who's not backward in coming forward?' said Gemma aside.

Linda addressed the young man.

'Excuse me, but do you know me? I don't think I know you.'

'No, I don't know you,' said the young man, 'but I've been overcome by a feeling that I'd like to.'

'Crikey, listen to him,' said Gemma, a teenager with style, and all four girls became involved with the interloper while the rest of the guests lingered to watch the pony and cart turn into the drive of Sammy's house far down the hill. It was a day for lingering in the sunshine, and for the intrigued bridesmaids to take stock of a young man not suffering from shyness or inhibitions.

'So what's your name?' He asked the question of Linda.

'Blessed impertinence,' said Gemma.

The young man said he was guessing that this was the wedding of Phoebe Adams, daughter of Mr Sammy Adams, well-known South London businessman.

'We're not telling,' said Jennifer.

'It's Linda,' said Emily, always inclined to make up her own mind, whether or not it was against the majority.

'What a pretty name,' said the young man, his smile exclusively for her. 'Well, I'm very pleased to meet you.'

'Come along, you girls,' called Annabelle. All the guests, except the bridesmaids, were moving back into the hall.

'I think you'd better go away before my father wants to know what you're up to,' said Linda to her admirer.

'You're right, I'm butting in,' he said. 'Still, how about if I call on you and introduce myself to your parents?'

'I can't believe I'm hearing this,' said Linda.

'Nor me,' said Gemma, fascinated by this prime example of how a bloke went about picking up a girl.

'You'd better buzz off before you get a black eye,' said Emily, 'and, anyway, we're all going back into the hall now.'

'Yes, goodbye,' said Linda, and she and

the other bridesmaids followed the rest of the guests into the hall. But she looked over her shoulder to see the young man going on his way. He was whistling.

'Crikey, Linda, you made a hit,' said Jennifer.

'But talk about his nerve,' said Gemma.

'Still, he was a bit of a looker,' said Emily.

Linda kept quiet. She preferred not to be the centre of attention.

Chapter Twelve

At her parents' home, Phoebe said goodbye and thanks to Mr Greenberg, telling him the ride had been terrific. Philip added his own thanks. Mr Greenberg wished them long life and happiness, and as he drove back to the hall to pick up his wife, even his beard wore a smile.

In the house, Phoebe ascended the stairs in billowing style, while Philip followed on. On the landing he kissed her, lovingly and with feeling. Phoebe said to mind her gown. Philip said he'd be happy to put it in an old oak chest and mind it for ever. It would always remind him of the day he acquired a bride, a lover and a cook. Phoebe told him he'd mentioned that in his speech, and it was no funnier now than then. Philip said he couldn't remember one word of his speech, because although the occasion had been really wizard, it had also left him a bit dizzy.

'When's your dad coming to motor us to the station?' he asked.

'In forty minutes,' said Phoebe.

'We'd better get changed, then,' said Philip.

'Yes, you there,' said Phoebe, pointing to what had been her brother Jimmy's bedroom, 'and me here.' She opened the door of her own room.

'Wait a bit,' said Philip, 'we're married now.'

'Yes, but I'm not used to it yet,' said Phoebe, 'so you don't think I'm going to undress in front of you, do you?'

'I could turn out to be a great help, and I could learn something about you,' said Philip. 'Something memorable.'

'Goodness me, I couldn't allow that,' said Phoebe, 'I've still got my full quota of modesty. Ask me again in a month or so. Go on, change in Jimmy's room.'

'Funny girl,' smiled Philip, but did as she wanted. One had to acknowledge that a bride could be shy, even if she did now own all his worldly goods and was due to share the honeymoon bed with him.

That took place late at night, in their room at a Salcombe hotel. Despite her declared modesty, Phoebe was a natural in her responsiveness, being healthy of mind and body. And Philip was already a worldly young man by reason of his

144

time in the RAF, which had included some bomber raids on Port Said during the brief war against Egypt. Not that his advances towards his bride were aggressive. He certainly didn't drop bombs on her. His flight was accurate but loving, his landing definite but gentle.

The evening's recreation capped the wedding celebrations for some of the young people. Giles, Emily, Gemma, James and Cindy all went to a dance in Brixton on the promise of being home by ten thirty. Although the band was only a local one, it wasn't half bad. The youngsters, together with two boyfriends of Cindy, swung and jived to the beat, and Emily was picked up by a Teddy boy whose prowess impressed her. He had a quiff to his hair like that sported by Tony Curtis, rising young Hollywood star. If Emily was impressed by his sinuous movements, he was even more impressed by her teenage allure and vivacity.

'Man, oh, man, you're something, baby,' he said in reckless abandon.

'You're not bad yourself,' she said, conscious that brother Giles was watching her. She took no notice of what might be bothering him. Her life was her own.

'What's your name?'

'None of your biz.'

'I'm Brad.'

'Brad?'

'Short for Bradley.'

'Is that a name or a town?'

'It's my baptismal.' His baptismal was actually Albert. Albert Thompson. But he called himself Bradley because he liked its American sound. Impressively, he executed a bit of a jig, perfectly in harmony with the beat, his drainpipe trousers clinging to his legs and a slight dent in his carefully moulded brilliantined quiff. 'So what's yours, Queenie?'

'It's not Queenie, I'll tell you that much.'

This friendly fencing went on for a few more minutes, by the end of which Emily had surrendered her name and Bradley had reset his quiff. The time was now coming up to ten o'clock, and some youngsters were beginning to leave in order to be home no later than the hour set by their parents. Somewhere out in the world was a youth movement advocating that young people should be free to set their own time. Everyone was a free individual, wasn't that so? Not yet, and not according to parents who believed they were still in charge of their children's comings and goings. But there was a movement, all the same, or the beginning of one.

★　　　★　　　★

At her home on Red Post Hill, Rosie glanced again at the lounge clock. Five minutes to eleven.

'Matt, what's happened to them?' she asked of her husband.

'I'm asking myself that,' said Matt, unwinding his sinewy frame from his deep armchair and coming to his feet. Four years older than Rosie, he was now forty-six, and the couple had reached their prime in a spirit of undemanding content. Any real worries they had concerned the future of Giles and Emily, for they were both aware of changing attitudes, and of the tendency of many young people to adopt a completely new way of life. And that new way did not appeal overmuch to either Rosie or Matt, for it seemed to be based on a lack of responsibility. It was a time when much was being made of the importance of young people's feelings, interests and expectations, and this was encouraging the young to feel important.

'Eleven o'clock is too late for a thirteen-year-old girl to be out,' said Rosie, never one to ask the unreasonable of her children.

'Well, at least we know Giles is with her,' said Matt. He waited several more minutes, then said, 'I think I'll phone Boots and find out if James and Gemma are back, and if they know what's happened to our two.'

To Rosie's relief, the missing pair arrived home then. Matt went to speak to them. She heard them in the hall. She heard Giles say something.

'I tell you, Dad, she's been a load of trouble.'

'No, I haven't, I just forgot the time.' That was Emily. 'Anyway, it isn't late.' It was ten past eleven. 'Not really late.'

'It's well over your time,' said Matt, and he returned to the lounge with the boy and girl following. 'Here they are, Rosie.'

Rosie was on her feet. She noted the apologetic look of Giles and a suspicion of defiance in Emily.

'What happened?' she asked.

'Nothing,' said Emily, 'we're home, Mum, aren't we?'

'Forty minutes late,' said Rosie, 'and that's not playing the game. What happened, Giles?'

'I blundered,' said Giles, a dark-haired, sinewy boy not unlike his rangy father. 'I let her disappear. Well, she was there one minute and gone the next, with a Ted who looked like Tony Curtis. And it was ten then, time for us to leave, along with James and Gemma. They stayed to help me find her.'

'I don't like the sound of Teddy boys who look like Tony Curtis,' said Matt.

'He was all right,' said Emily, 'and I didn't

disappear with him. We just went with the swing. Then I forgot about the time. Anyway, as I said, it's not really late. There were a lot of other young people on our bus.'

'Not as young as thirteen, I hope,' said Rosie.

'Well, I don't know what any of them thought of the way Giles went on at me, like an old fusspot,' said Emily.

'Giles had the responsibility of finding you and getting you home,' said Matt. 'Don't let it happen again. I expect your Aunt Polly worried about Gemma and James being late.'

'Crikey, Dad, I hope you're not going to be a fusspot too,' said Emily.

'Watch out for me being a tough one myself if it does happen again,' said Rosie.

'Do I always have to have Giles with me?' asked Emily.

'Yes, you do,' said Rosie.

'To my sorrow,' said Giles, who considered that being responsible for a sister as awkward as Emily was a bit of a burden for a brother. But there it was, while she was still so young he had to keep an eye on her, and to make sure she didn't get involved with the wrong kind of person. It was a parental dictum. Giles understood that. Emily, however, thought it had something to do with Queen Victoria and covered-up table legs.

Chapter Thirteen

Sunday morning.

Susie and Sammy, at breakfast, were fully aware that their home was going to be quieter now that all their children had lives of their own. Quietness was much valued by some people, but not necessarily by parents who had enjoyed the sounds of buoyant offspring growing up, never mind the moments when the sounds and the buoyancy were a bit primitive.

'I'm feeling – I don't know what I'm feeling,' murmured Sammy.

'Flat?' Susie was sympathetic.

'Something like that,' said Sammy.

'Never mind, Sammy, it was a lovely wedding,' said Susie.

'Except it's made today feel a bit half-baked,' said Sammy. 'They've all left us now, Susie. Daniel, Bess, Paula, Jimmy and Phoebe. We're going to miss Phoebe like we've missed the others.'

'I know that, Sammy love,' said Susie, 'but we've still got each other.' She smiled. 'And the business.'

Sammy perked up.

'That's a point,' he said. 'Better than just sitting around, you doing knitting and me twiddling me thumbs. I've got to be thankful for that. Listen, d'you think Phoebe will make it with Philip?'

'Make what, Sammy?'

'Happy ever after.'

'Of course she will.' Susie was definite. 'Those two were made for each other.' She smiled again. 'Sammy, you may be a tough businessman, but you're still an old softie.'

'Hope they'll get some decent married quarters,' said Sammy.

'I'm sure they will, they're getting officers' quarters, aren't they?' said Susie. Phoebe was going to travel up to Philip's station two days after they returned from Salcombe. 'Which reminds me, we'll have them with us for the weekend when they get back.'

'So we will, at the end of the honeymoon,' said Sammy. A little grin flitted. 'Newly-weds being a bit quick off the mark, Susie, I wonder how soon we'll be talking about more grandchildren?'

'It's not something you need worry about,' said Susie.

'Except that more grandchildren really will make me feel old,' said Sammy.

'Oh, you'll cope with that as long as you can still keep your eye on the business overheads,' said Susie, 'and in any case, you've still got a few unwrinkled years in front of you.'

'I'm obliged to hear you say so, Susie.'

'Don't mention it, Sammy.'

At ten fifteen Annabelle answered a knock on her front door. A smiling young man in a sweater and slacks greeted her.

'Good morning, am I addressing Mrs Harrison?'

'I'm Mrs Harrison.'

'Hello, Mrs Harrison, I'm Nigel Killiner, how d'you do?'

'I'm very well, thank you,' said Annabelle, 'but what brings you to my door, might I ask? I'm sure we don't know each other.'

'I had the pleasure of meeting your daughter yesterday,' said the young gent called Nigel, 'and I wondered if she—'

'Excuse me, but my daughter was at a wedding yesterday,' said Annabelle, 'the wedding of my son. So I don't think you could have met her.'

'Oh, it was like this,' said Nigel, and explained in winning fashion exactly how he had met Linda, one of four bridesmaids, pointing out she had been in possession of the bridal bouquet at the time. Annabelle, studying the caller with suspicion, said she didn't consider that a proper meeting, much more like a piece of cheek.

'I see your point,' said Nigel, 'but I couldn't help myself. It's strange how a chap can plan his day in very conventional fashion, and then have it all changed by something that can rise up out of nowhere. I don't want to be pushy, but is there any chance of seeing your daughter this morning?'

'Not as far as I'm concerned,' said Annabelle, 'and you're definitely being pushy.'

'I don't mean to be,' said Nigel, not in the least put down, 'I'm simply hoping to get to know your daughter, and wondered if I could do that in a walk round the park with her this afternoon. Or does she happen to be involved in a serious relationship?'

Well, thought Annabelle, I don't know if I trust this specimen and his barefaced cheek.

'Who's that, Mum?' Linda herself appeared in the hall. Spotting the young man on the doorstep, she blinked and said, 'I don't believe it.'

'Good morning, Linda,' said Nigel, noting how summery she looked in a dress of apricot, 'I've called to see if you'd like to come for a walk round the park with me this afternoon.'

'Beg pardon?' Linda fell a victim to astonishment.

'That's if you're not otherwise engaged,' said Nigel.

'Oh, really?' said Linda.

'Let me introduce myself. I'm Nigel Killiner—'

'Thrilled, I don't think,' said Linda, defending her sense of what was right and proper. 'Kindly don't bother me.'

Annabelle hid a smile. Her daughter, caught off guard at first, was now on her mettle as a well-brought-up girl not given to falling for a smoothie.

'Linda, I think I can leave you to deal with this young man,' she said. 'If he persists, call your father.'

'Believe me, I don't bite,' said Nigel.

'My father does, and so do I,' said Linda.

Annabelle, moving aside, then did her stuff as a wise mother, particularly as she quite liked the look of the young man. True, his impertinence was outrageous, but some girls responded more to that kind of approach than to a conventional one.

'Yes, I'll leave you to deal with him, Linda,' she said, and went back to her kitchen.

'How d'you feel now about a walk round the park this afternoon?' asked Nigel of the young lady who had apparently taken his fancy more than somewhat.

'The same as I did when you first mentioned it,' said Linda, 'that I can hardly believe I heard right. And nor can I hardly believe you've got the nerve to actually come knocking.'

'I felt I had to,' said Nigel, who seemed likely to remain on her doorstep unless a typhoon carried him off. He happened to be the kind of bloke who, once he'd made up his mind about something, didn't easily give up. 'You sure you wouldn't like to take that walk with me?'

'I feel amazed that you think I would,' said Linda, not prepared to conjure up a typhoon herself. Well, she didn't often have this kind of intriguing cut and thrust with someone on the family doorstep, especially on a Sunday morning. A girl had to see it through before going off to church with friends of her own sex.

'You can trust me, you know,' said Nigel, who had no complaints about being kept where he was. It could turn out to be a kind of starting point to the parlour and to other things, and she really was worth the effort involved in taking his time. 'I'm entirely respectable.'

'Oh, really,' said Linda. 'How do I know you're not some kind of lunatic?'

'Well, I can tell you I'm not certified,' said Nigel. 'I'm twenty-six and a schoolteacher.'

'You're what?' Linda goggled.

'A schoolteacher. At a local—'

'Never mind.' If there was one thing Linda was certain of, it was the conviction that she wasn't made to be any teacher's girlfriend. Teachers were all right in their way and very useful to the community, but, from what she could remember of them during her schooldays, too much like their profession. They sort of talked at you. Which was just what this one had been doing to her. He might be a personable young man, but she could easily imagine that a walk round the park with him might be like a history lesson. 'Good morning, thank you for calling, Mr Kilner.'

'Killiner.'

'Good morning, Mr Killiner,' said Linda, and that was her cue to close the door on him. But it didn't happen. Hesitation raised its head, which gave Nigel the opportunity to ask her if she'd like him to call some other time. 'Certainly not,' she said. 'Oh, well,' she added weakly, 'what time this afternoon did you have in mind?'

'For walking you round the park?' said Nigel, looking surprised and pleased all at once. 'I could call for you at three, say.'

'I think you'd better come in and meet my dad,' said Linda.

'Pleasure,' said Nigel, and finally vacated the doorstep as Linda took him through the house to the garden, where Nick was doing something to the mower. Linda introduced her visitor. He was on easy terms with her dad inside a couple of minutes. Nick, like Annabelle, thought him an agreeable bloke, even if he had been a bit barefaced in his approach to Linda.

'So what's the proposition?' Nick asked the question of his daughter.

'Oh, a walk in the park this afternoon,' said Linda.

'Well, if that means the two of you want to get to know each other, go ahead,' said Nick, who thought that a boy-meets-girl event didn't always have to be in strictly approved circumstances. As for Annabelle, when told that the walk round the park was on, she raised no objections. She had decided that the agreeable side of Mr Nigel Killiner more than made up for his cheek. She was, however, surprised to know he was a schoolteacher.

'I don't think many schoolteachers have come knocking uninvited on our door,' she said to Linda after he had gone. 'It seems you made quite an impression on him yesterday.'

'D'you think so?' said Linda, not at all displeased. 'I'm just hoping that my time in the park this afternoon won't be like a history lesson, or how to find the square root of sixty-six.'

That raised a smile in Annabelle.

'Go and tell your father he can come in from the garden, that his coffee's ready,' she said.

'Yes, all right, then I'm off to church,' said Linda, thinking that her mother was inclined these days to give orders instead of making requests. Her dad usually made light of it, saying that slightly bossy mums compared very favourably with the occasional housewife who ran off with the milkman.

'Well, old sport,' said Polly to her husband in the balmy air of the afternoon, 'what d'you think of these?'

They were both in their large garden, James and Gemma being out. Polly, wearing a smock over her dress, was inspecting her runner-bean seedlings. Boots, in an old shirt and old slacks, was hoeing around a long bed of early green peas.

'What do I think of your runners?' Boots smiled. From the early days of their marriage, Polly had taken to gardening, although this was confined mainly to vegetable plots. She thoroughly revelled in the rewards of her labours, and always talked of the harvests in the possessive way of a lady who had personally nursed them from seeds through to fruition. 'Your runners, as usual, Polly, look as if they mean to grow ten feet high. And your early peas will be ready to pick any moment, if not sooner.'

'Well, keep hoeing, old scout, and you shall be served the first mouthful,' said Polly, carrying her years commendably well. The sunshine was kind to her. At her age, the bright light might have shown up natural defects. But Polly had the kind of application and approach to her physical self that ensured a happy degree of preservation. A few crow's feet around her eyes she could put up with. The lines that defaced many sixty-year-old women were still struggling to surface on Polly. This eased certain worries. As Boots's wife, she had a dread of hearing herself referred to as the old lady in his life.

On the other hand, Boots himself had said she was growing old gracefully, and that he hoped he was too. If not, the reverse might come about, and he might be referred to as the old man in her life. He laughed now as those thoughts came back to him.

'What's funny?' asked Polly, noting with a frown that one bean seedling had been under night attack from slugs.

'A politician in charge of a grocer's shop,' said Boots.

'A comedy of errors? We could all laugh at that,' said Polly. 'By the way, what did you think of Gemma's account of how Giles lost young Emily for half an hour last night?'

'I thought it a much longer account than the one James gave us,' said Boots, turning weeds so that their roots were unmercifully exposed to the sun. 'It was Gemma who told us that Emily insisted she wasn't lost, she was with a new friend.'

'A Teddy boy,' said Polly. 'Was that a happy revelation, d'you think, or a gruesome one?'

'I couldn't say unless I knew the chap,' said Boots, 'but I understand Teddy boys on the whole are quite harmless, that they're society's peacocks.'

'In which case, perhaps Emily was a little dazzled by the feathers,' said Polly. 'I say, old love, look at this seedling – the abominable slugs have made war on it.'

'Well, slip out after dark tonight with a torch and a slug-crusher,' said Boots. 'That's the best time to catch them, after dark.'

'I know,' said Polly, 'I know from bitter experience that they wait until night falls before they emerge from hiding. That way they escape being noticed. Flossie recommends buying a pet tortoise.' Flossie Cuthbert was their daily help. 'Tortoises, apparently, are natural destroyers of the abominable. Slugs are not only a curse, they're also repulsive.'

'Created on one of nature's bad days,' said Boots.

'By the way,' said Polly, 'if Emily did get dazzled by the peacock and his feathers, Rosie could have early problems as a caring mother.'

'Rosie will cope,' said Boots, 'so will Matt. Have we had a pot of tea yet?'

'Not yet,' said Polly.

'Well, I'll go and do the necessary,' said Boots. 'You stay here writing love letters to your beans.'

'Kind of you since I need all this fresh air,' said Polly, now hoeing the bed. 'I can't take wedding revelry as well as I used to. How did I manage to escape a hangover?'

'No problem to any woman who was a Bright Young Thing in the Wild Twenties and patronized forbidden nightclubs,' said Boots. 'That's not to say I don't feel for your slight frailty today.'

'Thank you, dear man,' said Polly.

'But I don't suppose the happy pair will be worrying too much about it,' said Boots. 'They're probably still riding white clouds through blue skies.'

'Very imaginative,' murmured Polly.

'However,' said Boots, 'if one of them should phone to ask, I'll tell them you and I are enjoying a garden party.'

And off he went to make a pot of tea, leaving Polly thinking that while it was absurd to claim that any marriage was made in heaven, there were some that were worth a celestial mention. Her own, for instance.

In Salcombe, the newly-weds, strolling hand in hand by the sun-dappled ocean, looked happy. And no, they weren't worrying about the folks or frailties back home. They were telling each other that they were very much in favour of the wedded state. Philip qualified the declaration by saying that for his part, it meant with Phoebe alone, of course. Phoebe said she was happy about that, and definitely in favour of current events.

'The wedding laws should be changed,' she added, 'so that happily married couples could do it more often.'

'It?' said Philip. 'Is there a law, then, about only doing it once a week? If so, that's news to me.'

'I meant, smarty, that happily married couples ought to be able to have a repeat wedding every anniversary,' said Phoebe, so taken with her present state that she was in earnest recommendation of the idea.

'Well, we're a happily married couple now,' said Philip, 'and providing the vicar can't think up any real opposition, there's nothing to stop us celebrating our wedding by doing it again every year and twice every leap year. We won't need an Act of Parliament.'

'Man, you're brilliant,' said Phoebe.

'Glad you think so, blossom. How about a Devonshire cream tea in that place over there?'

'Lead me to it, Sir Lancelot.'

'This way, then, missus.'

Chapter Fourteen

Boots was placing the sugar bowl on the tray when into the kitchen by the back door came Gemma, young, skittish and, in a dress of light yellow, looking like the spirit of summer, even if rain had been forecast for tomorrow morning.

'Oh, hello, Daddy, are you making tea?' she asked, tossing her handbag onto the dresser. Gemma rarely had much to do with acts of slow deliberation.

'I'm making a mid-afternoon pot for the workers,' said Boots. The time was twenty to four. Full tea, Sunday tea, would be at five thirty. 'You're home early, aren't you, poppet?'

'Well, my girlfriend Sarah found a new heart-throb in the park, and James is doing hammer-and-tongs tennis stuff with three other guys,' said Gemma. 'So I've come home to take my record player into the garden and put on some of my Bill Haley numbers.'

'Bill Haley?' said Boots, pouring boiling

water into the teapot. 'Is that the man who rocks around the clock?'

'Yes, isn't he great?' said Gemma.

'Not in the garden on a Sunday afternoon,' said Boots. 'Doesn't he know about English Sundays?'

'I don't think he knows about them being sacred to Grandma Finch,' said Gemma, taking a look at a tin of biscuits.

'And to me and your mother, and most of the neighbours,' said Boots. 'Would you mind sparing us Bill Haley?'

'Is that a desperate request, Daddy?' asked Gemma, selecting a biscuit and biting into it.

'Absolutely,' said Boots, picking up the laden tray.

'Oh, all right, then,' said Gemma, 'I'll come out and share the pot of tea with you and Mum.'

'Bring another cup and saucer, then,' said Boots, 'and that tin of biscuits.'

Over the pot of tea around the garden table, Gemma said she was afraid Sarah Maggs, a schoolfriend, was going down the path of no return.

'Oh, dear,' said Polly, sipping tea with all the gratitude of a woman enjoying a perfect summer Sunday. Long gone were the days when restlessness afflicted her. 'Is it already fatal, Gemma?'

'She can't stop running after every boy she sees, poor thing,' said Gemma. 'I keep telling her to wait for the right one. We all ought to do that. It's my belief that if you go looking, you end up with the wrong one. Whenever I do any looking myself, say at dances, I almost always end up with some kind of freak. You know, the kind of freak we all feel sorry for – Daddy, have you picked up a chest cold?'

'Not that I know of,' said Boots.

'Well, something made you cough,' said Gemma, a girl with a happy belief in herself. 'Anyway, I don't feel any great need to have a boyfriend yet. My most genuine feeling is that boys are too young to be really interesting, whereas I'm sure adult males can appeal to a girl's intellect. That's important, our intellect.'

'It's important to me to know you have some,' said Boots.

Gemma smiled kindly at him.

'Did you mention adult males?' said Polly, fascinated by her daughter's social philosophy.

'Yes, young men who've spent their time sensibly growing up instead of playing about,' said Gemma. She glanced at Boots and made a thoughtful aside. 'Like Daddy did, I'm sure.' Boots coughed again. 'I expect he was very interesting to girls as an adult male.'

'Girls?' Polly laughed. 'Don't you know

that before he was twenty-one, he became the father of your half-sister Eloise by a French war widow?'

'Oh, yes, I know all about that,' said Gemma. 'It just shows the difference in male appeal between blokes who never grow up and those who do. I think I'll wait for the time when I can expect one or two really grown-up fellers to cross my path instead of looking for them now. At fifteen, a girl can afford to wait. Mummy, are you trying to say something?'

'Nothing that can't be left unspoken on a peaceful Sunday afternoon,' said Polly. 'But I wonder, do girls find James too young to be interesting?'

'Oh, some get soppy about him,' said Gemma, 'like Cathy Davidson and Cindy Stevens. You remember Cathy, don't you, who lives in Paris now with her mother?'

'I remember her mother all too well,' said Polly. 'We had to put a twenty-four-hour guard around your father to keep her from getting her hands on him.'

'Well, Cathy hasn't written to James for ages,' said Gemma, 'and Cindy's devotion only lasted about a month or so. Cindy just likes lots of strings to her bow.'

'Quality with quantity, or just as they come?' asked Boots.

'I couldn't say,' said Gemma. 'It all amounts to what I've been talking about, that at fifteen we're simply not old enough to form serious relationships.'

'So you've decided to wait a few years before committing yourself to someone tall, dark and – um – mature?' said Boots.

'I'm sure that's sensible,' said Gemma. 'Where are you going, Mummy?'

'Well, darling, fascinating as your dreams are,' said Polly, on her feet, 'I think I'll come down to earth by getting back to my onion bed.'

Linda's walk in the park with Nigel Killiner was not, after all, turning out to be like a history lesson. Nigel was proving to be far from a bossy teacher. The outing was actually fun, for he was full of the kind of light-hearted banter to which a young lady was readily responsive. She especially liked his anecdotes about certain schoolkids, the kind destined, he said, to be a danger to civilization if they weren't that already. What could be done, he asked, about boys who turned classroom wastepaper baskets into obstacles intended to trip him up and disable him? Linda suggested they should be reported to the headmaster or to their dads. Dads, she said, could always deal properly with misbehaving sons. Her own dad, she said, had always known how to make her brother Philip behave, which had helped him to accept discipline when he joined the RAF.

The park was a sunny retreat for people on this Sunday afternoon. Social mores might be changing, and radically, but Ruskin Park on a summer Sunday still drew the young as well as the old. Nigel and Linda, sauntering in close company along the paths, looked as if they had been friends for ages. Certainly Linda felt very much at ease with Nigel now, and listened absorbed as he told her he was delighted to know her brother was in the RAF. The RAF, he said, was a service he had always admired, and might have entered himself if he hadn't preferred to make his contribution to society by becoming a teacher. Mind you, he added, that preference had taken its course before he realized some schoolkids spent their time thinking up ways and means to inflict teachers with permanent injury.

'I think you must have more than your fair share of those at your school,' said Linda, smiling.

'Believe me, every school has always had more than its fair share,' said Nigel, and went on to say that in his opinion this was how the Empire was made, by unruly Britons overcoming uncivilized natives. Which was as far as any kind of dreaded history lesson made its appearance, for Nigel seemed to be fully aware that a young lady should be entertained, not treated as if she needed to be educated. He asked Linda what kind of a job she had, and when she told him she was a copy typist with a firm by Camberwell Green, he said he thought her more suitable for work as a window dresser for clothes shops. Linda, of course, immediately asked him why he thought that.

'Well, it's a matter of being visibly decorative,' he said.

'Visibly what?' asked Linda.

'Decorative,' said Nigel. 'And in a shop window, so that passers-by could have the pleasure of confirming first impressions.'

'First impressions of what?'

'That you're a very attractive girl,' said Nigel, 'and I hope I'm not offending you by saying so.'

'No, thanks for your compliments,' said Linda, 'but I don't think I'd want to put myself in a shop window for people to look at. I'd feel like a dummy.'

Nigel laughed. They kept to their leisurely walk, along with other people. The peace and calm of the park invariably induced users to relax, to enjoy a Sunday stroll in place of a weekday hustle and bustle. Nigel said really attractive girls shouldn't appear in shop windows for everyone to gawp at, and that if he ever had the good fortune to be attached to one, he'd like to think the last kind of job she'd want would be as a window dresser. Linda pointed out he'd just suggested that was where she should be, in a shop window and visibly decorative to the public. That was what he had said, visibly decorative. Nigel assured her he'd spoken without thinking, that girls as attractive and charming as she was didn't belong to the public, like Marilyn Monroe and other Hollywood female stars. Linda said she couldn't bracket herself with Marilyn Monroe, not in a month of Sundays. She supposed he simply meant she was entitled to her own private life, as everybody was.

They carried on in this way for some time until Linda said she was going to get embarrassed if they didn't talk about anything except herself. Nigel said the subject wasn't embarrassing to him, that from the moment yesterday when he first saw her, she had made her mark on him, and so had her nice personality. Did she mind him saying so?

No, she didn't mind too much, she said, except that considering this was the first time she'd been out with him, it really was a bit embarrassing to have him talk about her looks so much. Nigel said he must apologize for that, and hoped she'd forgive him. Linda said she didn't think it was serious enough for him to ask to be forgiven, only that she'd like it if he would spare her blushes.

'Oh, right,' said Nigel with a touch of briskness, as if that was now the key to their relationship. 'I fully understand, I suppose I was jumping the gun a bit, and being too personal. But to me it doesn't feel as if we've only just met, it feels as if I've known you for ages. I'll have to take care that I don't make myself as indigestible as some precocious schoolkid. I've met more than a few of that ilk in the short time I've been teaching.' That led him into more droll anecdotes.

In the sunshine of the park, Linda allowed herself to be entertained. If his interest in her was rather pronounced, well, it wasn't actually so embarrassing as to make her run for home, and at least he wasn't like some fellers whose only interest was in themselves. Also, she liked his way of speaking. It made him sound nicely educated, which one would expect of a teacher. But he wasn't a posh person. Which reminded her that the Adams family didn't encourage posh persons to enter their ranks, although Aunt Polly, very posh, had been allowed in, and Uncle Boots was known to have been referred to as Lord Muck in his young days. But, of course, Uncle Boots could get away with anything.

She asked Nigel about his family. His parents, he told her, lived in Hampstead, his father a City stockbroker, his mother a star turn in creating stunning floral arrangements for the glorification of the local church. His sister was at Durham University. He himself lived in lodgings in Bessemer Road, close to his school. His landlady was a good sort, but didn't encourage visitors. He hoped, he said, that none of that put Linda off him, and wondered if they might meet again next Sunday afternoon.

'Oh, if you'd like that, yes,' she said, 'and when we go back to my home in a few minutes, would you like to stay for tea with me and my parents?'

Nigel expressed positive delight, and when he took her home she had no trouble in persuading her parents to let him stay for tea. In fact, Annabelle and Nick were happy enough to accept the company of this engaging young man who had obviously made a hit with Linda. And the fact that he was a schoolteacher did away with any thoughts that his background might be suspect. Although Annabelle and Nick both had cockney antecedents, they'd become middle class in their outlook and way of living, and as parents they liked to be sure that a newcomer was suitable enough to begin a relationship with their daughter, whether serious or casual.

Over tea, they found Nigel all of suitable in his conversation and behaviour. He entertained them much as he had entertained Linda, with anecdotes about uncivilized schoolkids, and he readily offered information about himself and his family in an amusing way. They didn't fail to notice that he had impressed Linda with his personality. Well, it was time she found a steady young man.

When he finally left to go home to his lodgings, he had fixed up to call again for Linda next Sunday. Nick then spoke to her.

'I think you might be at the beginning of a heavy relationship,' he said with a bit of a teasing grin.

'Not heavy, I hope, Dad,' said Linda, 'I couldn't cope with anything like chain mail.'

'Chain mail?' said Annabelle.

'Yes, that's heavy,' said Linda, who felt she'd enjoyed an unusually entertaining day, and was already looking forward to next Sunday.

'Hello, yes?' Rosie, answering the phone on Monday evening, found herself communicating with a young baritone voice.

174

'You're not Emily, are you?' it said.

'No, I'm not Emily, I'm her mother.'

'Howd'youdo, lady. Could I speak to Em? Tell her it's Brad calling. Bradley Thompson.'

'Are you the young man she met at the dance hall on Saturday evening?'

'None other, lady. What a shindig. We merged.'

'Merged?'

'You've heard about soulmates?'

'I have.' This was Rosie's first social encounter with a Teddy boy, a phenomenon of the Fifties, and she was feeling her way, although not without a sense of amusement. 'But at a mere thirteen, Emily is nobody's soulmate, nor is she ready to merge, not even with Elvis Presley, every girl's dream, I believe.'

'Elvis we all dig, don't we? And I'd still like to talk to Em.'

'Very well, Mr Thompson, I'll—'

'It's Brad, lady. Mr Thompson, that's my old public bar.'

'Pardon?'

'My pa, lady. Could you get Em on this piece of equipment?'

'Hold on.' Rosie placed the receiver down and climbed the stairs in search of Emily. The girl was up in her room, doing her homework while listening to a pop record. 'Emily, a new acquaintance of yours is on the phone. Bradley Thompson. He wants to speak to you.'

'Bradley Thompson?' said Emily, frowning over a mathematical question. She was never on friendly terms with mathematics. In her opinion, mathematics represented something totally gruesome in the life of any schoolgirl. She would have been quite happy for the subject to be exclusive to boys, never mind that up-and-coming female undergraduates would have considered that unacceptable. 'Who's Bradley Thompson?'

'You met him, I believe, on Saturday evening,' said Rosie.

'Oh, him,' said Emily, apparently not impressed.

'I also believe he was the chief reason for your late arrival home, an event that's not to be repeated,' said Rosie.

'Oh, he's all right,' said Emily. 'For about an hour. Still, I'll go down and talk to him.' When she arrived at the phone, she picked it up and said, 'This is Emily Chapman. Who's that?'

'Brad.'

'The Brad who talks like the Lone Ranger?'

'Sure is, man.'

'Well, don't ring me, Ranger, I'm too busy doing homework in the evenings to take phone calls. If you want to see me, see me at the dance hall on Saturday. I'll be with my brother.'

'Brother? Em, that's tough on any doll.'

'I keep telling my mother that. It makes no difference. Goodbye.'

'Man alive, Em, I thought we had something going.'

'Yes, I'm going,' said Emily, 'back to my homework. See you Saturday evening, perhaps.'

'Hold on, Em—'

But this time Emily hung up. Her interest in Brad seemed to have been very short-lived. Actually, she felt he could be a stepping stone to more exciting heights. Teddy boys had a kind of relationship with up-and-coming bands.

Her mum and dad, however, happily assumed that some precocious Teddy boy was not their daughter's idea of teenage romance.

Chapter Fifteen

Mr Sidney Witchet, a retired clock and watch repairer, lived in an avenue off Denmark Hill. His wife having died five years ago, he had sold his business, with the shop and the goodwill, for a very tidy sum. That, added to the savings which he and his late better half had made, provided him with sufficient interest to enable him to live comfortably.

Some men are notably handy around the house. Some are hopeless. Mr Sidney Witchet was among the former, and he soon taught himself to cope with cooking, washing, ironing and other domestic chores. He was accordingly much admired by a number of neighbouring housewives, and pointed out to their husbands as an example of just how useful a man could be. Such husbands naturally came to look on Sidney Witchet as a pain in the elbow, although their wives said some lonely widow might be lucky enough to catch his eye. Not if she's a

Winnie, said one husband. Who wants to be known as Winnie Witchet?

It was true that Mr Witchet, born in Peckham of cockney parents, had known the trials of kids making fun of his surname during his schooldays. 'Oi there, watch it, Witchet.' Or, 'Was yer granddad a widget, Witchet?' Or, on the football field, 'Come on, kick it, Witchet.' Lots of that kind of stuff went on, so later in life, when he had improved himself and was doing well in his trade, with his own shop, he and his wife moved out of rumbustious Peckham to sample the more peaceful surroundings of the Denmark Hill area. He left behind kids who were as saucy about his name as those of his schooldays. ''Ere, Mr Witchet, me ma's got the fidgets. Can yer mend her?'

In the lower-middle-class area, Mr Witchet blossomed, along with his wife Amy. It was a sad day for him when she died, but he came out of mourning to apply himself to his life as a widower, overcoming each little problem in sterling fashion. He was essentially a man of positive qualities, with a great deal of self-belief. Uncharitable acquaintances sometimes referred to him in terms that implied he'd turned into a pompous old parrot.

He had just passed the age of sixty when, on this morning in June, he left his house at precisely ten thirty to call on a near neighbour. He was carrying a bunch of multicoloured sweet peas, cut from the early-flowering plants in his garden. Arriving at the neighbour's door, he knocked.

The lady of the house, Mrs Lizzy Somers, answered the summons and found the portly but healthy-looking gentleman on her doorstep.

'Good morning, Mrs Somers,' he said, lifting his trilby hat, 'might I be so bold as to suggest you could accept these flowers from my garden? I'm sure you must still be a grieving woman, but feeling just a mite better now, I hope, which might help you to enjoy these sweet peas.'

'Well, it's very kind of you, I'm sure,' said Lizzy, 'and I don't know I could have turned down such a nice present at any time. I can smell the scent from here.'

'Do me the honour of accepting them,' said Mr Witchet, and pressed the bunch into her hand. 'You might have noticed that although I attended Mr Somers's funeral, I've refrained from calling on you until now. I pride meself on knowing when to leave a sad neighbour to her grief, and when to offer her a consoling hand. Might I suggest that your feelings as a newly widowed woman have taken a turn for the better? I don't mean, of course, that you're over your loss. That can't be. Knowing Mr Somers as a good neighbour and an upright man, as I did, I'm sure it'll be a long time before you manage to get over your grief. As I daresay you know, it took me more than a while to get over all the grief when my dear wife passed on. However, in taking it on meself to call today—'

'Yes, it's really very kind of you.' Lizzy, thinking it was time to interrupt her talkative neighbour before he overwhelmed her, broke in gently but firmly. 'But I'll never come to terms with losing Ned.'

'Ah,' said Mr Witchet, and his homely features took on a very visible expression of sympathy. 'Might I say I can understand that, seeing I still miss the late Mrs Witchet?'

'I'm sure,' said Lizzy, wondering how to get rid of the man. He and his wife had been near neighbours for many years, and although she and Ned had never had much in common with them, neither had they found any real fault in either. Mind, Ned had once said it was a matter of guesswork as to who turned into an old woman first, Sidney Witchet or Amy Witchet. Well, both liked to be heard.

On the other hand, both were useful people, Mrs Witchet being adept at sewing and em-broidery, and Mr Witchet being a very good gardener. Since losing his wife, his gardening had become his major recreation, and he was well known for offering surplus vegetables to his immediate neighbours. They naturally spoke highly of him, thereby exacerbating the unkind feelings of those husbands who had to listen to their wives singing his praises.

'Well, it really is kind of you to think of me and to give me these lovely sweet peas,' said Lizzy in an effort to close the conversation, 'and I do appreciate it.'

Mr Witchet's plump but firm-bodied frame seemed to expand in pleasure.

'Might I be so bold as to offer my services whenever you need any kind of help around the house?' he said. 'If I do say so meself, I can handle most problems – mind, I'm sure Mr Somers always could, knowing him as I did, but now you're alone – well, as I say, if you do need any help in the house or in the garden—' Mr Witchet paused to let a new thought take root, but Lizzy cut in before he could elaborate.

'Well, thank you, Mr Witchet,' she said, 'but my family look after any little problems I have about the house, and my eldest son and his wife look after all the heavy work in the garden.'

'Mrs Somers, I couldn't be more pleased for you,' said Mr Witchet. 'It's comforting for me as a neighbour to know your family take a helpful interest in your life as it is at present, but any time there's a kind of emergency I'd be pleased to come along double quick and offer my services. You need only ask.'

'Well, thank you, Mr Witchet,' said Lizzy again. 'I'll remember that.' Which meant she'd remember not to ask, for however well meaning he was, he wasn't her first choice for help with her boiler or her electric toaster. 'Good morning to you, and thank you again for calling and for these sweet peas. I'd best find a vase for them right away.'

For some reason, Mr Witchet consulted his watch.

'Ah, yes, it's coming up to elevenses time, I see,' he said.

'Oh, is it?' said Lizzy, suspecting he was angling for an invitation to coffee. He was on barren ground there. She still wasn't up to entertaining neighbours, close or otherwise. Ned's death continued to give her painful moments, and only members of her family were of any comfort to her. In the matter of elevenses, she had a sure feeling that if she did invite Mr Witchet to join her, it might take all day to get rid of him. 'Time does fly, doesn't it?' she said busily. 'I'd best finish tidying my living room. Good morning, Mr Witchet.'

'Good morning, Mrs Somers,' said Mr Witchet, and offered a friendly smile. A woman passing by saw the sturdy man of sixty in company at the open door with a comely woman. Lizzy at the near age of fifty-nine was still attractive, and the passing woman no doubt thought the man was aware of it. He looked as if he was. The woman smiled and went on. Mr Witchet said, 'Might I take meself off in the hope of being allowed to call again?'

'If you don't mind, I'm not up to regular visitors yet,' said Lizzy. She said a firm goodbye and closed the door.

Sidney Witchet, thinking that the newly widowed Mrs Somers was standing up bravely to her loss, departed like a man whose morning had been very enjoyable, even if he hadn't been invited in for coffee. On reaching home, he inspected his garden and wondered if the lady would like a selection of his vegetables from time to time. Neighbourly gestures were part of the pleasant side of life, and would probably be very much so to a still grieving widow, especially when coming from a widower who had known his own sorrows.

Lizzy, having found a vase for the sweet peas, made a colourful arrangement of them. Aware of the fragrance of their scent, she told herself Mr Witchet really had been very kind. Then she forgot all about him.

★   ★   ★

That evening, on his way home from the office, Boots dropped in on Lizzy. He'd been doing that regularly since the death of Ned. He had an abiding affection for his sister. During their growing years, especially the years when they were aware that life was a struggle for Chinese Lady, their ever-enduring mother, their relationship had been close and confiding. It still was.

'Well, Lizzy?' he said, when she opened her door to him.

'Oh, I'm all right, Boots, and it's nice to see you,' she said. 'Come on in, I've been watching Wimbledon.'

It was the first week of the All-England Lawn Tennis Championships, and as usual, the BBC television service was covering the event. Lizzy didn't know much about tennis, or who was who in the game, but she did like watching it on the television and hearing the commentator make his occasional reference to the Wimbledon speciality of strawberry and cream teas.

'What's on at the moment?' asked Boots, following her into the living room.

'It's a men's singles match,' said Lizzy.

Boots looked at the flickering images of two players battling it out on the famous Centre Court, which was bathed in hot sunshine. Despite previous forecasts of rain, the weather had become tropically hot and dry, and although the television set could only transmit its pictures in black and white, some of the atmosphere of the Centre Court on a sunny day came through.

'That's Lew Hoad,' said Boots, referring to the player about to serve. Lew Hoad was a young Australian tennis star and favourite for the Wimbledon title.

'Oh, yes, I know some of the names,' said Lizzy. 'Isn't Mr Hoad a handsome young man?'

'I haven't taken much note of his looks,' smiled Boots. 'My Wimbledon fancy was for the young American lady, Gussie Moran, who turned up a few years ago wearing specially designed Centre Court panties. The press at once labelled her Gorgeous Gussie, but the Wimbledon committee fainted to a man. I think she only wanted to show there was more to tennis than racquets.'

'And strawberries and cream?' said Lizzy, as she and Boots stood watching the screen.

'I wonder if Chinese Lady was right when she recently complained to me that very soon nothing in this country will be sacred,' said Boots. He and his sister and brothers still used the long-standing nickname for their mother. 'If so, then we'll be seeing strawberries and cream sailing to and fro over the net instead of tennis balls.'

186

'That'll be the day,' said Lizzy. 'Boots, would you like a drink?'

'Thanks, Lizzy, but no, I'll wait until I get home,' said Boots. His sister always made the offer whenever he dropped in and he always made the same response. His homecoming drink was one he ritually enjoyed with Polly. His was a whisky, hers a gin and tonic. Lizzy understood that.

'What made Mum complain about nothing being sacred?' she asked.

Boots waited until huge applause from the Centre Court crowd for a spectacular rally had stopped echoing around the room. Then he said that Chinese Lady found it difficult to accept the behaviour of modern young people, particularly their tendency to consider themselves outside the conventions practised by their elders. That wasn't exactly how she put it, of course, he said. Lizzy said no, that she'd bet what Chinese Lady did say was more like the young people will all end up in purgatory if they go on as they are doing.

'True, that was more like it,' smiled Boots, sitting down.

'Well, I must admit some of them do go a bit wild,' said Lizzy, switching off the television. It seemed somewhat antisocial to have it on while she and Boots were chatting. 'Especially

187

at these concerts when they all climb over one another to get close to singers like that young man Lonnie Donegan who plays a washboard of all things.'

'I don't think Chinese Lady regards Tommy Steele as a singer,' said Boots. 'I think her idea of a singer would be Paul Robeson or Peter Dawson.'

Lizzy said she was pretty sure that that would make her grandchildren suggest their grandmother was a bit ancient. Boots said it was quite possible they'd suggest he was too, since he shared Chinese Lady's opinion on who could be called a singer and who couldn't. Lizzy said that what bothered her was the feeling that many young people sort of looked at anybody over forty as if they didn't belong, or were too old to matter. Boots said he had no objection to being left alone by young people of the helter-skelter kind, as long as the other kind didn't disappear when they saw him coming. He said he thought present trends only marked the beginning of social change, and there was always the hope and possibility that this beginning represented a false alarm.

'Oh, that's what you hope, do you?' said Lizzy.

'I simply hope young people looking for new excitements don't mistake quantity for quality,' said Boots. Then he asked where the scent was coming from.

'From those sweet peas,' said Lizzy, indicating the vase of flowers that stood on a table inside the bay window. 'Aren't they lovely?'

'Delightful,' said Boots. 'Are you growing them this year?'

'No, these were given to me this morning by a neighbour,' said Lizzy. 'Mr Witchet.'

'Witchet?' said Boots.

'Yes, Sidney Witchet,' said Lizzy.

'I think I've heard of him,' said Boots, 'I think Ned mentioned him once or twice as a neighbour.'

'Yes, he and his wife moved here about fifteen years ago,' said Lizzy. 'Ned and me never got round to entertaining them, though. They were just neighbours, and we just said hello to each other whenever we passed by. Mrs Witchet died a few years back, and Mr Witchet's looked after himself ever since. Everyone says he's very capable. He called this morning to ask if I needed any help, which I don't, seeing my family, especially Bobby and Helene, are all very helpful. Still, it was kind of him to offer, and I was pleased to have the sweet peas.'

'I'm sure.' Boots mused. He might have suggested the offer of help and the gift of sweet peas pointed to something more than a wish to be a good neighbour, but he knew Lizzy wouldn't go along with that idea, particularly as she would consider Ned wasn't yet cold in his grave. Lizzy had the same kind of conventional attitudes as Chinese Lady. She would probably wear some kind of mourning black for years, just as their mother had following the death of their soldier father in 1908.

Not under any circumstances would Boots have attempted to change his sister's outlook, but he had a feeling Mr Witchet might have that in mind himself. When a widower bearing gifts calls on a widow suffering loneliness, one should sit up and take notice, but refrain from interfering. Boots stood up. 'Well, I'll shoot off home now, Lizzy. Everyone's pleased to know you're managing, and I'm delighted that Bobby and Helene are such a help to you. If they're not around any time you especially need them, give me a buzz.'

'I will,' said Lizzy, and saw him out. As she watched him walk through the open front gate to his parked car, she thought, as she often did, how well his years sat on him. His tall figure was as fine as ever, his gait long-legged and easy. He turned before he entered the car, and made a hand gesture of goodbye.

'So long, sis,' he called.

'Bye,' called Lizzy. She did not close the door until she had seen him drive away.

The house seemed lonely and quiet then, and not for the first time during these recent months, she experienced the pain of loss as if it had happened only yesterday.

Chapter Sixteen

'There you are, Polly.' Boots handed his life-loving wife a gin and tonic, iced.

'Thank you, darling,' murmured Polly. This was something that had become very enjoyable over the years, the custom of marking Boots's arrival home from the office with a glass of what-you-fancy for each. She watched him sip his whisky. 'Chin-chin, old sport,' she said, and raised her glass to her lips.

'Where are the twins?' asked Boots.

'Up in their rooms, doing their homework,' said Polly. 'As befits a boy and girl who wish to follow in their father's footsteps and become wise and clever.'

'Who thought that one up?' asked Boots. 'Whoever did, I forbid it. Better for sons and daughters to carve out their own way of life than to try to emulate their fathers. Fathers generally are far from clever, and wise only after the event. They escape falling over their own feet only with the help of their wives.'

'Save my soul,' said Polly, 'your modesty alarms me. Gemma and James are fortunate enough to have a remarkable father, and if either of them takes on only your ability never to flap, I'll be happy for him or her. As it is, they're both coping with the kind of things that affect all young people.'

'Such as?' said Boots.

'Well, Gemma, as you know, has made up her mind that tall, dark and handsome men only appear to young ladies who wait, and James has developed the useful gift of avoiding commitments.'

'Very sensible at his age,' said Boots.

'Very,' said Polly. 'You and I, old love, can thank the gods that our twins aren't giving us the problems that I think Emily is going to give Rosie and Matt. By the way, what did Lizzy have to say?'

'That she had a visit from a neighbour who brought her flowers and an offer of help whenever she needs it,' said Boots, and went into a more detailed exposition. Polly asked if he knew the man.

'I only know his name is Witchet,' said Boots.

'Witchet?' said Polly, a gleam in her eye. 'Is there anyone living called Witchet?'

'This one is Sidney Witchet,' said Boots, and

Polly might have fallen about if it hadn't meant her gin and tonic would fall with her.

'Sidney?' she said. 'Sidney Witchet?'

'We all have our disbelieving moments, old girl,' said Boots. 'Enjoy yours.'

'Well, I ask you, old bean, Sidney Witchet?' said Polly.

'I knew a man in the army by the name of Peregrine Windybank,' said Boots.

'Good grief, is that possible?' asked Polly.

'Everyone called him Curly,' said Boots.

'How did he come by Curly?' asked Polly.

'He was bald,' said Boots. 'I've a suspicion that Mr Sidney Witchet is likely to become a new card in Lizzy's life, although I don't think she knows it. Or would even want to know it.'

'Save her,' said Polly.

'Lizzy,' said Boots, 'is quite capable of saving herself. Further, I wouldn't dream of interfering.'

'Saving dear Lizzy from anyone by the name of Sidney Witchet couldn't be called interfering,' said Polly. 'Not under any circumstances.'

'Nevertheless, I shall stand aside,' said Boots, quite sure that Lizzy could see Witchet off if the gent got too close.

It was Emily's dad, Matthew, who next had the pleasure of hearing a young baritone voice when he picked up the phone at eight that evening.

'Hello, it's Brad here – who's that?'

Matt, as much in the picture concerning this character as Rosie was, said, 'Are you the young man who kept my daughter out late last Saturday evening?'

'It wasn't late, was it?' said Brad, sounding youthfully untroubled. 'I mean, it was nothing like three in the morning. Hey, could you be Em's dad?'

'Not could be,' said Matt. 'I am. So let me take this opportunity of reminding you of what my wife told you last evening, that Emily is a mere thirteen, and any time past ten in the evening is late for her to be out. Ten past eleven is too late.'

'Mister, you're serious?' Brad now sounded astonished.

'I've never been more so,' said Matt.

'Hey, man, that's sensational. I guess it's tough being a parent. Anyway, can I talk to Em?'

'She's watching television, but I'll ask,' said Matt, acknowledging that even at only thirteen, Emily had a right to make certain decisions for herself. He called her. In response, Emily yelled back from the living room.

'What's up, Daddy?'

'There's an acquaintance of yours on the phone. He says he's Brad. He'd like to talk to you.'

'Oh, him.' Emily raised her voice again and yelled, 'Tell him I'll see him at the dance next Saturday evening. I don't want to talk now.'

'If you heard that,' said Matt down the phone, 'you'll know the answer to your request was no.'

'Little Prairie Cloud no feeling too good?' suggested Brad, one of whose heroes was Geronimo. 'Oh, well, she's still a great number. Could I talk to her ma instead?'

'Would you like to repeat that?' said Matt.

'I talked to her last night,' said Brad, 'and I figure she's great too. Sounded as if she could rock around the clock all night. That's style, man. Could she spare five minutes for another talk?'

'Don't push your luck, sonny,' said Matt, 'keep your head and stay alive. Goodbye.'

'Hey, man—'

But the phone was dead, and Brad's evening had turned out blank.

While Rosie listened with interest to Matt's recital of the phone conversation, neither Giles nor Emily were diverted from their enjoyment of the television programme until their father reached the point when Brad, **turned** down by Emily, had asked if he could speak to their mother instead.

'Tell more,' said Emily.

'Tell all,' said Giles, grinning at his mum.

'I can hardly wait myself,' said Rosie, whereupon Matt let them all know that Brad considered Little Prairie Cloud, Emily herself, to be a great number surpassed only by Heavenly Cloud, her mother. Giles fell about, Emily had fits, and Rosie regarded Matt with a mixture of suspicion and amusement. Matt played the final card by informing her that Brad reckoned she could rock around the clock until breakfast time with the best of the dolls. That put the whole family, including Rosie, into hysterics, which meant that Matt had garnered something uplifting out of a phone conversation irksome at times.

'All this, Rosie, reminds me that there's an old Dorset saying,' he said.

'There always is,' said Rosie, 'but can we be spared on this occasion?'

'No, let's have it, Dad,' said Giles.

Matt recited.

'Down by Dorset in the west,
Dads be helpful, but mums be best,
And when the tinkers do pass by
They'll take mums dancing on the sly.'

'That's as cock-eyed as all your other Dorset sayings,' said Rosie, 'but tinker fits.'

'Fits who?' asked Giles.

'Young Mr Impertinence,' said Rosie. 'Emily, keep your distance from him.'

'Stop fussing,' said Emily, whose vision of life embraced wider horizons than were good for a girl of only thirteen. But then in this day and age, other young girls felt they were already adult enough to run their own lives. This included the freedom to go to pop concerts every night, including Sundays. 'Brad's not evil, Mum. More of a laugh, really.'

'A scream, apparently,' said Rosie drily.

'Come dancing with us on Saturday evening, Mum,' said Giles, 'and you can find out for yourself.'

'I'm touched by your offer, Giles,' said his mum, 'but I think I'll give it a miss and stay home with your dad.'

'Lucky old Dad,' said Giles.

Chapter Seventeen

The following day, Sammy drove to Southend-on-Sea, taking Rosie and Rachel with him, as promised. Southend, on the Essex bank of the Thames estuary, did claim to be 'on-Sea', and no-one had ever lodged a legal complaint, so it lived merrily on as a seaside holiday resort for London cockneys year after year. Highly prized were the town's shellfish, particularly its cockles and mussels, and the cockneys' love of fried fish and chips was abundantly catered for. So was their liking for funny hats printed with catchphrases such as 'Kiss Me Quick' or 'Chase me, Charlie'.

Southend pubs did a roaring trade in the evenings, and in pre-war days many a rosy-faced female party had been caught doing a knees-up while rolling back to a boarding house. Come to that, such goings-on still happened. In the Kursal, a place of entertainment well patronized in the evenings, visitors could ride carousels or much livelier contraptions, participate in a coconut shy, have their fortunes told or guess their own weight in return for a prize. It was always very jolly, and on any fine evening, the shrieks of ladies trapped in speeding machines that played havoc with their dresses could generally be taken as signals of dire distress. Not that this kind of SOS ever resulted in a rescue. No, under the delighted eyes of male spectators, they had to endure the full ride for which they had paid.

'Elsie, what happened that we had to pay for being on show like that? I've never blushed more in all me life.'

'Well, I tell yer this much, Glad, I dunno why we let Albert and Ronnie talk us into it in the first place. Now everyone in Southend that ain't short-sighted knows the colour of our bank holiday knickers.'

The day was fine, the weather still hot, the crowds and players at Wimbledon in for a sweltering time, and when Sammy reached Southend the colourful holiday scenes, touched with summer's warm light, at once smote the eye in happy fashion. Not that the resort was crowded. That wouldn't be the case until July and August, the school holiday period, when the boarding houses would be full to over-flowing with London families. In these post-war years, the place was as popular as it had ever been.

The time was ten twenty. They had left early in order to give themselves a few enjoyable hours in the town, along with an inspection of the acquired shop. It being the first time Rachel and Rosie had seen Southend, they took in all they could as Sammy slowed and found a parking place in the main esplanade, which overlooked the beach and the sea, or, more correctly, the swirling waters of the Thames estuary. Still, it seemed like the sea. Sammy and his passengers alighted. Rachel and Rosie resumed their survey of the scene, that of strolling visitors, a cheerful promenade, a man leading donkeys down to the beach, and shops whose wares were on outside show. Such wares seemed, at first glance, to consist mainly of painted buckets, castle-building spades, funny hats and beach towels. These represented popular holiday offerings.

'Sammy,' said Rosie, 'it seems a happy place.'

'Southend,' said Sammy, 'has never been known to sulk, even on wet August bank holidays. But it does get a bit ratty if anyone suggests its sandy beach is made up of Thames mud. Come on, let's have coffee before we go and look at our holiday-wear shop.'

That was what they were there for, to inspect

the dress shop acquired by the property company for the benefit of Adams Fashions. The present proprietors, a young couple, would hand over the premises at the end of June. Running it with local staff from July through to September represented a new development for the company, that of entering the summer-wear market particular to seaside holiday resorts. Some shops in some resorts, such as Brighton or Blackpool, could make a small fortune from mid-June to mid-September.

Sammy had parked opposite a cafe called Sailor Joe's, and he headed straight for it, followed by Rachel and Rosie, both of whom looked nicely attired for the outing. Sammy had said they didn't need to dress up, that Southend wasn't as fashion-conscious as Ascot or a Buckingham Palace garden party, but neither Rachel nor Rosie would have dreamed of dressing down. For that matter, Sammy himself didn't believe in any female woman looking like a jumble sale, and accordingly Rachel in a stylish dress of a creamy coffee colour and Rosie in elegant light blue were highly acceptable to his critical eye. They also aroused the interest of a couple of old-age pensioners, male gender.

'There's a bit of all right, Fred. Two bits, you could say.'

'I ain't looking too hard, Bert, or I'll have one of me turns.'

'Go on, chance it. It wouldn't be a bad way to go, giving your mince pies a genuine treat. They're prime, them ladies.'

'I'd go up and give 'em me compliments if I was twenty years younger, but I ain't, so I won't.'

Sammy reached the cafe and opened the door. He held it for Rachel and Rosie, and they entered. The place was surprisingly attractive for a cafe. Most were plain and practical. This one was nicely appointed, and on the tables only cruets were visible. There were no bottles of ketchup keeping company with other condiments, and there were no table stains that needed cleaning.

A number of customers were present, including two young men and two young ladies at a table for four. While enjoying coffee and fruit buns, they were indulging their collective sense of humour. Their witty sallies and gusts of laughter were running around the cafe like titters around a court. With other customers in a genial conversational mood, the atmosphere was lively without being raucous. Rachel noted a waitress service, unusual in the general run of practical establishments. Sammy, once he had seen that the ladies were seated at a vacant table, excused himself for a moment.

'I'm just going to have a word with Sailor Joe,' he said, 'I knew him when he had a whelks stall down East Street market.'

'I have a permanent impression that all the people you knew in old Walworth ran a whelks stall in the market,' said Rosie.

'Whelks happened to be highly popular, along with jellied eels,' said Sammy. 'Order coffee for me when the waitress arrives, would you?'

'With a buttered fruit bun?' said Rachel, studying the menu.

'Good idea, it's been a long drive,' said Sammy, and took himself to the counter, behind which stood the proprietor, a large middle-aged bloke in a white apron and a chef's hat. 'Watcher, Joe,' said Sammy, 'how's business?'

Joe Plummer, known as Sailor Joe in his Walworth days because of his rolling gait and his shipboard talk, fixed a searching eye on the man in a light grey suit, trilby in his hand. A happy grin arrived.

'Well, blow me across the briny,' he breezed, 'if you ain't Sammy Adams as ever was.' He reached over the counter and shook hands. 'How are yer, matey?'

'Still up to me eyes,' said Sammy. 'How's yourself and how's the missus?'

'I'm shipshape,' said Sailor Joe, 'but Maggie's

204

putting on a bit of weight. Too many tasty vittles coming out of our galley. Still, her waist-line don't stop her doing her afternoon bingo at thruppence a card.' He glanced across at the table where the waitress was taking an order from Rachel. 'Susie looks like she's changed a bit,' he said.

'Eh?' said Sammy, then realized an explanation was necessary in order to let Sailor Joe know he didn't have a mistress, and that he hadn't brought one with him. In any case, a Southend landlady could spot an immoral intention as soon as the guilty parties arrived on her doorstep. Straightaway she'd send them packing. Sammy's explanation was accordingly hasty but clear. It embraced the purpose of his presence in the town with two members of his staff. Sailor Joe looked intrigued.

'It's a fact?' he said. 'You're taking over Warner's Wardrobe?' That was the present name of the shop, which name Sammy was going to change to Adams Fashions. Adams Fashions had style and gave a bit of class to a label, and he knew there was no reason why a bit of class shouldn't go down as well in Southend as in Torquay. There were people everywhere who knew quality was more lasting than the cheap.

'Yup, it's a fact, Sailor,' he said.

Sailor Joe showed another grin.

'So you're going to operate in my harbour? Welcome aboard, shipmate,' he said, at which point the waitress arrived behind the counter to prepare two trays, one in respect of Rachel's order, and the other in respect of a new customer.

'One ham sandwich, Joe,' she said, 'with mustard.'

'Got you, Queenie,' said Sailor Joe. 'Give us a minute, Sammy.'

'See you again before we leave,' said Sammy, and rejoined Rachel and Rosie. They were chatting away in easy fashion, enhancing the lively atmosphere of the cafe. All was redolent of the summer day and of vibrant Southend, and the sudden sounds of fire engines racing by outside seemed all part of the bustling day rather than an intrusion.

'Here we are,' said the waitress, arriving with a tray. From this she set out cups of coffee with saucers, sugar bowl, jug of milk, a dish of buttered fruit buns warm and fresh, with plates, dessert knives and paper serviettes. All of which confirmed Sammy's belief that if a cafe could promote a bit of class, so could a dress shop.

A yell of laughter rang out from the witty quartet. Infectious, it made other customers smile.

'Someone's happy,' said Rachel.

'They're on holiday from Barking,' smiled the waitress, 'and enjoying themselves.'

'I don't know Barking,' said Rosie, 'is it enjoyable to leave it behind?'

'Seems like it,' said the waitress, departing. She stopped to speak to a new customer as he came in. Sammy, Rachel and Rosie all heard him say, 'Woolworths, so I was told.'

Everyone looked up, and Sailor Joe said, 'You telling us those fire engines were heading for Woolworths?'

'So I heard,' said the new customer.

'It's all hands to the pumps, then,' said Sailor Joe.

A lady member of the quartet said, 'My dear old mum grew up on nothing over sixpence.'

'Well,' said one of the young men, 'it looks like it's all going up in smoke. Come on, finish coffee and let's take a shufti.'

The four were up and away a minute later, all keen to see a branch of the famous high-street store ablaze. Sammy, Rachel and Rosie remained to enjoy their coffee and buns at leisure. When they did leave, Sammy exchanged a few more friendly words with Sailor Joe, who supposed he'd see him regularly once he'd set up his shop, and that from the cut of his jib he was obviously worth a bob or two. Sammy said that if Sailor was referring to his suit, it was one he'd just redeemed from Camberwell pawnbrokers.

'Pull the other one, me wooden peg,' said Sailor Joe.

Sammy, accompanied by Rachel and Rosie, left with a grin on his face. He always enjoyed a bit of repartee with old associates.

'Right, ladies,' he said, 'this way to the shop.'

'We're not going to race down to the fire at Woolworths?' said Rosie.

'I'm leaving it to the fire brigade,' said Sammy. 'Let's head for the shop.'

They began their walk in the bright sunshine, the shop in question being located in a side street some way down. Rachel and Rosie did a little window-gazing here and there, and Sammy did not hurry them. There was no need, and further, the idea was for the ladies to explore Southend. He himself peered ahead from time to time.

'What are you looking for, Sammy?' asked Rachel.

'Well, as I recall,' said Sammy, 'Woolworths is down there somewhere, but there's no sign of a fire or fire engines. I can see smoke, but it's well to the left.'

'I can smell it now,' said Rachel.

'There, look,' said Rosie.

208

The smoke was drifting lazily above buildings to dirty the sky, and something made Sammy pick up the pace.

Ten minutes later, and still in company with Rachel and Rosie, he was part of a crowd watching firemen directing their hoses to douse the last of any burning embers of Warner's Wardrobe. Woolworths my aching foot, thought Sammy, that bloke who mentioned it in the cafe had a fit of mishearing.

The shop was a drenched, smoking ruin, equipment and stock all consumed. Mrs Phyllis Warner, wife of the owner, Bill Warner, was talking to Sammy. She was tearful as she told him she had no idea how the fire started, but thought it might have been due to a woman customer who went into the cubicle to try on a dress. She was smoking a cigarette.

'Thinking back, Mr Adams, I'm sure she didn't have the cigarette when she came out. I'm terribly upset, for Bill and myself, and for you – it's ruined your plans.'

'They're up the spout all right,' said Sammy, grimacing. Only a short while ago, the bright atmosphere of the seaside town had warmed the cockles of his heart. Now, everything relating to the main purpose of his visit lay under collapsed ruins and drenching water. Ninety-nine corblimey curses, he thought.

'What about the insurance, does it cover fire?' asked Rosie.

'It's a fact it does,' said Sammy. The property company had taken over the insurance cover on the day purchase was completed, with the priviso that Warners could have up to the end of June to sell what they could of their stock. 'But I ask meself, Rosie, how much of a consolation is that at this particular moment? And I answer not much. Still, I'll feel better in a month's time. There's always someone more unlucky, someone who's forgotten about insurance cover.'

The hoses were shut down then, and two firemen made a close inspection of the blackened ruins. The crowd began to break up as people drifted away.

'Mr Adams, I'm terribly sorry,' said young Mrs Warner.

'I share your headache,' said Sammy.

'Fires do happen,' said Rachel, 'but my life, this one has really wrecked the premises. I should be upset? I am, especially for you and your husband, Mrs Warner.'

'I must go home and phone Bill,' said Mrs Warner, her tearfulness on the brink of a breakdown. 'You'll contact the insurance company, Mr Adams?'

'I'll talk to my son and his co-director as soon as I get back to the office,' said Sammy. 'They'll be in touch with you, since part of the deal was that the insurance would cover cost of any ruined or stolen stock, and that we'd pass the reimbursement to you, right?'

'Bill and I will be grateful you agreed to that clause,' said Mrs Warner. She eyed the smoky ruins of what had once been a dress shop catering for the kind of visitors who were always looking for bargains rather than anything expensive. The fact that the shop had been sold and she hadn't long to go as its proprietress seemed of little consolation to her at this moment. A sigh escaped her, and then, with some murmured words of goodbye to Sammy and his companions, she turned and left.

'We should be sorry for her and ourselves for this kind of day, Sammy,' said Rachel.

'Right on,' said Sammy, grimacing again. He took a last look at the blackened ruins, from which the final wisps of smoke were escaping, then had a word with the fire brigade's chief officer, letting him know one of his firms, Adams Properties Ltd, owned the shop, such as it was right now. He was told that only an official investigation could determine the cause of the fire, and that the owners would be advised of the findings. 'Well, I've had other corblimey upsets in my time, Chief, so I daresay I'll get over this one.'

'All in a day's work for us, sir,' said the chief officer.

'Good luck,' said Sammy, and left, in company with Rachel and Rosie. They were both very sober.

'What do we do now, Sammy?' asked Rosie. 'We're hardly in the mood to go paddling or to wear funny hats.'

'Well, we need something to take away the nasty taste of burnt smoke,' said Sammy. He looked at his watch. Eleven forty. 'I know just the place, a pub that'll serve us a plateful of shellfish, together with rolls and butter. It'll also serve wine to you girls and a tankard of its best brew to me. D'you fancy the prospect? We'll take our time and head for home afterwards.'

'Lead on, Macduff,' said Rosie.

'If I'd been born a Macduff,' said Sammy, 'I'd be wearing a Southend kilt.'

Chapter Eighteen

Sammy and the ladies arrived back at the Camberwell offices at mid-afternoon, enabling Rosie to get home before her son and daughter returned from school. She was always adamant about that.

Sammy and Rachel looked in on Boots to give him the news of the fire. Boots expressed sympathy for their spoiled outing, but was philosophical about the event.

'Well, it's just another shop, Sammy, it's not your family home, or mine. Or Rachel's.'

'Thank you for that thought, Boots,' said Rachel.

'Hold on,' said Sammy, 'things ain't as casual as that. We've got to wait for the inquiry to tell us how the fire started, then sort out the insurance and consider whether we rebuild the shop or sell the site. Right now, there's no prospect of opening up until next year.'

Boots thought about all that.

'Sammy,' he said, 'don't we have an agreement with the Warners to reimburse them for loss of stock in the event of burglary or a fire prior to our taking over?'

'Is that a question or a reminder?' asked Sammy.

'Yes, we do have that agreement, Boots,' said Rachel.

'We all thought it a fair clause,' said Sammy.

'Well, I wonder,' said Boots, 'what happens if the investigation discovers the fire was started deliberately? That would point to arson and the Warners.'

'Look, I haven't spent the morning getting a headache just for you to give me another one,' complained Sammy.

'My life, Boots,' said Rachel, 'are you implying that the Warners may have lit the bonfire themselves in order to earn the reimbursement from the insurance company?'

'It'll be from us,' said Boots, 'after the insurance company has paid up, but of course it won't pay a penny if the fire was started deliberately.'

'That's it,' said Sammy, disgusted, 'you've definitely given me a headache on top of the one I've had since this morning. No, listen, I know the Warners, both of 'em, and I'd swear they're as honest as Chinese Lady and her vicar. In any

214

case, you're only talking about a figure that wouldn't amount to more than a few quid. Well, comparative, like.'

'Very true, Sammy, if the Warners' claim for lost stock turns out to be modest,' said Boots.

'That's a point,' said Sammy.

'So is the possibility that the loss of stock was self-inflicted by the Warners,' said Rachel. 'We'll need to look carefully at the amount they claim. My life, Sammy, if arson is proved, the insurance company won't pay a penny, either for lost stock or ruined property.'

'Rachel,' said Sammy, 'it's bad enough listening to Boots, without you putting the wind up me as well. I'm going to have a word with the property company's joint managing directors.' He was referring to his son Daniel, and Boots's son Tim. Together, they had turned the property company into what Sammy called an asset with rounded corners and no sharp edges, which meant highly profitable and a valuable contributor, along with Adams Enterprises and Adams Fashions, to the personal prosperity of every family member who worked for the companies or had shares in them. Sammy, as the founder of the business, modestly accepted the largest percentage as his due, despite the fact that Chinese Lady frequently told him he'd turned out to be an implorable profiteer – she meant deplorable – and she could only hope no-one else in the family would turn out the same.

Tim and Daniel listened to him retailing the happenings in Southend, and what Boots had implied in regard to the Warners. Tim said his dad must have been looking on the black side of things for the first time in his life. He thought that perhaps at sixty, the old lad was losing a bit of his bottle. Sammy at once said that if Boots lived to be a hundred, he'd still have all his bottle, and would take it with him when he did go. Tim said it simply wasn't worth the risk for the Warners to have fired their stock themselves. They'd get very little out of it. Sammy said they were his sentiments entirely, but there was always the chance of something dubious about some shop fires. Anyway, the next step was to contact the insurance company, which induced Daniel to unconsciously echo Rachel's declaration that not a penny would be paid unless the investigation into the cause of the fire came up with the right answer.

'Don't I know that?' said Sammy. 'Anyway, have a dicky bird with them. Let them know about the fire and ask for a claims form.'

'Dad, you're teaching us to suck lemons,' said Daniel.

'Well, I had some of that myself in me

younger days,' said Sammy. He brightened a little. 'Still, Southend wasn't all bad news. Rosie, Rachel and self enjoyed some nourishing cockles, mussels and shrimps at a pub that poured me a tankard of its best brew. All right, then, I'll leave the pair of you to start the ball rolling in respect of the fire.'

'Much obliged,' said Tim, smiling.

'And never mind your sorrows, Dad,' said Daniel, 'you look in great shape.'

'I don't know how I've managed that,' said Sammy from the door. 'Not considering I've had the kind of day I want to forget.'

Over supper with Boots and the twins that evening, Polly said it wasn't often that Sammy, in his business career, had been stopped dead in his tracks.

'On this occasion,' said Boots, 'it's not Sammy, it's the company. The Southend shop prospect is now flat on its back in the middle of the town.'

'I've never been to Southend,' said Gemma, by way of a mild complaint.

'I could say the same,' said James, 'but I won't.'

'The fact is,' said Boots, 'if there's any suggestion of arson, there could also be a suggestion of collusion between the Warners and the company.'

'I say, old thing, that's a bit pessimistic,' said Polly.

'Dad, collusion's a crime,' said James. 'Under certain circumstances, that is.'

'That's pessimistic, you gloomy boy,' said Gemma.

'Hear, hear,' said Polly, 'except I exclude gloomy boy. And let's banish pessimism. This family has managed to do without it ever since you and James were born.'

'What about the time when Daddy had chronic dandruff and we all thought he'd have to shave his head and go about bald?' said Gemma. 'It was gloom all the time.'

'That was when you were nine,' said Polly, 'and it wasn't Daddy's head, it was Uncle Tommy's, and he didn't have to shave it. Your Aunt Vi cured the problem by giving him a medical shampoo every night for weeks.'

'Good old Aunt Vi,' said James.

'Further,' said Polly, 'I would never allow your father to develop anything as frightful as dandruff.'

'But what about if it crept up on him when you weren't looking?' said Gemma.

'I'd rely on you and James to give it the old one-two,' said Polly.

'Where'd you get that from?' asked James.

'Well, dear boy,' said Polly, 'it could be the

old heave-ho, not the old one-two. Whichever it was, I think I heard it on *The Goon Show*.' *The Goon Show* was a hugely popular radio programme. It featured four comedians, Michael Bentine, Spike Milligan, Harry Secombe and Peter Sellers, every one of them as zany as a cross-eyed parrot, and so excruciatingly funny off the cuff that they frequently departed from their script. 'Yes, I'm sure it was a Goon thing,' murmured Polly.

'Mummy,' said Gemma, 'if it came out of *The Goon Show*, it's just a big laugh.'

'Oh, well, never mind, ducky,' said Polly, 'it all sounds better than a discussion on the Southend shop fire, and I'm sure we've all helped to make your father more cheerful about the future.'

'I'm sure myself, that with my kind of family I'll never feel the need to leave you. I won't emigrate to Australia,' said Boots. 'Or Canada. Or New Zealand.'

'Or even Clapham Common,' said James.

'It's a promise,' said Boots.

'And so say all of us,' sang Polly, James and Gemma in concert.

'What's next?' asked Boots, noting that the repartee hadn't interfered with anyone's appetite. Sliced choice ham, with a mixed salad and hot new potatoes, had vanished from every plate.

'Oh, yes,' said James, 'what's for afters, Mum?'

As usual, their daily maid, Flossie Cuthbert, had prepared the supper before leaving, and Polly had only needed to serve it. However, she did know what the dessert was.

'Peaches with ice cream,' she said.

'Great,' said James.

'Goody,' enthused Gemma, and no-one said anything about the fact that they knew the peaches had come out of a can. One couldn't always get fresh and luscious imported peaches.

'And what do you say, Boots?' smiled Polly.

'What's one more shop?' said Boots.

At a little after eight, Giles Chapman answered the ringing phone.

'Yes, hello?' he said.

'Who's that?'

'Oh, I just live here,' said Giles. 'Might I ask who you are?'

'Hey, Buster, you're not the brother of that doll name of Em, are you?' asked the Teddy boy who called himself Bradley Thompson.

'I've got a sister called Emily,' said Giles, 'but I don't know how much of a doll she is, just that she talks too much when the radio's on.'

'Do us a favour and bring her to the phone to

do some talking to me, would you, man? I'd like a cosy chat with her. Tell her it's Brad.'

'Wait a bit and I'll see,' said Giles. He put the phone down and went into the living room, where his parents and Emily were watching a television programme on the life and death of an African lion. 'Emily, it's your funny friend again, Brad Whatsisname. He'd like to have a cosy chat with you.'

'I'm sure he would,' said Rosie, 'and I forbid it here and now.'

'Tell that precocious young man that Emily's too young for the kind of caper he's got in mind, and that she is not going to speak to him this evening,' said Matt.

With which message Bradley Thompson had to be content, although he assured Giles that come Saturday evening he'd rock around the dance hall with Em until closing time.

'You make it sound like a pub,' said Giles.

'That'll be the day, man,' said Brad, 'when your sister and me can legally prop up a bar.'

'In the Last Chance Saloon?' suggested Giles.

'You bet,' said Brad, and Giles hung up.

'Honest, I just don't know why everyone fusses about Brad,' said Emily as the family watched the doomed lion begin its last attempt to oust stronger rivals. 'Or treats me as if I'm only six years old. But anyway I wanted to see

221

this telly programme all the way through, and if I hadn't said so before, which I know I have, I'll see him at the Saturday dance.'

One of a certain man's favourite ways of acquiring what didn't belong to him was to go to any of London's main railway terminals, buy a platform ticket and wait for a train to come in. He would then make a quick sortie along the platform, using keen and greedy eyes to spot anything passengers might have left behind, usually in an overhead rack. Whenever an item was noticed, he'd take a quick look around to make sure no railway official was watching, then dart into the compartment and snatch what was there for the taking. Mostly it was something like an umbrella, a parcel or a man's hat. Parcels could turn out to be nice surprise packets, while umbrellas could always be passed on to hawkers in street markets, for something like a bob a time. The hawkers, of course, would sell them as second-hand goods in first-class condition, which some of them often were.

Recently, on separate occasions, he'd come into nefarious possession of a very smart umbrella, a superior raincoat and a bowler hat. He was minded to visit one of London's busy Sunday markets to barter them for a quid or two. Instead, however, he decided to pay a return visit to a certain house near Herne Hill, south-east London. Yus, he'd do that, and maybe pick up a useful item or two. Well, he owed the woman of the house a bit of misfortune. He'd suffered painful headaches for weeks ever since the morning when she'd bashed him with a saucepan. Bloody cow. It was people like her that made life difficult for a bloke whose last job as a Government-directed farmhand had come to a finish at the end of the war. Well, after all that suffering as sweated labour, up at dawn and out in the fields for a back-breaking twelve hours every day, he was finished for any other work. For years now he'd had to live hand to mouth, like, and didn't get any help or sympathy from them toffee-nosed people at the employment agency, except an offer to put him in the way of starting a new career as a navvy. He always asked if they were offering to pull the shutters down on his suffering life.

That's it, he thought, that's what I'll do. I'll try that house again, even if only for the pleasure of paying that woman out for what she'd done. She needed to be out shopping, of course, and with luck, she might be.

So he set out from his grubby room in a dosshouse on a bright but chilly morning.

'Where are you off to at this time of the morning?' asked the bloke who acted as warden.

'To see an old friend.'

'Didn't know you had any.' The beery warden grinned. Well, it was something to see Dodgy Dan going forth wearing a fine bowler, a posh raincoat, and carrying an umbrella. Usually he looked what he was, a tramp on the make. Still, no questions of a meaningful kind were ever asked of the inmates. So off went Dodgy Dan, free as air.

His get-up, of course, meant that outwardly he was very unlike the tatty old figure of before. No-one who had seen him on that previous occasion would recognize him now, even if he hadn't bothered to shave for a couple of days or so.

The scene in Kestrel Avenue, near Herne Hill railway station, was peaceful in the well-known way of lower-middle-class suburbia. That is, there were no hollering street kids kicking a ball about, and no rent collectors hammering on the doors of defaulting tenants. The only movements of any note were those of a housewife carrying a shopping bag, and of a car coming out of a drive to turn in the direction of Herne Hill. From the far end of the avenue, a respectably dressed man on the corner was watching.

He saw the car turn right into Herne Hill, whereupon he entered the avenue to follow in the footsteps of the woman with the shopping bag.

She was well ahead of him, but he made no move to catch her up. Indeed, when she too turned right into Herne Hill, he stopped at the gateway of a particular house. Looking around, he noted the convenient absence of people out and about, then made his way up the drive to the front door. He knocked, and, while apparently waiting for an answer to his summons, turned to take a look up and down the road. All was still clear, and with no-one responding to his knock, he used the side path to walk round to the rear of the house.

He moved slowly and silently up to the edge of the kitchen window. He hesitated a moment, then leaned to look through. It was immediately clear to him that the kitchen was unoccupied, which, on top of the fact that his knock had not been answered, convinced him there was no-one at home. Setting the umbrella aside, he drew a crowbar from the deep pocket of his raincoat, only to tense and stiffen as he heard someone knocking on the front door. Although the sound did not reach his ears loudly, it was all too recognizable as a demanding rat-a-tat. He stayed where he was, unmoving. He thought he heard footsteps on the path then, and he certainly heard a voice.

'Excuse us, missus, are you there hanging out a bit of washing in the sun? Parcel for yer.'

Dodgy Dan scurried into the nearest hideaway, the garden shed. A postman, coming round by the side path, took a look at the garden and the empty washing line, decided the lady of the house was definitely not at home, and left. Dodgy Dan re-emerged and ventured to put himself at a point on the side path from where, craning his head, he was able to observe the morning scene again. He saw a post office van moving away, while across the road a housewife was putting an empty milk bottle on her doorstep. That done, she went back into her house and closed the door.

The coast was clear again, but Dodgy Dan waited a few more minutes before going to work.

Meanwhile, Mrs Patsy Adams, American daughter-in-law of Sammy and Susie Adams, was driving to the shops and the local post office. Suddenly she slowed down and brought the car to a stop. Oh, shoot, she'd forgotten the letter she'd written to her good old pa last night. It needed an expensive stamp and an air-mail sticker, and then posting. She turned the car round and drove back home.

Entering the house, she went straight to the kitchen. The letter, she knew, was on the kitchen table. About to pick it up, she became aware of an unfamiliar noise, a creaking and straining of the back door. She yelled.

'Who's there?'

A bowler hat appeared at the left-hand edge of the kitchen window. She didn't recognize the hat, but she did recognize the face beneath it, a swarthy face, unshaven and bristly. Startled eyes peered into hers, then the bowler hat turned at speed and Dodgy Dan, a greasy old piece of work-shy humanity, made a run for safety towards the back wall of the garden.

Patsy, hollering in good old American fashion, unlocked and wrenched open the back door, seized the nearest weapon and ran out in punitive pursuit. She caught the bloke as he was scrambling up and over the ivy-covered brick wall. She struck. A heavy, old-fashioned wooden rolling pin assaulted his purloined raincoat exactly where it covered his backside. He bellowed with pain, and again when a second strike landed quite ferociously. He fell over the wall, which wasn't part of his escape plan at all. The tarmac surface of a path came up and bruised him horribly, which, on top of the pain in his injured male behind, caused him to emit a hoarse cry of agony. Also, the bowler hat fell off. A shout reached him from the other side of the wall.

'Stay there, you punk! I'm coming after you!'

He didn't wait to find out whether that was true or not. Despite his injuries, he upped and bolted, even though every yard he covered hurt him disgustingly. It was all too much like that first time, when she went for him with a saucepan. Bugger this, he thought, what a cow. Females like her ought never to have been invented. This is the last time I want anything to do with her and her shack. She ain't fit to know. She's cost me an arm and a leg. Well, a prime bowler hat and a nearly new umbrella. It ain't my day.

Patsy, returning to her kitchen, spotted an umbrella on the path, obviously left behind by the injured party. She then noticed the edge of the door was scarred from wounding treatment by a jemmy or something similar.

'Who'd have thought it?' she asked herself. 'When I was young and naive, I used to think this little old island was full of eccentric but harmless old buffers with moustaches. I didn't know a thing about thieving old tramps in bowler hats. I guess there's always something new to learn about everything.'

★   ★   ★

She had a story to tell Daniel when he arrived home from his office. He listened, then inspected the scarred door and asked her if she'd called the police. No, she hadn't. She didn't think she needed to, since she was sure there wouldn't be a third visit from the great and lousy unwashed.

'What makes you sure?' asked Daniel.

'Well, Daniel old boy,' said Patsy, taking off Aunt Polly, 'I guess I didn't hit the blighter hard enough the first time. I know I did today, the second time. He won't be able to sit down for a jolly old month. Oh, and we've won an umbrella and a bowler hat, so chin-chin, old top.'

'Get you, cookie,' said Daniel. 'I'll have the door seen to. But next time stop to think what might happen if the great and lousy unwashed turns on you. I'm dead against anything happening to my favourite wife. I mean, favourite wives aren't on sale in London markets at bargain prices.'

'I guess not,' said Patsy, 'but behind a closed door you might get one for fifty dollars. That's if you won't mind her being about ninety, with dentures and a wig, but good references.'

'Somehow,' said Daniel, 'I don't think I'll swop one like you for someone like that.'

'That's it, thrill me,' said Patsy.

Chapter Nineteen

Charlie Ellis had an instinctive affinity with a camera. His professional name was Morton Fraser, and his studio was in the West End. That is, in a room above a shop in Soho. He had good contacts, mainly Continental. With the assistance of a ferry, he usually took the negatives across the Channel himself. A fellow couldn't always rely on the post office not to nose into a packet destined for Denmark and marked 'Holiday Snapshots'. Some interfering GPO blighter had caused Charlie to be informed that the export of obscene material was illegal, and that he was liable to prosecution for attempting it. Be warned, that was the message.

If photographs of a model doing a cute striptease in her hot kitchen while baking a cake were obscene, then the law lords of Great Britain were silly old buggers. Fortunately, once across the Channel a bloke didn't run up against that kind. The law lords of the

Continent had a broader outlook, and a mistress or two in some cases. As for Continental men, they were highly appreciative of eye-winking ladies of a photogenic kind with no inhibitions in front of a camera, and no objections to decorating spicy French magazines. They particularly appreciated the UK variety, especially those who could, in their looks, be classed as English roses.

Charlie had just found a perfect example. Well, no, he couldn't claim that credit. That belonged to a photographer name of Amos Anderson, who had a studio in some London backwater called Camberwell Green, and did weddings, portraits and kids. And as a sideline he did pin-ups, mostly of girls in swimsuits. Charlie knew Amos. They'd studied photography at the same polytechnic. In later years, he'd told Amos more than once that his kind of studio work was all right, but after a lifetime at it, ten to one he'd still be riding on buses instead of having his own limousine.

Now, however, Amos had found a real earner in the shape of a piece of local talent called Maureen Brown. He'd photographed her as everybody's girl next door, but with a saucy touch to the poses in the way of a breeze-blown dress. Result? He'd actually got the photographs published in a national daily and elsewhere.

Further photographs of her had popped up in weeklies and magazines, all credited to Amos Anderson. Each one made Charlie feel that Continental eyes would see the girl as a typical English rose.

Metaphorically licking his lips, he eventually phoned his old polytechnic buddy.

'Good morning, Anderson Studio here,' said Amos's lady assistant. 'Can I help you?'

'Yes, you can put me through to Amos. Tell him Charlie Ellis, an old friend, is calling.'

'Ever so sorry, Mr Ellis, but he's in the studio at the moment. He has a sitter.'

'Well, good for him. As soon as he's free, would you ask him to give me a ring?' Charlie quoted his phone number.

'Yes, I'll ask him, Mr Ellis.'

Amos rang back half an hour later.

'What's brought you out of the woodwork, Charlie?'

'Glad you asked, mate. How's business? Making your fortune yet?'

'Not yet,' said Amos.

'Told you years ago weddings don't rate an apartment in Monte Carlo or even a seaside shack in Sussex. Listen, I'm interested in this girl you've found, the one you've labelled as everybody's girl next door. Smart touch, that. And you've used a genuine pin-up angle with the flirty dress and the leg showing. Start her off with that before we get into real money with swimsuits. Listen, where can I find her?'

Amos, not in the same league as Charlie, seeing as he was basically a decent bloke with a sense of what was fair, if businesslike, baulked at that request. He knew Charlie Ellis as a gifted professional but with the kind of Continental contacts that meant he turned out photographs fit for export but unfit for home consumption. He was always sailing close to the wind. Amos was pretty sure that what he had in mind for Maureen would end up in the naughty magazines of Holland, Denmark and elsewhere. She'd be paid well, but it wouldn't do much for her career in the UK. As things stood she was earning steady money, which he paid to her out of the sale of her photographs. Maureen was under contract to him. He'd been sharp enough to see her potential. He now informed Charlie that Maureen was exclusive to himself, and he was keeping it so.

'Now, now, Amos, come on,' said Charlie, 'you can lend her out to an old friend, can't you? I'll pay you a fee, of course, and you wouldn't stand in the way of her earning her own fee from me, would you? Just give me her phone number and then later on we'll talk about what she can earn for you and me both.'

'Not if she's going to end up glazing the eyeballs of every dee-oh-em on the Continent,' said Amos, dee-oh-em standing for dirty old man. 'And in my book, her earnings come from poses that don't give her the wrong kind of label. Clean earnings for her and me I like, don't I?'

'Course you do, Amos, course you do,' said Charlie. 'Where would we be without the little darlings?'

'I'd be where I am now, wouldn't I?' said Amos. 'With my usual earners.'

'I'll be fair to the young lady and to you,' said Charlie.

'Being fair ain't going to include making Maureen stand on her head in a party frock, no, man,' said Amos. He went on to say that Maureen came of a respectable family, and photographs of her for permissive Continental publications were out as far as he was concerned. So no, he wasn't going to give Charlie her phone number, her address or permission to sell any photographs of her, not unless he saw them first.

'Here, hold on,' said Charlie, 'I know she's under contract to you, but shouldn't you give her the option of deciding for herself. But all right, okey-dokey, you've got a point. I'll let you see the contacts first, then, and if I could say fairer than that, I'd be everyone's Father Christmas.'

'Mrs Anderson and self don't do Christmas,' said Amos, a follower of Moses. 'But I should trust you?' Charlie had made his own point in saying Maureen had a right to decide for herself, providing Charlie would guarantee straight poses and no dubious stuff. 'Can I trust you?'

'Course you can, Amos, course you can,' said Charlie. 'Don't you and me go back to the polytechnic as student mates with only pennies in our pockets? Come on, what's her phone number? I could find out from some other source, y'know, so do me the favour.'

'I'm thinking about it,' said Amos. The most important thing was for him to make sure he definitely saw the contact sheets himself before giving permission to sell any of the photographs. 'All right, you give me sight of the contacts as soon as they're ready.'

'Promise,' said Charlie.

'All of them,' said Amos, 'and my fee for giving you permission to photograph her will be five guineas, which is fixed and non-negotiable.'

'That's tough on me, but all right,' said Charlie. 'We can all earn some useful lolly on your girl next door, and I do mean lolly and not peanuts.'

★ ★ ★

Maureen took two phone calls later that day. The first was from Amos, who told her that a photographer from town, Morton Fraser, would be contacting her with a view to arranging a sitting. Maureen responded with enthusiasm. Being a glamorous pin-up model was great. Amos said make sure he doesn't pose you in a way your parents wouldn't like. Some photographers who concentrated exclusively on glamour, he said, asked more of a girl than was decent. Maureen rushed in to say oh, she wouldn't ever do anything exotic in front of a camera. She meant erotic, but exotic sounded in keeping, so Amos let it go and assured her he was going to vet all the shots before he allowed Morton Fraser the legal right to sell any.

'Morton Fraser's a posh name,' said Maureen. 'Is he posh?'

If Charlie Ellis is posh, thought Amos, I'm baby Moses in the bulrushes, which I know I'm not.

'No, he's not posh, Maureen, just a good photographer with a lot more outlets than I've got. You're earning a few guineas fairly regular at the moment, and Charlie will—'

'Charlie?'

'Mmm?' said Amos. 'Oh, yes, that's his middle name but he doesn't use it profession- ally, which I wouldn't myself if it was mine. It

236

ain't got enough dignity for a professional man. Anyway, he'll help you earn more than a few guineas at a time, and if I didn't think he would, I'd have turned him down. Looking after your interests is a serious responsibility of mine, and don't we know it?'

Maureen said she was happy at the way he looked after her, and that Morton Fraser sounded ever so promising. What she would like, she said, was to see herself on the front page of a classy magazine. Amos said a cover girl, eh? Not half, that's what we'd both like, he said.

'Crikey, you bet,' said Maureen.

'Well, we know, don't we, that a model who's made a front cover is a model who's close to regular top earnings,' said Amos. 'So when Fraser gets in touch with you, play a bit hard to get. That'll up the ante.'

'Oh, I'll look after my interests,' said Maureen.

Her second call was from Charlie himself, who came across as a very friendly-sounding bloke and who introduced himself as Morton Fraser, West End photographer.

'West End?' said Maureen, thrilled. 'My manager, Mr Anderson, mentioned you worked in town, but he didn't say West End.'

'Haven't you heard of me?' asked Charlie, letting his tonsils sound surprised.

'Well, no, I can't say I have,' said Maureen. 'Mind, I could've done, except it's sort of escaped me.'

'I forgive you,' said Charlie. 'But I'm sure you've seen photographs of Rank film starlets in your newspaper or magazines.'

'Oh, yes,' said Maureen.

'Well, every time you've seen one, you've been looking at my kind of work,' said Charlie.

'Crikey, I've seen some of those starlets on the front cover of *Filmgoer*,' said Maureen.

'If I photographed Diana Dors tomorrow, it wouldn't be the first time,' said Charlie, on easy terms with a porkie.

'Diana Dors? Oh, crikey, imagine that,' said Maureen. Diana Dors was a bit more than a starlet. She was well on her way to becoming the UK's favourite blonde bombshell. 'Mr Fraser, are you phoning about giving me a sitting?'

'So I am, girlie,' said Charlie. 'How will next Tuesday suit you? Say two in the afternoon at my studio?'

Maureen said that would suit her fine, and how long would the sitting be? Charlie suggested it could well be two hours, and Maureen asked what the fee would be per hour. Charlie said he'd pay her five guineas for the session, which delighted Maureen considering Amos had told her some photographers only paid one guinea an hour. She ventured to ask this West End professional who had photographed Diana Dors if Mr Anderson would also receive a fee, seeing she was under contract to him. Charlie said she and Amos, and he himself, were all expected to earn something from the sitting.

'Oh, who do you expect to sell the photos to?' asked Maureen, thinking of the front covers of famous magazines like *Vogue*.

'Not to a tuppenny-'apenny comic,' said Charlie. 'But first let's see how the pics turn out, right? Next Tuesday, then, at two?'

'What kind of outfits d'you want me to bring?' asked Maureen. 'I've got some lovely dresses.'

'Don't you worry about that,' said Charlie, 'I'll supply the costumes from me studio wardrobe, every item clean and laundered. You just bring yourself, eh? Good-oh.'

But Maureen asked what kind of costumes did he have in mind? Charlie said highly fancy and very chic. And Maureen said she was in favour of anything chic, as it helped a model to look high-class. Apart from her latest poses in a sweater, all her sittings for Amos had required her to do leggy shots, since that was how he had first brought her to the attention of some news-papers and magazines. Sitting on a gate with the breeze lifting her dress. Amos said every girl next door ought to have legs like hers, but liked the fact that hers alone were special.

'Oh, all right, Mr Fraser, I'll be at your studio at two next Tuesday afternoon,' she said. 'What's the address?'

'It's Old Compton Street,' said Charlie, and gave her the door number.

'I don't think I've ever been in Old Compton Street,' said Maureen. 'It's in the West End, is it, like you mentioned?'

'Is it?' said Charlie. 'It is, and no more than a stone's throw from good old Piccadilly Circus. Nor is it here today and gone tomorrow. From Monday to Monday, every day of the year, it's where it is now, next to Shaftesbury Avenue, and if I could say fairer than that I'd be every-one's guide to the bright lights.'

'Oh, I know Shaftesbury Avenue,' said Maureen.

'Then I'm glad for both of us, girlie,' said Charlie.

Over the phone, they parted company on very sociable terms, each looking forward to meeting the other next Tuesday.

Of course, Maureen's parents, Cassie and Freddy Brown, wanted to know all about their daughter's latest booking, and when she told them it was to be with a real West End photographer, they both wished her luck, except that Freddy spoiled it a bit by asking what an unreal West End photographer was like.

'Is that supposed to be funny, Dad?' said Maureen.

'No, just something I thought I'd ask,' said Freddy.

'Well, now you can answer it yourself,' said Cassie. 'Maureen and me both like a laugh.'

Neither she nor Freddy had had any objections to Maureen giving up a boring old office job to become a pin-up model. They both took pride in her looks and her figure, and went happily along with her dreams of becoming as popular as a Rank film starlet, or as glamorous a cover girl as Diana Dors. Diana Dors always seemed to photograph with a saucy twinkle in her eyes and lots of uplift. Still, saucy pin-up girls had been part of the social scene since the heady barrack-room days of the Second World War, when American soldiers and sailors pinned up photographs of Betty Grable, the Hollywood film star, and men of the British Eighth Army adopted the German Afrika Korps's dream girl, Lili Marlene, as their own pin-up in the shape of an artist's impression.

So Maureen was in good company, really.

'D'you know how much you'll be paid for the sitting?' asked Freddy, who liked to feel sure she'd always receive her fair dues.

'Five guineas,' said Maureen.

'Bless my dear old dad,' said Cassie, 'that's as much as some workers earn in a week.' Her dear old dad, known as the Gaffer, still lived with them, and had taken to spending part of his pension playing bingo regularly at the local hall. 'That pleases you, Maureen, I'm sure.'

'Oh, not half, Mum,' said Maureen, 'and think what I might earn if Mr Fraser helped me to become a cover girl. Well, he must have the right kind of contacts, being a well-known West End professional.'

'Is he well known?' asked Freddy.

'He told me he was,' said Maureen.

'I don't think I've heard of him,' said Freddy.

'Nor me,' said Cassie.

'Well, he was a bit surprised when I told him I hadn't heard of him meself,' said Maureen. 'I expect he meant well known in the West End, and we're Walworth.'

'I've been Walworth all my life, except when I was in Burma with the old 14th,' said Freddy.

'Oh, we're proud of you, Dad,' said Maureen.

'Both of us,' said Cassie, 'and my dear old dad too.'

'I wasn't asking for compliments,' said Freddy. 'Still, you can all put something extra in my stocking come Christmas. Anyway, Maureen, you go ahead next Tuesday and then let me and your mum know how it worked out.'

'Righty-oh, Dad,' said Maureen, chuffed at developments.

Chapter Twenty

It was Matt's dubious pleasure to pick up the phone that evening and to hear that Emily's Teddy boy was on the line again.

'Hi there, it's Brad here – can I talk to Em?'

Matt let the phone shift from his ear for a moment while he regarded the instrument as if he was losing faith in its usefulness. Then he spoke.

'Brad there,' he said, 'this is Emily's father here, and I'd like to know if we're to expect a phone call from you every evening for the next ten years.'

'Hey, man, is that what you'd go for?' said Brad.

'It's what's bothering me,' said Matt, 'and I'm not sure it isn't bothering Emily.' As soon as the phone had rung a minute ago, she had said if that was Brad, tell him she was busy doing her homework.

'Believe me, Mr Chapman, sir,' said Brad, 'I

don't go in for bothering people. I'm a genuine good guy, and both my parents like me. I could grow on you, given time, like. So can I talk to Em?'

'My daughter,' said Matt, 'is busy doing her homework. After which, she'll be just as busy making a dress for her favourite doll.' That wasn't actually a prize porkie, but an attempt to capitalize on the fact that Emily had made a dress for one of her dolls when she was nine, and that she was still only thirteen.

'No kidding?' said Brad. 'Well, man, I grew up with a teddy bear myself, and I think it's still somewhere around in my family's shack. But listen, are you telling me that my sugar baby actually does homework? School home-work?'

'My daughter is not your sugar baby,' said Matt, 'but yes, I assure you she really does do school homework. What do you do?'

'Plumbing.'

'Plumbing?'

'Sure,' said Brad, 'glad you asked. Well, strictly, I'm an apprentice. Mister, you positive I can't talk to Em?'

'Quite positive,' said Matt.

'OK.' Brad sounded philosophical. 'Saturday evening, then.'

'Do me the favour of co-operating with my

son to make sure Emily is back home by not later than ten thirty,' said Matt, with a touch of parental severity.

'Ten thirty?' said Brad. 'That's no time. Still, early birds can still swing.'

Burn my Sunday shirt, thought Matt, plumbers' apprentices weren't like this one in my day. They were too busy fetching tea for the plumber to make phone calls, and too simple to make weird ones.

'Goodnight, young man,' he said, and hung up.

'Hello there,' said Rosie, when he rejoined her in the lounge. Giles and Emily were in occupation of the living room, doing their homework. Giles was industrious as a scholar, while Emily thought society ought to have invented a more entertaining alternative to schools. 'What kept you?' asked Rosie.

'A plumber's mate,' said Matt.

'A plumber's mate?' Rosie smiled. 'Is that something to do with the precocious Teddy boy?'

'The young gent informed me he's apprenticed to a plumber,' said Matt.

'I'm glad to know there's something in his favour,' said Rosie, 'since I had the impression that his main activity was standing on street corners.'

'Well, he told me he's a good guy, and that both his parents like him.'

'Really?' Rosie was amused but not a little sceptical. 'Well, I beg you, Matt, not to let him into the house if, instead of making phone calls, he rings our doorbell.'

'Better if you hadn't said that,' murmured Matt, switching on the radio, 'it's tempting Providence.'

The following day Mr Austin Cobb, manager of the claims department of the relevant insurance company, telephoned the offices of Adams Property Company Ltd and asked to be put through to Mr Tim Adams. Connected, he informed Tim that the insurance company would send an official to work in concert with the investigators of the fire. He also said a claims form was on its way, but that there was little point in completing it until the cause of the fire was known.

'Thought you'd say that,' said Tim. The fire and the destruction of the Southend shop was less of a headache to him than to Sammy. He considered only an earthquake under his living-room floor could spoil his daily delight in the fact that Felicity's blindness was gradually curing itself. All the years when the world had been a blank to her were coming to an end, and against that a shop was only a shop to a firm that already had a dozen. However, Uncle Sammy seemed to have taken the loss and the implications personally. 'Mr Cobb, how long do these fire investigations take, do you know?'

'The time taken varies. It's always governed by circumstances. You understand, Mr Adams?'

'Yup, I understand only too well,' said Tim. 'But I'd be obliged if you'd keep in touch.'

'If you're asking for a daily bulletin, it's against the rules.'

'I learned when I was still young that there are rules and rules,' said Tim.

'Of course,' said Mr Austin Cobb, 'so shall we say a bulletin once in a while?'

'That's fair,' said Tim.

'I'll be in touch, but it's certain that in the event of the cause of the fire being acceptable, settlement will still take time.'

'I'll bet Christmas,' said Tim, 'and who's going to quarrel with that? Only Mr Sammy Adams, our managing director.'

'I've heard of the gentleman.'

'So has everybody here in Camberwell,' said Tim, and closed the conversation on a cordial note. He'd won a small concession from the manager of the claims department, and that was as much as he could hope for. He let his co-director Daniel know of this, then went to talk to Sammy. Sammy wasn't so much concerned with bulletins as with the fact that the powers-that-be were going to turn over every spot of ash in the burnt-out shop. It meant, he said, that the cause of the fire was considered suspicious.

'Uncle Sammy, you know better than that,' said Tim. 'All destructive fires have to be investigated, and no insurance company will settle a claim until the cause has been discovered.'

'Well, I do know it, sunshine,' said Sammy, 'and I'm much obliged to you for reminding me. No, my big worry is if the investigation rubs off on us and some interfering newspaper hound turns it into a story. You know what editors are like, they'll print anything that smells a bit. My dear old ma, Lady Finch, won't let any paper into her house except my step-dad's *Telegraph*. That way she doesn't have to read about things like some bloke in Croydon turning into a woman. She'd throw up at that kind of stuff. I tell you, Tim, what with the headache that kept me awake when the garment union was threatening a strike, and now this new headache over who done what in respect of the fire, it's not been my year.'

'Well, hard luck, Uncle Sammy,' said Tim, 'but I don't think you'll go under, whatever happens. You've survived too many crises to let this one turn you grey. Which reminds me, d'you realize that you, Uncle Tommy and Uncle Boots don't have a single grey hair between the three of you?'

'Nice of you to mention it,' said Sammy, 'and might I point out that it's due to all of us being healthy, hardworking and honest since we left school. Of course, personally, I could say that being up to my ears in work every day is what keeps my loaf too busy to grow anything but me natural hair.'

'Grey hair's natural,' said Tim.

'Yes, but you know what I mean,' said Sammy. 'Now, about the insurance company and our claim. Keep after them.'

'Will do,' said Tim, 'and I'd better get back to my desk now.'

'For any special reason?' asked Sammy.

'Yes, I'm up to my ears,' said Tim. Sammy watched him leave and thought there goes a chip off Boots, the old block. And at thirty-six, he looked not unlike his dad at that age.

The phone rang in the Chapman family's home that evening.

Rosie twitched.

'Can it be?' she asked.

'Him?' said Giles.

'Him,' said Rosie, whose maternal instincts cautioned her to protect Emily from the advances of the Teddy boy who had phoned every evening so far this week.

'I'll go,' said Emily, 'otherwise there'll be more fuss.'

As soon as she picked up the hall phone, a well-known voice reached her ear.

'Brad here – who's that?'

'Me,' said Emily.

'It's you yourself, you doll?'

'Yes, and what d'you mean by phoning us every night?' demanded Emily.

'I've got this urge to talk to you,' said Brad, 'and I've got to do it over the blower on account of not being invited to drop in by your ma or your pa. I guess parents live in a different world, I guess they're all still waltzing or foxtrotting. That sure is sad, baby.'

'Don't call me baby—'

'Sugar doll, then?' suggested Brad.

'Not that, either,' said Emily, 'and stop talking like Frank Sinatra. And don't try to get me on the phone every night, because it's playing on my mum's nerves. She's beginning to twitch each time the phone rings.'

Brad said he was sorry to receive that piece of news because he was sure her ma was pretty nice, even if she was still stuck on waltzing.

Emily said not to keep phoning, then. Brad said he'd like to write to her once a day instead of phoning, except that his writing wasn't all that hot. Emily said to remember she'd only seen him once, last Saturday, and because of that she didn't need to be written to, whether it was hot or cold. Brad said she was real cute for her age, and was it true she was only thirteen? Emily said she was actually nearly fourteen, and would be when her birthday arrived in August.

'Well, that's great, baby,' said Brad. 'We'll go places one day. By the way, how's your pa's plumbing?'

'Do what?' said Emily.

'I could come and look it over if it's a mite screwed up in places, like you've got a toilet that won't flush properly,' said Brad. 'Me and plumbing, we're already buddies. I'm getting to know all the wrinkles, and I sure would be pleased to look at your pa's system and let him know if anything needs the expert attention of Jeremiah.'

'Who's he?' asked Emily.

'The plumber I'm apprenticed to,' said Brad. 'A genuine guy, except he's another one who's still into waltzing.'

'Forget plumbing and my dad's system,' said Emily, 'and meet me at the dance on Saturday. That's all.'

'Hey, give us a break, Em, I'm—'

'Goodnight,' said Emily, and hung up. She returned to the family in the living room.

'It was him?' said Rosie.

'It's not my fault he keeps ringing,' said Emily. 'Oh, he made an offer, Dad. He offered to come and look at your plumbing in case it wasn't working properly.'

'Your mother has instructed me never to let him into the house,' said Matt. 'The boy's a wrecker of nerves.'

'Still, he seems to be getting on well in his plumbing job,' said Emily, 'and he's a great rock 'n' roller.'

'So there you are, Dad,' said Giles.

'Matt,' said Rosie, 'I've a feeling that the young people are taking us over.'

'Burn my Sunday socks,' said Matt, 'is there a future for you and me, Rosie?'

'Only if we don't give in,' said Rosie.

Chapter Twenty-one

Saturday, and Phoebe and Philip were on the way home from their honeymoon. They'd enjoyed a lovely week, including the fascinating aspect of getting to know each other as well by night as they knew each other by day. Well, what else would the world have expected of them as newly-weds? However, Philip had to report back to his squadron on Monday, and Phoebe, happily, was to go with him, for the housing officer had arranged for them to occupy married quarters. Philip had said this would be in the form of a house, one of several available to married couples. Phoebe was talking about that now, which reminded him to remind her of what he had already told her, that she wouldn't have to worry about being suddenly overwhelmed by housework, because she'd be receiving help from his batman.

'Well, imagine that,' said Phoebe amid the rhythmic sound of the smooth-running train that was carrying them to London. 'It would be like having a servant while I'm still young and active instead of old and arthritic.'

'Just the job,' said Philip, 'so we'll hang onto him. We have to remember that at your age and under present circumstances, you never know when you might need someone to lend a hand with the Hoover.'

'Why?' said Phoebe, too entranced by love's purple horizons to be as quick on the uptake as she usually was.

'It does happen to wives,' said Philip, and Phoebe did catch on then.

'Oh, help,' she said.

However, she wasn't the only Adams bride who had called theatrically for help at some time or other. Adams bridegrooms were an adventurous lot.

Saturday evening, and the dance at a hall in Brixton was swinging, the young people rocking and jiving. Dance halls generally were becoming the haunt of the young, and only rarely on Saturday evenings were there occasions when an old-fashioned band played old-fashioned music for old-fashioned couples. The latter weren't necessarily aged, but even a husband and wife in their mid-twenties were counted as old hat if they still preferred the foxtrop to jiving.

The band this evening was hot stuff, made up of four young men and a young woman vocalist who owned a powerful pair of lungs. She belted out the numbers, the microphone trembled, and the sounds bounced back off ceiling and walls, adding continuous echoes to the recreational buzz.

Giles was swinging it with Cindy Stevens. Cindy, in her assertive way, was intent on drawing him into her exclusive circle of boyfriends who would, in a manner of speaking, eventually bow down to her. Giles, however, while thinking Cindy the tops in looks and style, wasn't the kind of young bloke who didn't mind being one of a crowd. This evening, for instance, Cindy had two other boys waiting for her to notice them. Giles, accordingly, was inclined to side with the non-committed.

'Giles, you're great, and you're swinging great, d'you know that?' she said.

'Pardon?' said Giles. It was difficult to hear, especially with the vocalist belting out one more number. He and Cindy had to shout at each other. 'What was that you said?'

'I said you're going great, Giles, you're the best.'

'It'll probably be a wet Sunday tomorrow, then.'

'What d'you mean?'

'Didn't you say there was rain coming from the west?'

'Would I say that? No, I said you're the best.'

'Pardon?'

And so on. It tangled up the dialogue, which suited Giles.

Emily, meanwhile, was jiving with young Bradley Thompson. Away from the four walls of her home, and her parents, she was more responsive to the Tony Curtis lookalike. They'd established a rapport based on hitting the rhythmic factor together, and Brad, who always had a lot to say, even when it was difficult to be heard, let Emily know in loud tones that she was the classiest ladybird of all time.

'You've got style, babe, as well as the same name as my grandma.'

'What? Oh, your grandma. Well, never mind her, I wasn't named after her.' Emily was fully aware that she'd been named after Uncle Boots's first wife. He was her grandpa actually, but she never called him that, and nor did any of her cousins. He was simply everyone's uncle, and she was pretty sure he wouldn't fuss about her social life, not like her parents did. He didn't fuss about anything, actually. 'Oh, watch your feet, d'you hear me?'

Her Teddy boy's feet were flying about.

'Come on, let's swing, Em,' he said, bawling

the words into her ear as he stepped up the rhythm.

'Don't go mad,' yelled Emily. He was all moving limbs and hips, the music and the beat sending him over the top. Still, it was infectious enough for her to match his gyrations.

They were surrounded by other dancers, the girls passing in and out under their partners' upraised arms and swinging their hips joyfully.

'I've got music in my hoofers, so go, baby, go,' said Brad.

'There's not enough room,' said Emily.

In the packed dance hall, all the young people needed more space.

'Give it a go, doll,' said Brad.

'Excuse me, mate,' said a vigorous bloke, 'you talking to mine?'

'Yours?' said Brad.

'My private doll. You don't want yer leg broke, do yer?'

'You bet I don't,' said Brad, noting that the private doll, a blonde, was closer to him than to her partner, such was the way the crowded hall jumbled people up. 'Believe me, I'm talking to nobody but my own ladybird.'

'Eh?'

'It sure is a great shindig,' said Brad, and went rocking with Emily, who told him he was bound to fall down a hole if he kept talking all the time. Brad said a load of silence always made him feel the cops were at his door and about to charge him with robbing a bank. Well, anyway, he made a gifted partner for Emily. His sense of rhythm matched hers, and that was something worthwhile in any boy. Too many of them couldn't shake a leg without falling over.

Not far from them, James and Gemma were going it with a girl and boy respectively. Gemma was alight with enjoyment, eyes sparkling, skirt swinging. James's partner was a girl he'd only just met. Or, rather, a girl who'd fastened onto him. James didn't mind. He took life, events and people as tolerantly as his dad. From time to time he cast a glance at cousin Emily and her Teddy boy partner. James had been asked by his mother to help Giles make sure that Emily was home by ten thirty, and thus save his Aunt Rosie a touch of the twitches. Giles himself was also keeping an eye on Emily to make sure she didn't suddenly disappear.

It so happened that at fifteen minutes to ten, Brad suggested to Emily that they leave now so that she'd be home as early as any parents could dream of. He'd mentioned, he said, that parents had a bit in common with the dodo, and it sure was best to keep them happy before they were only history.

'I don't want to leave yet,' said Emily.

'How about if we took a taxi ride to your ranch?' said Brad.

'Do what?' said Emily, using her elbows to make space for her swinging hips.

'I'm flush,' said Brad, 'I picked up my pay yesterday afternoon. It wasn't a fortune, but it wasn't peanuts, either. Well, plumbers' mates are valuable to plumbers, and if a plumber's got his own business, he'll slip you a dollar or two. So how about a taxi ride, babe?'

The thought of a ride in a taxi instead of on a crowded bus won Emily over, and she left the hall after first letting Giles know that Brad was taking her home this minute, and in a taxi.

'God's honour?' said Giles.

'Yes,' said Emily.

'Sure,' said Brad, and Giles felt tickled by the possibility that his mum and dad were going to come face to face with Emily's Teddy boy. It wouldn't, he supposed, be something they'd welcome, although it might give his dad a chance to let Brad know in no uncertain terms that his relationship with Emily wasn't what her parents wanted at this time in her life.

The fact was, of course, that like many parents, Rosie and Matt weren't too much in favour of the burgeoning social changes that were giving young people an overblown sense of their own importance, and leading them into foolish or reckless behaviour.

'Well, good heavens, Emily,' said Rosie a little later, 'you've made up for last Saturday.' The time was ten twelve. 'Is Giles with you?'

'No, he'll be home at his usual time,' said Emily. 'But Brad's here, he brought me home in a taxi. Come on, come in, Brad, and meet my mum.'

Brad entered the hall, and Rosie did indeed come face to face with Emily's Teddy boy, whose dark shiny quiff was undisturbed by the evening's exertions. His light brown thigh-length jacket was single-breasted and fastened by one button only. His double-breasted fancy waistcoat of maroon bore gleaming brass buttons. The collar of his white shirt was adorned with a dark brown bow tie, and his dark brown drainpipe trousers clung to his legs all the way down to his crêpe-soled suede shoes. However, he had surprisingly pleasing features, which cancelled out the suspect aspects of his outfit. His smile indicated he didn't feel in the least nervous. Rosie decided to be welcoming.

'Good evening,' she said.

Brad was taking stock of Emily's Ma. He hadn't expected to see a quite lovely woman with massed hair the colour of golden corn, and blue eyes that could mesmerize a guy in two shakes of a gee-gee's tail. She didn't seem at all the kind of woman to come down hard on her daughter for being a bit late home. No, she looked a knockout. Brad judged her to be about thirty-five. She was actually forty-two. He himself was sixteen. Coming to, he said, 'Good evening to you too, lady.'

'So you're Mr Bradley Thompson,' smiled Rosie, recognizing his voice.

'Lady, I don't go with mister, call me Brad, and I've got to say it's great to meet Em's mother. I kinda like mothers, I've got one of my own, and she's a real sweetie most times.'

'There are other times?' said Rosie, with Emily looking on.

'Only when she knows Aunt Totty is going to call,' said Brad. 'Aunt Totty kinda rubs Ma up the wrong way, and Ma's a mite difficult to live with then.'

'Who'd have an Aunt Totty?' said Emily, and took herself abruptly off to enter the living room and let her dad see she was home early, and therefore no-one need fuss.

'Well, Brad,' said Rosie, 'come in and meet Emily's father. He'll be happy to know you brought her home in a taxi.'

'I guess she's worth a cab now and again,' said Brad, 'she's a great girl and a great rocker.'

'And a young schoolgirl.' Rosie's reminder was gentle but pointed.

'It hardly notices,' said Brad airily, and followed Emily's striking mother into the living room.

For the next several minutes he made himself known to Emily's parents. If they thought his Teddy boy outfit was a bit bizarre, they were pleasantly surprised by his social graces. His habit of using American terminology was accepted by Rosie as part of his obvious desire to be noticed. Matt thought it the sign of a young man hooked on Hollywood Westerns. But for that matter, all kinds of people of all ages liked Westerns.

Emily played a looking-on role, and from time to time her expression conveyed a rebuke to her parents on the lines of 'There, now you can see why you don't have to fuss.'

After ten minutes, Brad was offered a cup of tea or coffee before departing. No, thanks all the same, he said, but his ma would have something for him, like a slice of pork pie and a glass of barley water.

'You can digest a slice of pie before you go to bed?' said Matt.

'No problem, mister,' said Brad. 'Ma's pies are digestible any time of the day. She's a natural in the kitchen, and could make a name for herself running a cookery class. Well, I guess I'll say goodnight now. Been real homely, meeting you both, and any other Saturday when I'm hoofing it with Em, I'll see she gets to her front door in good time.'

'Don't get smart,' said Emily, and saw him out. On the doorstep he bent and gave her a kiss. 'And don't take me for granted,' she said.

'I'll call you,' said Brad.

'You'll drive Mum and Dad dotty if you phone next week as much as you did this week,' said Emily, at which moment Giles appeared. He grinned to see Brad and his sister.

'OK?' he said.

'Sure,' said Brad, 'a great evening, and I kinda like your parents. So long, Em, so long, man.' Off he went.

'What a character,' said Giles.

'He's all right when he's not talking too much,' said Emily. 'Listen, you're getting a bit close to Cindy Stevens, aren't you?'

'Well, she's grown up in pretty good form,' said Giles. He closed the front door and went to show himself to Rosie and Matt, with Emily following. His parents told him about their meeting with Bradley Thompson, and how he had arrived with Emily in the full regalia of his outfit. They didn't seem as if they'd met a bit of a layabout, which was what they had thought he might be. And they'd been quite impressed by his good manners, even if he did talk like a cowboy. Rosie said the young man had proved quite likeable, and Matt said he might well become an asset to civilization once he dropped his Teddy boy outfit off London Bridge and passed his plumbing exam.

'He won't drop his outfit off any bridge,' said Emily, 'he'll live with it for years. Crikey, don't you know Teds feel they belong to a club, and clubs can last for ever, can't they?'

Rosie had a sudden mental picture of Bradley as a bridegroom, all togged up in his long jacket, his drainpipe trousers, a waistcoat like a purple sunset and a wedding-day shine to his quiff.

'Well, for his own sake, I hope he grows out of it,' she said.

'Anyway, Mum,' said Giles, 'you and Dad didn't find him such a bad bloke?'

'In future,' said Rosie, 'I'll do as I usually do, reserve my judgement on people until I've actually met them.'

'There you are, Emily,' said Giles, 'Brad's been approved by Mum and Dad as your boy-friend.'

'No, he hasn't,' said Matt, 'he's on probation until your sister's out of her school uniform and either at university or in a job.'

'But I'll be fourteen in August,' protested Emily.

'That's no age,' said Matt, now a heavy-handed father but a cautious one. 'There's an old Dorset saying.'

'There always is,' said Rosie, 'and how many times have I told you that every one's a shocker?'

Ignoring the opposition, Matt recited in his native county's accent,

'Down by Dorset, so they say,
Perky chaps roll in the hay,
Enticing girlies every day
To join them in their saucy play.'

Emily giggled.

Rosie said, 'That's the daddy of all shockers, but I think it means keep away from boys who talk like cowboys, Emily.'

'Brad's just a laugh,' said Emily. 'I thought you could see that while he was here.'

'Well, you can go dancing with him,' said Rosie, 'but your dad and I still want you home by no later than ten thirty on your dance nights.'

'But like I mentioned, I'll be fourteen soon,' said Emily crossly.

'Yes, very young,' said Matt.

'I'm going to bed,' said Emily, 'it's no fun down here.' And off she went without saying goodnight, leaving Rosie wondering how it was that she and Matt were troubled by a rebellious daughter. The answer, she thought, lay in the fact that many modern teenagers were beginning to regard parents as out of touch with developing trends.

Chapter Twenty-two

The following day, Sunday, saw Nigel Killiner and Linda promenading again in Ruskin Park. He found it easy to talk to her, and in the sunshine of the afternoon, she found it easy to listen. After a while, however, Nigel encouraged her to tell him all about herself. What were her favourite recreations, for instance?

'Oh, I don't have what you call recreations,' she said, the flared skirt of her summer dress lightly whispering. It was no more given to making itself loudly heard than Linda was herself. 'I mean I don't play tennis or anything like that, and I don't go on country rambles. I help my mother with the cooking sometimes, and listen to gramophone records on the radio.'

'You're a home girl,' smiled Nigel, looking pleasantly relaxed in an open-necked beige sports shirt and navy blue slacks. He was bare-headed, and the widow's peak of his black hair was well defined. It gave his comfortable look a tidy appearance. 'I read somewhere that home girls get full marks as housewives.'

'Really?' said Linda. 'I might get to be a housewife one day, so tell me more.'

'I would,' said Nigel, 'if I knew more about home girls and housewives, and a lot less about cheeky schoolkids. It's my sincere opinion that most of them should never have been born.'

'Oh, that's a bit hard on them,' said Linda, enjoying the stroll, the park and the company she was keeping. Nigel really was entertaining, and despite what he had just said, she could imagine there were moments in class when his pupils were either tittering or laughing at his sense of humour. 'You make allowances for most children being naturally precocious, don't you?'

'If I didn't,' said Nigel, 'I'd end up as a cross-eyed patient in a home for the deranged.'

'How sad,' said Linda, smiling. Nigel reciprocated. Round the park they strolled, and round again, along with other leisurely promenaders, and Linda wondered if Nigel was beginning to regard himself as her beau. She was ready to have him do so, even though this was only the second time they'd been out together. Bless me, she thought, have I met my fate or does he just like walking and talking in a park on a Sunday? Certainly, neither last week nor this week had he suggested taking her dancing or to a cinema or a theatre. Of those pastimes, she felt Nigel, as a schoolteacher, would opt for a theatre, which a lot of people would consider a bit more cultural than a dance hall or a cinema.

'Penny for your thoughts,' said Nigel, and she realized she'd been musing for a couple of minutes.

'Oh, I was just thinking it'll be teatime soon,' she said.

'Good point,' said Nigel, 'let's go to the tea rooms.'

Linda said they didn't need to do that, because when he took her home he could stay for tea, like he had last Sunday. Her mother had said so. Nigel said her mother was very hospitable, and he'd be delighted to stay.

At this point, two boys, both about ten years old, approached at a run, their smothered mirth suggesting they had just teased a girl or two. On they came, and one glanced at Linda and Nigel as he rushed by. He called, 'Oi, Killy, where'd yer get yer filly?'

'Who's a clever bloke, then?' called the other.

Both boys kept going and disappeared, leaving Nigel to make the kind of comment Linda expected.

'There you are, Linda,' he said, 'that's a

definite example of two young specimens who should never have been born.'

'Oh, well,' said Linda, 'you can't stop boys catcalling. Most of them have their rowdy years.'

'What d'you say, shall I walk you home now?' asked Nigel.

'That's a very sudden offer,' said Linda, 'but I suppose it's time we did think about leaving.'

So they walked to the gate, from where Linda caught a glimpse of the two boys. They were pointing at Nigel and laughing. I suppose it is funny to them, she thought, a schoolteacher walking me round the park, like boy meets girl. Nigel, however, took no notice of the pair, apart from saying he'd sort the terrible twins out at school tomorrow. Linda asked were they twins? Yes, said Nigel, in that both of them were a pain to everyone else.

They left the park to walk to Linda's home. There Nigel was given a hospitable welcome by Annabelle and Nick, who were quite happy for him to stay to tea. Annabelle was happy because a schoolmaster was the epitome of respectability, and Nick was happy because Linda was. It was obvious she was enjoying the prelude to what might become a romantic relationship. Society might be changing, but some young women still thought in romantic terms.

So tea was served in the open air of the sunny garden. The conversation flowed, Nigel again encouraging Linda to put in her tenpenny-worth, and Nick, a football fan, talking about the local amateur club, Dulwich Hamlet, until Annabelle reminded him this was the cricket season, and football was out of order.

Linda ventured to tell her parents that two of Nigel's pupils had catcalled him in the park.

'In the park on a Sunday afternoon?' said Nick with a broad grin. 'That'll alarm the park-keepers. They'll think about smothering the kids for the sake of peace and quiet. It's always been that way in Ruskin Park. As far as I know, they've never allowed any kind of high jinks, especially on a Sunday. What will you do to those kids, Nigel?'

'Smother them and save the park-keepers a job,' said Nigel good-humouredly, and that raised a laugh.

Annabelle took covert note of the developing relationship between Linda and her school-teacher friend, and she thought how well matched they were, the amenable nature of her daughter complemented by Nigel's easy approach to life and people.

The chink of cups and saucers, the appeal of home-made scones and cake, and four people all in tune with the sunny afternoon, made for very pleasant moments. By the end, Nigel was as comfortably ensconced as if he were one of the family. Before he left, he asked Linda if next Sunday, for a change, she'd like to go with him to Hyde Park. Linda enthused at the idea, and said that in Hyde Park they could count on the absence of rowdy kids from his school.

'That's a point,' said Nigel.

'But what about young rowdies from other schools?' she asked.

'Don't tempt Providence,' said Nigel.

That evening, Joe Chambers asked his wife Lily, not for the first time, if she had something on her mind. It was, he said, making him feel he wasn't there. Lily came back with the riposte that more often than not he actually wasn't there, he was either doing overtime or playing darts.

'Overtime pays,' said Joe. 'Come on, there is something on your mind, so give.'

'Well, if you must know,' said Lily, 'it's my housekeeping money. I've been sure for some days that somewhere or other I either lost a ten-bob note or had it pinched. Mind, I don't know how it could've been pinched because it was in me purse and me purse was in me handbag, and no-one could've got at any of the money unless they pinched the purse out of me handbag, but it's still there.'

'You sure the ten-bob note was there in the first place?' said Joe.

'There, I thought losing it might upset you,' said Lily, and continued with her fairy story. 'I've been worrying about it since it happened, and it's not doing my peace of mind much good.'

'Well, cheer up and start living again,' said Joe. 'What with your wages and mine, plus a bit of overtime, you don't need to make yerself sick over ten bob. It's not as if you lose it every week. Forget it, eh?'

'Oh, all right, thanks,' said Lily. 'I didn't like having to tell you because it makes me look careless, and after all ten bob is ten bob, not fourpence. Still, if you think I needn't worry, I won't, but I'll be a lot more careful in the future.' She carried on in this vein, swamping Joe with words, most of which began to go in one ear and out the other, while all the time her mind wasn't on any ten-bob note, but Mr Sammy Adams. It was no good, she'd fallen in love and something had to be done about it. Lord, if only she could be sure she wouldn't be interrupted if she spoke to him in his office again, then she'd have a go.

She looked up as her flow of words, all for Joe's benefit, dried up, and what did she see?

She saw Joe with his head on his chest, fast asleep, the *News of the World* on his lap.

Husbands. What got into them that they couldn't talk to their wives?

Monday morning, and Sammy and Susie were at King's Cross railway station with Phoebe and Philip. Sammy had made the journey in his car so that he and Susie could see the young people off to begin their new life. The train was in and waiting, emitting little puffs of restless steam as if impatient to get going. Phoebe was by no means impatient herself. She was facing up to the wrench of saying goodbye to her adoptive parents in the knowledge that her home would no longer be with them. Like Rosie, the adopted daughter of Boots and his first wife Emily, Phoebe had known years of caring love, the kind that fully compensated for an unhappy beginning to life.

'I'll write lots,' she said, her eyes visibly misty.

'And there's always the phone,' said Susie.

'Do we have the phone?' asked Phoebe of Philip. She looked engaging in a light summer coat and a pillbox hat, and he looked like every girl's lanky dreamboat in his RAF uniform and cap.

'Yup, we have the phone,' said Philip, 'and we pay the bills.'

'Oh, phone bills are never much,' said Phoebe, 'and anyway, I can reverse charges when I phone Mum and Dad, can't I, Dad?'

'Be my permanent guest,' said Sammy, who knew when a financial outlay was worthwhile. He had a bit of a lump in his throat, while Susie was as misty-eyed as Phoebe.

'Phoebe kitten,' said Philip, 'I think we'd better do our boarding act. The train's due out in a few minutes.' He had a first-class railway warrant for both of them, and had already taken their luggage to the relevant compartment.

'Oh, I suppose we'd better,' said Phoebe. She gave way to emotion then by closely hugging her parents in turn, and hanging onto each of them for a few seconds. Her goodbyes were somewhat muffled. So were Susie's. And Sammy had to cough to clear his lump.

'Good luck, pet,' he said. 'Good luck, Philip.' He shook hands with his new son-in-law.

'Thanks a bundle to both of you for giving me Phoebe,' said Philip, and kissed Susie before shepherding his bride onto the train. The platform was clearing of passengers, and the guard had his flag and whistle at the ready. As

276

Phoebe entered the compartment she had a sudden attack of nostalgia for the life she was leaving behind. She let down the window, put her head out and smiled wet-eyed at Sammy and Susie, who were close by.

'Love you, Mum, love you, Dad,' she said huskily.

'It's always been mutual,' said Sammy, who had another lump in his throat as Susie reached and touched Phoebe's hand.

A whistle sounded, the engine blew steam and the train began to move. Philip and Phoebe were both at the compartment window, waving to Sammy and Susie.

There they go, thought Sammy.

It's their own lives now, thought Susie.

We've seen them all go off to their own homes, said Sammy to himself. Daniel and Patsy, Bess and Jeremy, Paula and her Italian heart-throb, Jimmy and Clare, and now Phoebe and Philip. I feel sort of deprived. He took off his hat and waved it as the train slowly disappeared and took Phoebe and Philip with it.

'Well, they're on their own now, Sammy,' said Susie.

'Susie, how old are you?' asked Sammy, as they left the platform.

'Gentlemen don't ask ladies their age,' said

Susie, 'especially not in public.' They were skirting numerous individuals weaving about in different directions. London railway stations always provided telling examples of how arriving and departing people could get mixed up with those merely waiting.

'Well, between you and me in private, Susie,' murmured Sammy, 'you don't look like anyone's middle-aged mother. No, more like a female woman of thirty, for which I admire you considerable.'

'Thank you, Sammy,' said Susie, 'but what's on your mind, if it isn't Phoebe?'

'Well, I was thinking, Susie, are we still young enough to start another family?'

People hurrying into the station turned their heads to look at two people coming out, a well-dressed man and a nicely dressed woman. The woman was laughing aloud.

In public.

Sammy drove Susie home, then went on to the Camberwell Green offices. Once there, he asked Tim and Daniel if they'd received any kind of official letter about the fire. The answer was no. Tim said it was a bit soon, anyway, and Daniel said the only official letter he wanted to arrive on his desk was the one advising them that the fire had started accidentally and they could therefore rightfully make their claim on the insurance company.

'I couldn't agree more,' said Sammy, 'you're a bright lad, Daniel.'

'I could point out I'm now thirty,' said Daniel, 'but I won't in case you don't believe it. Did Phoebe and Philip catch their train on time?'

'In good time, actually,' said Sammy.

'How was their honeymoon?' enquired Tim.

'Don't ask me,' said Sammy, 'send them a postcard care of the RAF and ask for an answer.'

Chapter Twenty-three

At the offices on Tuesday, Sammy and Boots were inspecting the conversion job that would turn the ground-floor shop and storeroom into a canteen and an extra office. The work was in its final stages, and Sammy and Boots both liked what they saw, the canteen invitingly bright and spacious, and the kitchen and counter clean and gleaming. Boots said he'd be happy to lunch there from time to time, but would keep mainly to his ingrained habit of enjoying a beer and a sandwich or a salad at the pub opposite.

'Well, I've got a habit of having to go out for business lunches now and again,' said Sammy, 'so would you mind telling me what ingrained means?'

'That one gets stuck in a groove,' said Boots.

'I thought so,' said Sammy, 'but I wouldn't use ingrained meself. I'm not educated enough. I'd just say what you just said, that I'm stuck with it.'

'So am I,' said Boots.

'Who's playing a comic?' asked Sammy. 'By the way, Rachel has found a woman who'll be assistant to the cook. It's all going well, no headaches at all – no, button up, I shouldn't have said that, it's a sure way to muck up progress.'

'Touch wood, old lad,' said Boots, and Sammy touched the main door. He wasn't keen on inviting trouble or any kind of a headache. He'd lived uneasily during the days when a strike was threatened, and he was now having to live with the consequences of the Southend fire. What else had given him a headache? Oh, yes, that peculiar female bookkeeper, Mrs Lily Chambers, a little while ago. Pity about her peculiarity, because she was a good worker.

He made his way upstairs to his office, and of all things, who should be waiting at his door but the funny female herself.

'Oh, good morning, Mr Sammy,' trilled Lily, 'I was hoping to see you as I've got something to show you.'

'A dubious bank statement?' said Sammy, as he entered his office.

Lily, following him in, closed the door and said, playfully, 'Oh, no, nothng like that. It's this.' She placed a Marks & Spencer carrier bag on the desk, reached into it and drew out something black and silky. She shook it out and Sammy found himself mesmerized by what it was, a black nightie trimmed with lace. 'Isn't it sexy?' said Lily, hoping there would be no interruptions.

'What's it doing in my office?' asked Sammy, squaring up to the necessity of giving her another talking-to.

Lily sighed, let her eyes go soulful, and whispered, 'Wouldn't you like to see me in it, Mr Sammy?'

'Where?' asked Sammy, as she placed the nightie against her female figure. The item was sexy all right. 'Yes, where?'

'Oh, we could go to a country hotel one evening when my husband's playing darts,' said Lily, proving that because Joe left her alone so much she'd gone potty.

'I'm not going anywhere,' said Sammy, setting aside good humour to make himself understood, 'but you'll be walking the plank if you carry on like this. I'm happily married, and I don't need any piece of sugar in a black nightie. The idea embarrasses me considerable. What's got into your brainbox, might I ask?'

'Mr Sammy, I'm in love,' said Lily.

'No you're not, and anyway it's not allowed, and I ain't in favour,' said Sammy. 'Put that nightie away and forget having a bit of what you fancy with me or any other bloke except your old man. Does he know about your problem?'

'No, course not,' said Lily, 'he's got his darts and I keep me problem to meself – oh, except now I'm sharing it with you.'

'Leave off and be your age,' said Sammy. 'And stop looking at me as if I've just been turned into a fruit bun. Go back to your work and make it your only interest in office hours. If you don't, I'll have to do what I won't want to do, and that's give you your cards.'

'Mr Sammy, you wouldn't do that, would you?' Lily looked upset, very. 'You wouldn't give me the sack, would you?'

'If you don't put that nightie away and out of sight,' said Sammy, 'it'll happen here and now.'

'Oh, that sounds awful hard on a girl,' said Lily.

'You're not a girl, you're a woman and your old man's wife,' said Sammy, 'and you're also a good bookkeeper. It's better you live with that than some cock-eyed idea about what you'd like to happen in a country hotel. Are you with me, Lily?'

'Oh, Lor',' said Lily, 'I didn't think it would come to this, Mr Sammy.' The black nightie was drooping forlornly, and Lily herself wasn't exactly at her brightest. 'I didn't think you'd talk about giving me the sack.'

'Well, I am, and I will if you don't get your head in order,' said Sammy, pretty sure that to be kind he had to be tough. He knew she enjoyed her job, and a threat to hand her a week's notice had every chance of scaring her out of her dotty notions. 'Now, go back to your desk and behave yourself.'

'Yes, all right,' said Lily, dreams of romantic high jinks crushed by this, the second time Mr Sammy had spoken to her in an unsympathetic way. She walked to the door, the nightie back in its bag, and she couldn't help thinking this was the one time when there had been no interruptions and yet it had all ended in a wounding negative.

However, once she was back at her desk, a succession of book entries played their soothing part, and the black silk nightie lay unseen and unspoiled in its carrier bag.

Joe was in when Lily arrived home from her job. He'd been working an early shift. Usually, on early shift, he stayed to do overtime. He hoped it would help them to save enough for a car. Not many postmen had a car in addition to a wife.

'Welcome home, me love,' he said, 'I've just made a pot of tea. Like a cup? Yes, course you would. Sit down and I'll pour you one.'

Lily blinked. She seldom received a welcome

like this. Her suspicions pointed her at a reason.

'Oh, I know what this is all about,' she said, 'you've got another darts match tonight and you know you're going off for the evening. Don't you care about leaving me alone so much?'

Joe poured the tea, put one knob of sugar in the cup, and pushed cup and saucer along the kitchen table in the direction of his wife.

'Come on, Lily,' he said, 'sit down and drink this. It's nice and hot and fresh. And listen, about darts—'

'I don't want to hear nothing about any darts,' said Lily, but she sat down. 'Darts are all you live for.'

'Only three times a week,' said Joe.

'Yes, and your overtime or your late shift at other times make sure I hardly ever see you of an evening,' said Lily. But she took a sip of the hot and welcome tea.

'Well, I want you to know I'm giving up darts,' said Joe.

'You're what?' said Lily.

'I'm resigning from the pub team,' said Joe.

'I don't believe it,' said Lily.

'I've been thinking,' said Joe, 'and I've decided it's up to me, as your lawful wedded, to spend more time with you. I went into Palmer's shop on me way home and ordered a television set on hire-purchase terms that won't do no harm to your housekeeping money, even if it sets us back a bit on getting a car. It'll be delivered and set up tomorrer. And tomorrer evening, you and me can sit and have our first telly evening together. How about that, eh, Lily?'

For about twenty seconds, Lily was lost for words. Then she said, 'We're going to have television and you're not going to darts any more?'

'That's it,' said Joe. 'Except for late shifts and when I'm doing a bit of evening overtime, I'll be watching the telly with you. As for me beer, I'll stock up with a few bottles of light ale.'

'What's brought all this on?' asked Lily, now making much of her cup of tea.

'I told you, I've been thinking,' said Joe, 'and I've concluded, Lily, that you're more important than me darts. It's a poor man who can't enjoy evenings at home with his better half, specially if he can still enjoy his beer.'

'I just don't know what to say,' said Lily, 'except are you sure you're all right and not feeling a bit queer, like?'

'I'm fine,' said Joe, 'and I don't have any quarrel with me thinking. So how d'you feel about things now?'

'I can hardly take it in,' said Lily. But she was conscious that Joe's words were softening the blow of being finally rejected by Mr Sammy. 'Well, having a television and you home most evenings is a bit of a surprise, I can tell you, but it's a nice surprise.'

'That's my girl,' said Joe. 'Listen, what's in that carrier bag?'

'Pardon?' said Lily.

'What is it, something you've bought for yourself?' asked Joe.

'Well, I'm glad you asked,' said Lily. 'It makes a nice change, being asked about me personal shopping. Yes, it's something I bought for meself.'

'Let's have a shufti,' said Joe.

'All right,' said Lily. Present circumstances being an improvement on what had gone before, she took the nightie out of the bag, stood up and draped it over her front. Joe visibly goggled.

'Eh?' he said.

'Like it, do you?' said Lily, feeling a whole lot better.

'Saucy sailors,' said Joe, 'it's a black French nightie. Lily, you going to bed in it?'

'Not now, not right now, but later,' said Lily.

'Not too much later,' said Joe. 'I mean, I can hardly wait, can I?'

'Well, I'm blessed,' said Lily, 'you're remembering I'm alive, Joe Chambers.'

Sammy, meanwhile, had said not a word to anybody about Lily Chambers being definitely off her rocker. He thought keeping it under his hat best for both of them, in the hope that what he had said to her this time would finally cure her of her desire for a bit of what she thought she fancied in a country hotel. Imagine her coming out with that in working hours.

Women. Mother O'Grady, what a funny lot they were. Except Susie, of course. And Phoebe had never been off her rocker. It had been a pleasure, having her and Philip at home for the weekend, even if a bit gloomy watching her disappear on that train yesterday. He hoped she'd like married quarters and not come up against too many rules and regulations. In the army, navy and air force, everything had to be done by numbers or regulations. It was a wonder that Boots's time in the army hadn't turned him into a filing cabinet.

Chapter Twenty-four

Tuesday afternoon.

In a photographic studio above an Italian grocery shop in Soho, Miss Maureen Brown, known to pin-up fans as London's girl next door, was getting ready for her sitting under the auspices of Mr Morton Fraser, whose real name was Charlie Ellis. The dressing room, brightly lit, was a welcome treasure trove, with its rich supply of all kinds of fine-quality cosmetics laid out on a dressing table. They enabled Maureen to ensure her make-up was perfect.

The first outfit awaited her. It was right up to the mark fashion-wise, a full mid-blue skirt, stiff petticoats, a black bodice-style top with a plunging neckline, black nylons, a white half-bra and frilly white panties. Everything was new, so Maureen had no qualms about wearing any of the items. She changed in front of a lovely full-length wall mirror, a great help in ensuring she was satisfied with her look. Her ponytail hairdo went perfectly with the outfit, although the plunging neckline of the top and the skimpiness of the half-bra revealed more of her bosom than she had bargained for. But she was not prudish about it. She supposed that while Amos liked to focus on her legs, of which he was proud, Mr Morton Fraser was going to help her show off her figure, of which he was admiring. On her arrival, he'd said he was dee-lighted to see her and to classify her as a 36–24–36 girlie. She asked how did he guess? Experience and sensitive eyesight, he said.

When she was ready, Maureen entered the studio. It was spacious, but the only furniture was a small corner table on which stood cartons containing rolls of film, a central round-topped table and an old-fashioned sofa with red and gold upholstery. There was also another full-length wall mirror to enable her to check her appearance from time to time. Mr Morton Fraser – Charlie Ellis – received her with hearty acknowledgement of her turnout.

'Girlie,' he said, 'you're great and we're going to have a great session. Sit your fair self on that table.'

'Sit on it?' said Maureen.

'Sure. Plant your derrière on it and cross your ankles.'

Maureen did as he wanted, and the session

began. He posed her this way and **that,** making the most of her legs before moving in on her tantalizing cleavage. The glamour came from her, and the studio soundtrack from him, for he talked all the time to let her know how photogenic she was. Maureen was sure the bodice-style top with its plunging neckline was committing her to the kind of poses new to her. The wall mirror confirmed it. Still, she was in the mood, a glamorous-minded mood. After all, cleavage was ultra glam, even if it wasn't quite in keeping with a girl next door.

He posed her next on the sofa, and in a kind of languid, feline way that made her look like an old-style Hollywood vamp, except that her outfit was far from old style. He began to take close-ups of her plunging neckline.

'Fantastic – great – super-duper – love it – don't go away – stay like that – got you.'

'Crikey,' said Maureen, 'I don't know what my dad's going to say about these kind of photos.'

'Take it from me, girlie,' said Charlie, 'it's your photographers and pin-up fans who'll make your career, not your dad.'

Maureen accepted that. She was, in any case, under the spell of a real West End professional. Her bus ride to Soho, her walk down Old Compton Street, and the fact that she actually had an appointment in the heart of London's glamorous playground, all planted the seeds of excitement. Well, Old Compton Street wasn't like Camberwell Green, where Amos had his studio, it was much more intriguing. Even the people seemed different. She'd noticed several Italian-looking characters, all of whom wore black trilby hats and shiny shoes, and one or two very flashy-looking women of indeterminate age. She wasn't so naive that she didn't know Walworth people would have called the latter tarts or old pros. Still, you couldn't deny everything had atmosphere, whereas the only places of interest in Camberwell were the Camberwell Palace theatre, two cinemas and a Lyons teashop.

After the sofa shots, her real West End professional photographer asked her to change into a second outfit of blue jeans and a red-and-white checked shirt, together with a half-bra the colour of golden wheat and a cowboy's hat. Maureen asked if jeans would look glamorous.

'They will, girlie, they will,' said Mr Morton Fraser, 'providing you don't do all the shirt buttons up, if you get me.'

'Oh, I get you,' said Maureen, 'it's more cleavage shots.'

'In your case, lovey, more is plenty, and plenty's not what every girlie can lay claim to.'

So she went back to the dressing room and changed outfits. She left the top three buttons of the shirt undone, did an unnecessary repair job to her make-up, put on the felt Stetson, regarded herself in the long mirror and returned to the studio, where Mr Morton Fraser again received her with enthusiasm.

'Well, here's a glad picture of a girl cowboy,' he said. 'All we need now is a horse.'

'Don't tell me you've got one here,' said Maureen.

'What I will tell you is that while we've got you, we don't need any gee-gee. See that chair, Gloria? Sit on it like a cowboy.'

'Gloria?' said Maureen. 'I'm not Gloria.'

Mr Morton Fraser shook his head at himself. A model who called herself Gloria was a do-it-all for the Continentals, one of his regulars.

'I'm not all there,' he said, 'I'm intoxicated, believe me, by how cute you look in that cowgirl outfit. Anyway, sit on that chair like a cowboy, eh?'

A pine chair with a low back had made an appearance. Maureen sat down on it like a cowboy, facing the back and planting her legs on either side of the seat. A new succession of poses began, all aimed at proving how cute a cowgirl could look in an unbuttoned shirt, a skimpy bra and a Stetson hat. The low back

of the chair left her shirt and cleavage un-
impeded, and she had the Stetson tipped back
to ensure no shadow darkened her face. Mr
Morton Fraser's enthusiastic verbosity accompanied every click of his shutter.

'I tell you no lie – that's the tops – love it, love
it – what kept you away from me, girlie? Turn
your head a little to the right – good on yer –
beautiful – take a bow.' And so on.

Maureen was used to a photographer's
verbiage, the kind that was supposed to make a
model feel she was the one he'd been waiting for
all his life. Even so, it was always helpful,
especially coming from this larger-than-life West
End bloke.

Having satisfied himself that he'd taken all
the shots he wanted of her as a cowgirl, he sent
her back into the dressing room to change
into her third and final outfit, an off-shoulder
low-cut evening dress of midnight blue, with a
narrow waist and flared skirt. The bra, matching the dress, was built-in, with the result that
the upper curves of her well-developed bosom
hardly hid their light under the midnight blue.

'Oh, help,' she murmured, studying her
reflection in the mirror, 'I hope he doesn't pose
me in a way that'll make me fall out. Oh, well.'
She made adjustments to the dress, to her hair
and to the dress again.

In the office, where three of the four walls sprouted filing cabinets, the photographer's assistant was busy cataloguing contact sheets. He looked up from his desk as someone entered.

'Afternoon,' said someone, 'I'm Amos Anderson. Is Charlie busy?'

'Mr Morton Fraser, if yer don't mind,' said Curly Harris, the assistant.

'Oh, Charlie's an old friend of mine, ain't he?' said Amos. 'He's spoken of me, I expect.'

'What did you say your name was?' asked Curly, dark, foxy and protective. This bloke could be a copper. Coppers in Soho were always poking their noses into some legit business. Well, any business was legit if it had customers.

'I'm Amos Anderson, a fellow photographer.'

'You're him?' said Curly. 'It's one of your models he's busy with just now, right?'

'I'm Miss Brown's manager,' said Amos. 'I'd like to see how she's getting on. My privilege. Can I go through?'

'OK, but knock first,' said Curly.

Amos went through to the studio. On the door was a notice in heavy black capitals.

KEEP OUT AT ALL TIMES

Amos knocked. He was there for a very specific purpose, having had second thoughts this morning about Charlie Ellis and the way he earned most of his bread.

'Whoever that is, bugger off,' called Charlie.

'It's Amos.'

'Eh? Look, I'm busy.'

'I know. I'm only here to see how you're getting on with my best model.'

The door opened, and Charlie thrust his head out.

'I'm doing great, she's doing great, we're both doing great, so what's your problem, old buddy?' he asked.

'No problem,' said Amos genially, 'I'd just like to sit in on a couple of shots, and see what she's looking like. I should have a personal interest in her promotion to a West End studio? I do, you bet.'

'All right, come in for a couple of ticks,' said Charlie, 'I'm just about to photograph her in classy evening gear. She's got a prize figure.'

'Yes, 36–24–36,' said Amos, and entered. Maureen was still in the dressing room, so he looked casually around. He noted the furniture and the corner table on which lay about a dozen completed rolls of film, some cartons containing new film, and, to one side, three more completed rolls. He further noted the full-length, highly polished wall mirror.

In came Maureen, looking stunning in the evening dress, the built-in bra giving her noble uplift. Amos had to admit she was glamour personified, with all the advantages of her nineteen tender years.

'Well, look at you, Amos, where did you come from?' she asked.

'Just passing by, so I thought I'd drop in and see how you were getting on,' said Amos.

'Well, that's ever so nice of you,' said Maureen, 'and I think I'm getting on fine. Am I, Mr Fraser?'

'Great,' said Charlie, 'you're top of the bill. And that outfit is just the job, and not half. I'll pose her conventional to start with, Amos. You take a seat on the sofa for a couple of minutes.'

'Sure,' smiled Amos, although he knew he'd been given his marching orders. Charlie didn't want anyone ferreting around, especially a fellow photographer. He posed Maureen standing, the round table behind her, her hands on its edge, her body leaning slightly backwards. This enhanced the uplift. Amos, seated on the sofa, smiled again. Charlie knew his stuff. Maureen looked like everybody's favourite pin-up for sure, the evening dress real flattering to her figure.

A knock on the door preceded Curly's voice.

'Hey, Mr Fraser, there's a client wanting to see yer.'

'I'm busy, he'll have to wait.'

'I know you're busy,' called Curly, 'and I

wouldn't be interrupting yer, only the client's come a long way and he's a regular.'

'Oh, right,' said Charlie, getting the message. 'Excuse me for a couple of shakes, Maureen, there's some clients some of us can't keep waiting. Amos, you're going now?'

'I'll follow you in a tick, won't I?' said Amos, coming to his feet. 'I need to get back to Camberwell pretty quick, anyway.'

'Right,' said Charlie. He gave Amos a look, and he glanced at Maureen. Both smiled in return, and out he went to see to the client who'd come a long way. From Amsterdam.

'Don't ask questions, Maureen,' said Amos. 'Just tell me what's on the other side of this wall mirror.'

'The dressing room,' said Maureen, 'with a matching mirror.'

'That's a fact, is it?' said Amos, and made a quick inspection of the dressing room. He noted the mirror, and then made a keener inspection of the one in the studio. He knew what it was all about then, a two-way contraption with a concealed button which, when pressed, would turn the studio mirror into a window. Charlie Ellis was down in the dirt. It was a disgusting practice, keeping models unaware that he was photographing them when they were dressing and undressing. And they remained unaware,

298

for such photographs were sold abroad by Charlie, and never seen in the UK. Amos wished he had never met the man. 'Change into your own clothes, Maureen,' he said.

'What?' said Maureen. 'But me and Mr Fraser, we're not finished yet.'

'Yes, you are,' said Amos, 'and if you need an explanation, little lady, just see this.' He found and pressed the hidden button, and the mirror became a window that revealed the brightly lit dressing room.

'Oh, the rotten swine,' breathed Maureen, 'no wonder he put me in different outfits so's he could watch me changing.'

'I hate to say so, but I think it amounted to more than a peepshow,' said Amos. He pressed the button again, and the window became a mirror once more. 'We're leaving,' he said, 'so go and put your own clothes on.'

Maureen, flushed with fiery anger and not a little humiliation, rushed into the dressing room. Amos looked again at the corner table on which lay about a dozen spools of completed film, and three to one side. He slipped the three into his pocket, and replaced them with three from the large number, of which there were actually fourteen. Charlie had done his pin-up work at length, and Amos didn't doubt that the contacts would all be acceptable.

Out came Maureen, ready and willing to leave. Quietly, Amos took her by the arm and they left the studio, bypassing the office and the subdued sound of voices, to make a silent way down to the exit at the side of the Italian grocery. Outside, in the busy street, Maureen drew a deep breath.

'Amos—'

'Wait till we're in my car,' said Amos, 'it's parked in Shaftesbury Avenue. I should be glad I decided to look in on your sitting? I am.'

'So am I, even if it means I won't get my fee of five guineas,' said Maureen, still flushed and angry.

'We'll see, we'll see,' said Amos. 'I wasn't born yesterday, was I, and nor were you.'

Chapter Twenty-five

On the way to Camberwell in his car, Amos explained exactly why it was necessary for Maureen to have nothing more to do with Charlie Ellis, who called himself Morton Fraser but was far from being a gentleman or even a reputable professional.

'In my pocket,' he said, 'I've got three rolls of film, which I suspect are shots taken of you through that two-way mirror while you were changing outfits. It's best you know that—'

'But if you knew he wasn't what he ought to be,' said Maureen, still very upset, 'why did you agree to me sitting for him?'

'I did think he was going to play straight with you, didn't I?' said Amos, driving with care towards Waterloo Bridge. Motor traffic in the West End and the City was far more intrusive than pre-war. 'About lunchtime today I had second thoughts. I began to worry, didn't I? Get up to Soho, I said to myself, and see what's happening with my girl next door.'

'I'm glad you did worry,' said Maureen.

Amos said that as soon as he saw that studio wall mirror and three rolls of completed film set aside, he had his suspicions. But he didn't want to create uproar, not on the premises he didn't, and decided it was best to do a quiet bunk with her when Charlie's absence offered the opportunity. She wouldn't have liked a stand-up set-to with everything being shouted out. That would have added to her embarrassment, wouldn't it? In his opinion, went on Amos, not half it wouldn't. Maureen said she was grateful to him for coming all the way to the studio to find out what was happening. But was he sure the three rolls of film really did have shots of her dressing and undressing?

Driving over the bridge, Amos said no, he couldn't be sure, so he was going to develop them and find out. If they turned out to be illegit photos of her, he'd destroy them.

'And I'll have a short word with Charlie, won't I?' he said.

'I think he's going to come after you,' said Maureen, as they entered Waterloo Road and headed for the Elephant and Castle junction. Post-war developments of bomb sites made their mark on the eye. 'I think he might turn out quite nasty, especially if you're wrong about the photos.'

'I've got instincts, ain't I?' said Amos. 'You bet I have, as well as knowing a bit about Charlie and how he earns the butter on his bread.'

'What d'you mean?' asked Maureen, not too knowledgeable about what some photographers could really get up to. But she was coming to realize that the highly dubious could exist along with the reputable. 'Yes, what d'you mean, Amos?'

'I mean, Maureen, that if these shots are what I suspect,' said Amos, 'then Charlie would have sold them to a Continental publisher of naughty girlie magazines, the kind that are banned in the UK, and you would never have known anything about it.'

'Oh, the rotten beast,' said Maureen, 'and would he have sold the decent shots to UK mags?'

'You bet,' said Amos, 'he had you looking like a hundred guineas in that evening dress. That wasn't for the sake of kidding you, he had legit earnings in mind as well as the other kind.'

'What upsets me as well as those mirrors,' said Maureen, 'is losing out on the five guineas.'

'I'll see to things, don't worry,' said Amos, feeling for her blush-making afternoon and her bitter disappointment. 'So we won't give up on that five guineas, you bet we won't. We might even up your dues.'

'Get more, you mean?' said Maureen. 'But I bet he's not going to pay me a penny now, not after me walking out on him.'

'We'll see, we'll see,' said Amos. She was back on her home ground as he entered Walworth Road, since she lived in Wansey Street, close to the town hall. 'Would you like me to drop you at Wansey Street?'

'No, I want to come to your studio with you,' said Maureen, 'because I've got a feeling you're going to develop those films as soon as you get there.'

'So I am, Maureen, so I am, ain't I?'

But when they reached his studio, his lady assistant, who was about to leave, since the time was just after five thirty, said that the phone had been ringing repeatedly for the last half-hour, and each call had been from Mr Ellis. Would Mr Anderson please ring him now? Amos said he'd see to it at once, and his assistant left. No sooner had she disappeared than the office phone rang. And it sounded like an angry ring. Amos looked at the instrument.

'You'll have to answer it,' said Maureen.

Amos picked it up.

'Anderson's photographic studio here,' he said, 'can I help you?'

The response was a tidal wave of foaming threats and oaths from Charlie, all on account of Amos having the gall to remove a model for no given reason while his back was turned, which was a bleedin' breech of professional etiquette and the law as well. For said act he could be sued down to the last coin in his bank account.

'And don't think it won't happen. What the hell did you think you were bleedin' doing?'

'I'll ring you and let you know,' said Amos. He had to get those films developed before he had the necessary ammunition to fire at Charlie, and that depended on whether or not the films were what he suspected they might be. He'd made a mental note of the fact that Charlie hadn't mentioned there were some missing. He hadn't noticed, obviously. 'Yes, I'll let you know in the morning.'

'You'll let me know now, you hear, you bugger?'

'Tomorrow morning,' said Amos, 'and don't try calling me any more, the phone will be off the hook. Sorry, Charlie.' And he put the receiver back to cut the call before placing it on the desk, where it lay looking as if it had fallen out of bed.

'What did he say?' asked Maureen.

'Nothing for your ears, m'dear,' said Amos. 'Now, you take it easy while I get busy in the darkroom.'

'Shall I make us some tea?' asked Maureen. She knew where everything was.

'What a great girl,' said Amos tenderly. 'One lump of sugar for me.'

Sometime later, in the office, he showed her several of the negatives, of which there were thirty-six in all. Maureen held them up to the light, since Amos had not printed any contacts. He wanted nothing to do with seeing the shots in stark black and white, not even as small two-by-two-inch contacts. Stark was the word all right, if the negatives were anything to go by. His eye was sharp and practised.

'Oh, Lor',' breathed Maureen. Just three or four negatives were enough to make out that she'd been photographed while undressing. In another one she was sure she was down to the nuddy. 'I'd never have believed anyone could take such a rotten advantage of a girl. He's disgusting.' Maureen was flushed again, very much so. 'Amos, what're you going to do with all these negatives?'

'First, I'll talk to Charlie tomorrow morning, won't I?' said Amos. 'Then at the right time I'll burn them.'

'You're not going to make prints, are you?' said Maureen. Amos gave her a sad look. 'Oh, sorry, Amos, you wouldn't have gone to all the trouble you did if you— Well, you know.'

'Look in again tomorrow morning about coffee hour,' said Amos, 'then I'll let you know how much Charlie is going to pay you for your time and trouble.'

'You think he'll do that?'

'Yes, I think so.'

'I'll get my five guineas?'

'More, I hope.'

'You'll frighten him?'

'I'll blackmail him.'

'Amos, you'll do that?'

'All's fair in war, ain't it?'

'Blackmail as well?'

'You bet, not half,' said Amos.

The phone call next day didn't take all morning. Amos had Charlie with his back to the wall in two minutes flat, which was pretty good going where fly Charlie was concerned. He was told he not only had to pay Maureen ten guineas or else, he also had to pay her twenty per cent of what he earned selling the straight pin-ups, again or else. Or else what? The negatives, said Amos, would be shown to Maureen's dad.

'You're a traitor to your profession, you bleeder,' breathed Charlie.

'And you, Charlie, you grieve me,' said Amos. 'You don't have any ethics or principles, and you know it. In view of which, I want a legal guarantee from you that you'll pay up.'

'Or Daddy's going to find out, is he?' That was a sneer from Charlie.

'Daddy will,' said Amos, 'and what you'll find out is that Daddy's got muscle.'

'Do I get those negatives back?' asked Charlie, rocking quite a bit.

'Is that a serious question?' asked Amos.

'Don't you have any principles yourself, you punk?' bawled Charlie. 'You nicked those films.'

'So I did, and it's your hard luck, ain't it?' said Amos. 'That's all for now. Just make sure I get that guarantee.'

'Sod you.'

'Or else,' said Amos, and closed the conversation.

When Maureen arrived at coffee time, Amos took her into the studio away from the ears of his receptionist, and told her that he'd talked to Charlie, and that Charlie was going to settle at ten guineas for the sitting and twenty per cent of what he earned for selling the straight shots.

'Amos, honest?' Maureen glowed.

'Honest,' said Amos, 'and I'm personally advancing you five of the ten guineas this morning. After all, it was my doing that sent you to Charlie.'

'Crikey, I'm thrilled about the money,' said Maureen, 'but I'd still like to dot that Charlie beast one in the eye.'

'Did you tell your parents anything?' asked Amos.

'Not likely,' said Maureen, 'or my dad would've gone out and bought a shotgun. I kept quiet about that mirror, I just said I hoped me poses in different outfits would come out great and get me on a front cover.'

'Wise girl,' said Amos, 'we don't want shotguns sounding off, do we? Shotguns are noisy. And damaging.'

'Oh, not half,' said Maureen. 'Amos, I'm ever so grateful for all your help.'

'I should turn a blind eye? Not on your life,' said Amos, and handed her five one-pound notes and five shillings as the promised advance on what she could expect to receive from Charlie.

'Oh, thanks ever so,' said Maureen, 'I'm feeling better now, Amos.'

'Good,' said Amos, 'feeling better is what we both like.'

Chapter Twenty-six

'Hi, sugar.' Brad was on the line.

'Mum said it was you again.' Emily was at the other end.

'She's a cookie, your ma,' said Brad.

'Don't you do anything of an evening except make phone calls?' asked Emily.

'I sure don't,' said Brad, 'I only call you, and it's more than worthwhile if your ma answers first. What a lady. Anyway, doll, what're you doing right now?'

'I'm just finishing my homework,' said Emily.

'School homework again?' said Brad. 'That's sad, baby, considering you're ready to make your mark on civilization. Say, when d'you leave school?'

'I'll be going on to higher education when I leave my present school,' said Emily. 'My parents think I'm just about bright enough for university.'

'Hey, baby, that's for eggheads,' protested

Brad, 'and you're no egghead. You're built for living.'

'Yes, but parents always have the last word until a girl comes of age,' said Emily. 'Most girls have to do what they're told, just as if they're still children. And parents always expect us to behave like they behaved a hundred years ago. Change passes them by, poor things.'

Brad said that sounded painful, and something he wouldn't have expected of her ma, who looked great enough to be able to rock around the clock with the best of guys and dolls, like he'd mentioned before. Emily asked if he had a fancy for her mum. Brad said that seeing she herself was the most fanciable doll in the UK, he didn't need to answer her question. It was just that her ma looked something special, considering she was a parent. Parents usually look old, he said. Emily said it wasn't that they looked old, it was more to do with them thinking old.

'I get you,' said Brad. 'Still, if yours feel you ought to try for university, I wouldn't say that was old thinking. More like good thinking.'

'Crikey, you said it was only for eggheads a minute ago,' protested Emily. 'Now you're talking as if you're on the side of parents.'

'No, I'm on your side, sure I am,' said

cowboy Brad, 'which is why I'm giving you the lowdown. Yep, I'm telling you university will mean you'll get to be more than a plumber's mate.'

'What's wrong with being a plumber's mate?' asked Emily.

'OK, I guess, if you get to be the plumber,' said Brad. 'But I wouldn't have minded having your chance to go to Eton.'

'Not Eton, you dummy,' said Emily, 'you mean Oxbridge. Besides, I want to make my own decisions about my life, and anyway, I can't stay here gassing all night. Bye for now, see you at Saturday's dance unless you're going to a Tommy Steele shindig with my mum.'

'Leave off about that and talk more to me,' said Brad, but there was no response from the other end of the line. Emily had hung up and gone back to her homework.

In another family home, Polly, while waiting for the nine o'clock news on the television, was asking the twins exactly what they thought of the odd young man who was apparently their cousin Emily's current dancing partner. She knew of the Teddy boy only by way of their mention of him.

'He's all right,' said James. 'I mean, he doesn't go in for robbing banks, just some cowboy talk, like cousin Daniel does at times, when he's talking American with Patsy.'

'His clothes are a bit freakish,' said Gemma.

'Freakish?' said Boots. 'Daniel's?'

'No, not Daniel's,' said Gemma. 'We're speaking of Emily's Teddy boy. But he seems all right to me.'

'What is meant by freakish?' asked Boots.

'Freakish, dad, means unusual,' said James.

'Boots,' said Polly, 'our children are doing shuddering things to the English language.'

'Might I point out, Mum,' said James, 'that in your time you did your particular thing, like calling fussy elderly blokes frightful old kippers?'

'She still does,' said Gemma.

'Change the subject,' said Polly. 'No, switch the television on, James, and let's catch the news.'

That did little good, for the main bulk of the news concerned what was known as the Cold War, the antagonism existing between the Western democracies and the Soviet Union bloc. Accusations and counter-accusations of espionage were never-ending, and since the whole thing had been going on almost from the moment the Second World War ended, boredom was now the principal reaction of many people to any mention of it.

Gemma said she'd go to bed unless she was

allowed to turn the set off. Boots said he'd prefer a silent set to his daughter's absence. Polly said asking for the news to be switched on was sometimes a ghastly mistake, so if James would care to switch it off, perhaps more could be told about Emily's Teddy boy. He was, after all, the first of his kind who had brushed up against Grandma Finch's redoubtable family.

James switched the set off. 'Well, there are a lot of them about. Perhaps everyone will end up wearing their clothes.'

'I don't think your headmaster will,' said Polly. James was attending Dulwich College. 'I won't. And your father certainly won't.'

'Mum, you can't buck a trend, you have to let it happen,' said James. 'Dad might be persuaded.'

'Daddy a Teddy boy?' said Gemma, and yelled with laughter. 'That'll be the day.'

'Take it from me, little lady, I'll fight any of it that appears in my wardrobe,' said Boots.

'What does Emily's odd friend do?' asked Boots. 'Or is he still at school?'

'He's apprenticed to a plumber,' said James.

'A plumber?' said Polly.

'Yes, he's a plumber's mate,' said Gemma.

'Well, if he qualifies,' said Boots, 'he'll be joining a band of blood brothers that our plumbing systems can't do without. As your mother will tell you, all a good plumber asks for is a pot of tea and the price for the job. By the way, James, are there Teddy girls as well as Teddy boys?'

'James, don't answer that,' said Polly, 'because if you do I'm afraid I'll have a sleepless night worrying about what Gemma will look like dressed as a Teddy girl.'

Young Mr Albert Thompson, who called himself Bradley, had no idea at all that his arrival in the life of Miss Emily Chapman was making him the talking point not only of her family, but the family of cousin Gemma.

At this moment, in company with a band of Teddy boy brothers, he was in Leicester Square. Moving as one in theatrical fashion over the pavement, they were showing off their feathers, much to the amusement and interest of a group of foreign tourists out to enjoy the atmosphere of the West End. On the whole, that was all a Teddy boy asked for, the public's admiration of his rig-out, although some nervous people were inclined to regard his exaggerated sartorial look as a sign of delinquency, the kind that posed a threat to law and order, and their personal persons.

To someone like that, Brad would have said something like this: 'Gee, man, cool your blood pressure.'

The following morning, Lizzy had a caller. Opening her front door, she found Mr Witchet on the step again, another bunch of colourful sweet peas in his hand and a neighbourly smile on his friendly face.

'Good morning, Mrs Somers,' he said, lifting his hat in a gesture of courtesy, 'how are we today?'

'I can't complain about my health, thank you, Mr Witchet,' said Lizzy, standing four-square at her open door in an instinctive posture that defied entry.

'Splendid,' said Mr Witchet. 'Might I be so bold as to offer you these sweet peas fresh from my garden?'

Lizzy could not refuse without being ungracious, so she said, 'That's very kind of you, Mr Witchet, they look lovely.'

'My pleasure,' said Mr Witchet, and handed her the bunch of fragrant blooms. 'May I ask how life is treating you now?'

'I'm managing, if that's what you mean,' said Lizzy, the sweet peas held close to her bosom, their scent delightful. 'Well, one has to manage.'

'Any little problems?' enquired Mr Witchet, portly self face to face, as it were, with Lizzy's comely plumpness. She had given up trying to reduce her figure, and accepted the fairly comfortable spread of middle age, since it was by no means excessive. 'I'd be happy to be of service at any time, Mrs Somers, which I might have mentioned before. Well, being a widower, I do have a special sympathy for widows and any of their problems.'

'Well, thanks, but like I told you, I don't have any problems that my family can't see to,' said Lizzy.

Mr Witchet nodded understandingly, his occupation of the doorstep again inviting a 'come-in' response.

'Might I be bold enough to offer to do any shopping you require?' he said. 'It must be an ordeal for you, I'm sure, facing up to the shopkeepers and their solicitations. It means a daily reminder of your loss, and I remember that for quite a time after me dear wife went I tried to avoid being reminded of it day after day.'

'Oh, I don't shop daily,' said Lizzy. A sound issued from her kitchen. Her kettle was whistling. 'Oh, there goes my kettle, Mr Witchet, it's boiling. Do excuse me— Oh, what's that?' The whistling had stopped, and a sharp little clattering noise reached her ear.

'Allow me, Mrs Somers,' said Mr Witchet, latching onto the opportunity to be of service as he stepped smartly past Lizzy and sped into her kitchen. Steam climbed to the ceiling from her newfangled electric kettle, the lid of which lay on the floor. He switched off the electricity supply and pulled out the plug. Then he made an inspection. The kettle was hot and empty. 'My word,' he said, as Lizzy entered, 'just as well we heard the noise, Mrs Somers. The kettle's boiled itself dry. The whistle should have sounded minutes ago. It's faulty.'

'I should have turned it off before I answered the door to you,' said Lizzy. 'Now look, my kitchen ceiling and walls are wet with steam.'

'Don't worry, my dear,' said Mr Witchet, 'we only need to open a window and let in some warm fresh air. As for the kettle, I'll take it home with me and see if I can spot the fault and put it right. I do pride meself on knowing a bit about these modern devices, which is all self-learned. Were you boiling water for some tea?'

'No, to make myself a cup of instant coffee,' said Lizzy. 'I'll have to use my old gas kettle.'

'No, sit yourself down,' said Mr Witchet, 'this has been a shock to you. These electric things are a bit complicated for ladies. Nothing like our old-fashioned stuff, eh, Mrs Somers? Allow me to boil your old kettle and make you your coffee while you take a rest. Go on, I insist. It's no trouble, and what are friends and neighbours for, I ask, in times of need?'

He talked Lizzy into a mind-soggy acceptance of his presence, his help and his provision of instant coffee for both of them, which they drank in her parlour. She had always referred to her front room as the family parlour, for that was what she'd grown up with in her Walworth days. It was instinctively shrewd of her to have Mr Witchet end up there, since the parlour had a much more formal air than her living room or kitchen.

All the same, Mr Witchet made himself at home without too much effort, causing Lizzy to wonder what excuse or reason she could find for getting rid of him. Not that he was an awkward old misfit. No, he had plenty to say about the problems of life for widows and widowers, and the odd ways of certain neighbours. Did Mrs Somers know, for instance, that Mrs McCorkindale of number sixty-two worked behind the bar of a pub in Brixton every evening, and that she dressed for the work in very fancy get-ups?

'No, I didn't know,' said Lizzy, thinking that Mrs McCorkindale, well into her forties, was a bit past togging herself up in fancy costume. 'What does Mr McCorkindale say?'

'According to my hearing, not much,' said

Mr Witchet. 'Well, since commercial television opened up a couple of years ago, he watches the ITV programmes every night and all weekend. His next-door neighbour, Mr Clements, says he's developed staring eyeballs, which I venture to suggest, Mrs Somers, is quite comical. More coffee, might I ask?'

'No,' said Lizzy, 'no, thank you, and don't let me keep you.'

Not until the parlour chiming clock struck twelve noon, however, did her friendly visitor take himself home, along with her new fangled electric kettle, and a promise to bring it back as soon as he'd repaired the fault, which he was confident he could on account of having a bit of a gift for such things.

Lizzy wondered how to keep him from crossing her doorstep when he did return. Her kettle, yes, she could let that back into her house, but she would rather not entertain Sidney Witchet again. He might be well-meaning, but he was definitely not her cup of tea. For that matter, there would never be anyone who could take the place of Ned.

Imagine Mrs McCorkindale working as a Brixton barmaid, and in fancy get-ups too. No-one could have looked or acted more respectable than that lady when she was out and about in the Denmark Hill area. But in Brixton these days, apparently, one just couldn't tell what some people could get up to. She'd even heard that Rosie's daughter Emily was actually going dancing there with one of those funny-looking Teddy boys.

Later that day, when Boots dropped in on his way home from the office, Lizzy told him how Mr Witchet had finished up in her parlour.

'That actually happened, did it, Lizzy?' smiled Boots.

'Well, like I've just told you, it wouldn't have happened at all if my electric kettle hadn't blown its lid off,' said Lizzy. 'Next thing I knew, there he was, in my kitchen making coffee and then in my parlour drinking it. What's going to happen when he brings that kettle back?'

'Tell him the neighbours have started to talk,' said Boots.

'Well, yes, so I will,' said Lizzy, 'what a good idea, Boots. That's bound to send him on his way.'

'He may need a little push as well,' said Boots.

'I don't like being unkind to people, especially if they think they're being helpful, but I'll have to give Mr Witchet a bit of a push if I feel I need to,' said Lizzy. 'Listen, lovey, I've been hearing things about Rosie's Emily, that she's actually taken up with a Teddy boy, and her still at school, would you believe.'

'Well, the twins have given Polly and me some information,' said Boots, 'and as we understand it, it seems that Emily and this lad get together at Saturday night dances.'

'Well, I don't know much about Teddy boys, except I heard they're not very respectable,' said Lizzy. 'And it's not as if I could phone Rosie or Matt and ask about the one Emily's friendly with. It would be like poking my nose in, which makes me remember we were always brought up to mind our own business.'

Boots, who rarely lost sight of the humorous aspects of life and people, said, 'Well, Lizzy, if our revered mother finds out Emily goes dancing with a Teddy boy, the heavens will fall. I'll wager she rates Teddy boys on a par with delinquent young Bolsheviks.'

'Oh, Bobby's told me they're not as weird as they look,' said Lizzy, 'they just like dressing up, he says. Oh, d'you know what Mr Witchet told me about a neighbour, Mrs McCorkindale?'

'No, I don't know,' said Boots, 'and I don't think I know the lady, either.'

'Well, she's always looked and acted very respectable,' said Lizzy, 'but it seems she does a bit of fancy dressing up as an evening barmaid in a Brixton pub.'

'Is that sensational?' asked Boots.

'No, not actually sensational, I suppose,' said Lizzy, 'but a bit of a shock because she's over forty and she's got married daughters.'

'Well, earning some lolly as a dressed-up barmaid could be counted as enterprising, I suppose,' said Boots. 'And good for a spot of gossip.' He smiled. 'I daresay Mr Witchet could let you know more about the lady and her Brixton outfits, given the chance.'

'He's not going to get any chance,' said Lizzy.

'That's the style, Lizzy, fight the good fight,' said Boots. 'Ned will be right behind you.'

'I'll always be sure of that,' said Lizzy.

Over drinks when he arrived home, Boots acquainted Polly with the details of Mr Witchet's successful entry into Lizzy's parlour. He painted the picture in light-hearted style. Polly demurred.

'Boots, you old horse chestnut, your sense of humour is out of order in this case,' she said. 'Your sister Lizzy is still a grieving widow, even if she doesn't show it as much as she did at first.'

'I wouldn't argue with that,' said Boots. 'We all still miss Ned, but there's something a little amusing about my sister's electric kettle going pop at a moment when the helpful widower was on her doorstep.'

'Utter disaster,' said Polly, 'and it's up to you to help her deal with the Witchet blighter before he takes up permanent residence in her parlour. Great mothballs, think what that could lead to. I demand appropriate action from you.'

'I think we can leave all necessary action to Lizzy,' said Boots. 'It won't be in the form of cutting the bloke dead. She's too nice to be as unkind as that. She's more likely to see him off by telling him the neighbours are talking about him. I suspect he doesn't want to be bracketed with Mrs McCorkindale.'

'Who on earth is Mrs McCorkindale?' asked Polly. Boots gave her the details, and she laughed so much that the twins came running down from their rooms to find out why their dearly beloved mother was having hysterics. They thought their father's explanation was on a par with rhubarb.

The ground-floor conversion job had been finished at the Camberwell Green offices, and the opening of the staff canteen was officially heralded by a speech of welcome from Sammy. He'd asked Susie if it should be him or Boots.

'I'll admit,' he said, 'that Boots, being

educated, is probably better at speechifying than I am.'

'Sammy,' said Susie, a light in her eye, 'much as I adore Boots—'

'Now, Susie,' protested Sammy, 'how many times have I told you it's not fitting for you to adore any bloke except me?'

'Be that as it may, Sammy,' said Susie, 'you'll make the speech, just like you did when Bert and Gertie Roper retired from the factory. You founded the whole business, you put all the profit-making ideas into it, and you thought up the conversion. The speech is your privilege, and anyway, Boots is the last man who'd push himself forward.'

So in the virgin atmosphere of the bright and shining staff canteen, Sammy addressed the multitude. That is, some thirty-odd staff, with just the switchboard girl left on duty. He said the management was pleased to offer its workers up-to-date amenities, such as what was usual plus a recent drying-out room for wet coats on rainy mornings, and now this canteen, which, he hoped, would feed them good lunches without giving them indigestion. So would they kindly note that the chef, Mrs Mary Tindall, wouldn't be dishing up any lumpy suet puddings. On which cue young Mary Tindall presented herself, complete with kitchen apron and chef's hat. Applause rang out, as well as one or two relevant questions.

'Will you be doing sausages and baked beans?'

'Sorry, I'm a chef, not a can-opener.'

'Will you be serving prunes with hot custard for afters?'

'Only by special request.'

Sammy, resuming his speech, said it wasn't compulsory to use the canteen, but he'd give it a month to see what the general figures for usage were. Mrs Tindall could then settle into providing for the average amount of food required, which would do away with a lot of leftover consumables and also look after the overheads. (Smiles of understanding travelled round the listening staff.) Oh, in respect of costs, Sammy went on, they all knew they'd only be charged nominal prices for their lunches, and now they might like to know everything on this first day was free.

'Spoken like a real gent, Mr Sammy.'

'Love it, Mr Sammy.'

'Happy day, Mr Sammy.'

And so on.

'Finally,' said Sammy, 'as today's the one and only first day, we're all lunching together. That's excepting Freda, who's looking after the switchboard and taking down phone messages.

For which, when she comes down to lunch herself, she can have a second helping of fruit pie, which I understand from Mrs Tindall is on the menu. After today, however, half of us will lunch between twelve and one, and the other half between one and two. The management couldn't afford for no work at all to be done for a full hour, especially if our competitors found out. Some competitors don't have any manners. That's it, then, enjoy your lunch with the compliments of the management.'

That was a signal for all present to give Sammy a ringing round of applause, then to see what was on offer on the day's chalked-up menu and to line up for counter service.

Sammy, Boots, Rachel, Rosie, Tim and Daniel, the management, in a natural gesture of what was right, brought up the rear.

Subsequently, an excellent meal was enjoyed by all, and both Boots and Sammy not only complimented the chef, they also complimented Rachel for finding her and hiring her.

'I should be happy for all of us?' said Rachel. 'I am, especially as she'll be with us for at least two years. That's a definite promise.'

'Definite promises,' said Sammy, 'happen to be a welcome change from all that's fell apart or gone down the drain this year. I've nearly been ill from me heartburnings and headaches.'

'Be of good cheer, Sammy, you're still on full charge, still on your feet,' said Boots.

'Yup, you're still alive, Dad,' said Daniel.

'I'm wondering,' said Sammy. 'Rachel, d'you think you could ask our valuable chef if there's any fruit pie left? I think I fancy seconds.'

Chapter Twenty-seven

On Saturday evening, Emily again spent most of her dancing time in company with Brad, which flattered him. Well, although she was still a schoolgirl, he could see she really did have all the makings of a great cookie. Rocking together, they were a smash hit with each other, and the only time Emily saw fit to disagree with him about anything was when he again suggested they should leave a little before ten in order to get her home well before ten thirty.

'No, I'm going to stay on for a while,' she said, 'it won't matter if I'm a bit after ten thirty.'

Brad said he'd more or less promised her parents to get her home well on time, and a bit after ten thirty would ruin things for him. Emily said that was his hard luck, especially as he'd made the promise without consulting her.

'D'you want to land me in the doghouse?' said Brad. 'If I get you home late, that's where your ma and pa will put me, in the doghouse, and without handing me a bone. So come on, baby, let's hoof it to the bus stop.'

'No taxi this time?' said Emily.

'Man, I'm short of bread this week,' said Brad, 'I had to divvy up for this new waistcoat.' His new waistcoat was purple and gold, and highly noticeable. Accordingly, it pleased his idea of trendy plumage and it drew attention. Emily thought it great, and said so. 'OK, then,' said Brad, 'no taxi tonight, so let's hit the trail on a bus and get back to the ranch pronto.'

Emily sulked for a minute or so, then said, 'Oh, all right,' and they detached themselves from the crowded floor. She caught sight of Giles, waved to him and indicated Brad was taking her home.

Giles, ready to follow on, bawled, 'OK, sis, got you.'

On the bus, she asked Brad if he'd ever been to Brighton. Brad said yes, his parents took him when he was ten, and he remembered living it up for the day in old-fashioned style, like going on the pier, having a trip in a boat called *Saucy Sally*, and eating fish and chips on the beach. He asked Emily if she'd been there herself. No, she hadn't, she said.

'I hear *Saucy Sally* has been pensioned off and that the place is now up and coming,' said Brad.

'I'll find out if I do go there,' said Emily.

Brad delivered her home to her parents well in time again, and they invited him in for a cup of tea and a slice of cake, which he accepted on this occasion. Rosie said nothing about the fact that his new waistcoat hurt her eyes, and Matt refrained from mentioning that his quiff had reached a memorable height.

It was when she and Matt were preparing for bed that Rosie said, 'Can that young man be true, Matt?'

'Not to look at,' said Matt, 'but apart from his waistcoat, he could be quite sound. He's keeping Emily up to scratch time-wise.'

'I feel there's something brewing in Emily,' said Rosie.

'Growing pains?' said Matt.

'Ask me another,' said Rosie.

Sunday in Hyde Park. July had brought breezy conditions that stirred the laden top branches of trees and caused well-dressed women to clutch at their hats. Old-fashioned hatpins were no longer in vogue.

Mr Nigel Killiner, strolling with his young lady, Linda Harrison, wore no hat. Neither did Linda. Hats for young men were out of fashion, and hats for young ladies were mostly seen only on special occasions. The breeze plucked at

Nigel's hair without altering the shape of his widow's peak, but it was playing havoc with Linda's untrammelled locks. They blew about her head and face. She laughed as she swept them aside.

'It hasn't been like this in our walks round our local park,' she said.

'You mean this isn't Ruskin Park weather,' said Nigel.

'Oh, the sun's out, and I'm not asking for more,' said Linda. 'I don't mind colliding with the breeze. If there are any cobwebs in my hair, they're being blown away.'

'You've got beautiful hair,' said Nigel, casting an admiring glance at the fair if wayward tresses.

'Well, thanks for saying so,' said Linda.

The crowds were turning London's premier park into a panorama of colour, life and movement. Its atmosphere was always that much more vibrant on Sundays.

'I must say I'm fond of parks,' said Nigel.

'Yes, I think you are,' said Linda, watching some young people dashing about. The fresh and sunny day, and the handsome park itself, did, she thought, invite energy to have a go. 'You're fonder of parks than cinemas or dance halls, Nigel?'

'I prefer the open air,' said Nigel, 'especially

in summer and especially with someone like you. But cinemas, yes, I know the kind of fascinating entertainment they offer, so would you like to see a film with me next Saturday evening?'

'I really would love to see *High Noon*,' said Linda, 'it's on at the Camberwell Green cinema all next week.'

'I've heard of that film,' said Nigel.

'Yes, it stars Gary Cooper and Grace Kelly,' said Linda, 'and it's the second time round in Camberwell. I suppose, as a teacher, you go in more for museums than films.'

'With you,' smiled Nigel, 'I'll be delighted to go in for *High Noon* next Saturday evening.'

'Oh, flattered, I'm sure,' said Linda.

'By the way,' said Nigel, 'I've spoken to my landlady about you, and she's agreed that as you're respectable and don't go in for high jinks at low dives, I can entertain you to tea in my rooms next Sunday afternoon. It'll be in return for having Sunday tea with you. Would you like to come?'

Linda said she'd love to see his lodgings, anyway, and to stay for tea. What was the address?

Nigel gave her the details, and Linda thought that at last something more personal than a walk round a park could be in the offing. She was still willing to be Nigel's steady. Would his landlady stand outside his door, however, listening to make sure nothing unrespectable was going on? She asked the question. Nigel laughed and said well, actually, the old girl would be out visiting her sister all that day. Would Linda mind about that?

'Not if I can trust you,' said Linda.

'A hundred per cent,' said Nigel. 'Come on, let's go to the tea rooms now and catch a pot of tea and a currant bun.'

Which they did, and very enjoyable it was too. Afterwards, Nigel took her home and they regaled her parents with an account of Sunday afternoon in Hyde Park before Nigel left to go home to his lodgings. He had some work to do on next week's lessons, he said. A teacher's spare time was never completely spare. There was always something getting in the way, such as working out a system that would make it easier to teach arithmetic to backward schoolkids. But he said so long to Linda and her parents in his usual easy manner, as if awkward schoolkids were really no bother at all.

During the evening, Annabelle, Nick and Linda watched television's most popular show, *Sunday Night at the London Palladium*, hosted by an ex-Army comic, Tommy Trinder. Some of its acts featured new stars of wit and modernity, as well as established stars of the fading music-hall world. The latter needed to be on top form to sustain their old-style acts, for their general popularity was falling way behind that of television presenters like Trinder and the increasingly popular Bob Monkhouse. Any Palladium number that featured Britain's blonde bombshell, Diana Dors, was received uproariously.

On this Sunday evening the show, as usual, went with a swing and a gallop. Many households owned television sets, and most watched the Palladium spectacular on the commercial channel, ITV. It was putting the BBC's Sunday nose out of joint.

While enjoying the show, Linda's mind frequently turned to next weekend and a possible new development in her relationship with her favourite schoolteacher.

Chapter Twenty-eight

It was Tuesday morning when Lizzy discovered that a knock on her front door heralded Mr Witchet calling again. She noted at once that he had brought back her electric kettle. This domestic appliance was actually one of the last items Ned had bought for her, telling her that its whistle would always alert her to its boiling point. In the hands of Mr Witchet, Lizzy felt it looked out of place. However, she didn't want it to remain faulty, and if he'd mended it, she'd be grateful. She liked using it daily in simple memory of Ned and the thoughtfulness behind his purchase.

'Ah, good morning, Mrs Somers, here we are again,' beamed Mr Witchet.

'And with my kettle, I see,' said Lizzy. 'Have you mended it?'

'I'm pleased to say yes,' said Mr Witchet, looking the part. Self-satisfaction always sat happily on his countenance. 'I do have a little gift for mending this, that and the other. In fact, of course, as you probably know, my most paying gift was the repair of clocks, watches and all kinds of timepieces, including, I'm proud to say, some very old and valuable Swiss cuckoo clocks that belonged to various customers of mine. If you happen to own one of these and you ever find it faulty, I'd consider it a privilege to repair it for you as an act of friendship. Well, of course, that applies to any clock – or watch – of yours that needed looking at, especially as I know how much the correct time means to those of us who live alone.' Mr Witchet paused to let Lizzy digest this opening speech and its message of good neighbourliness and possible honourable intention.

Lizzy, who had suspected his intention from the beginning, said, 'Well, I think everyone likes to know what the correct time is. I mean, the wrong time isn't much good to anyone, is it? But thanks ever so much for mending the kettle.' She took it from him. 'It was one of the last presents Ned gave me, so I'm grateful.'

Mr Witchet beamed.

'Shall we test it?' he asked, looking ready to step in. His portly outline was in the forward position in a manner of speaking.

Lizzy, glancing over his shoulder, gave a start. 'Oh, dear,' she said.

'What's wrong?' asked Mr Witchet.

'I think Mrs Palmer's curtains moved,' said Lizzy, drawing back from her open door in what seemed like an attempt to efface herself.

'Beg pardon?' said Mr Witchet.

'Yes,' said Lizzy, knitting her brow in worry, 'I think she's noticed you from behind her curtains, I think perhaps you're being talked about.'

'Talked about? Me?' Mr Witchet looked startled.

'I expect it's only a rumour,' said Lizzy, casting another glance and doing her best to appear upset for him. 'But I did hear Mrs Palmer's been talking.' Which was no lie. Mrs Palmer was known to talk every day, just as everyone else did, apart from those unfortunate souls born dumb.

'She's been talking about me?' said Mr Witchet, casting his own uneasy glance at the curtained windows across the way.

'I expect it's only a rumour,' said Lizzy again. 'But she might have noticed you knocking at my door just recent.' Half of her was now behind it. 'Oh, dear, she might also have noticed how you call on other ladies.'

Mr Witchet's healthy complexion paled slightly.

'But only to make a little gift of vegetables or suchlike,' he said.

'I expect it's being invited in that Mrs Palmer might have noticed,' said Lizzy. 'Some people gossip about that sort of thing in an unChristian way. I'm sure nothing's ever happened that's been unmentionable. Still, I'd best not invite you in. Mrs Palmer might still be looking to see if I do.'

Mr Witchet quivered.

'Yes,' he said. 'I mean no – that is, yes, I see. People gossiping. I never – well, we don't want that – no.' He proved then that although he liked to be regarded as upright and reputable, qualified to talk about his neighbours, he didn't at all favour being talked about himself. Flapping a bit, he removed himself from Lizzy's doorstep with the haste of a man who had no designs on the widow, none at all. He accompanied his departure with several agitated words. 'Yes, I'd better go, Mrs Somers – your good name and mine – most upsetting – I wouldn't like to think . . .'

His voice, slightly hoarse, trailed off.

'Goodbye,' called Lizzy, most of her respectable self well behind the door now. Her word of farewell and her cautious effacement plainly implied she'd prefer it if Mr Witchet didn't come back and get both of them talked about.

Boots had been right. His sister had known the best way of keeping the widower from her door, leaving herself content with her memories of Ned.

On behalf of Maureen, Amos Anderson received a cheque for ten guineas from the chastened Charlie Ellis, together with a guarantee of straight dealing. He also sent contact sheets of the acceptable photographs he'd taken of Maureen. Nice, thought Amos when he noted how Charlie had brought into being the distinctly appealing nature of her cleavage. One had to hand it to him. He knew how to pose a model.

Amos banked the cheque and phoned Maureen. When she subsequently arrived at his studio, he gave her what was still owing to her, five guineas, and told her that Charlie would definitely divvy up in the event of selling any of her photographs, the straight ones. Maureen was delighted at having received a full ten guineas. Not only was the amount handsome, it also went more than a little way towards curing her feelings of mortification.

'Amos, d'you think he might get me on a front cover?' she asked.

'A front cover we'd like, you bet,' said Amos. 'Here, take a look at the contact sheets.'

Maureen took a look, and a second look.

'Crikey, is this me?' she asked.

'If Charlie sold one of these for a front cover,' said Amos, 'it could match you with a Rank starlet, or even Diana Dors.'

'Diana Dors?' breathed Maureen. 'She's me dad's favourite pin-up after me mum.'

Amos coughed.

'Your – er – your mother does pin-up poses?' he said.

'No, course she doesn't, you daft thing,' laughed Maureen, still entranced by the contact sheets. 'It's just what me dad calls her. Well, she's always been attractive-looking and still is. Mind, I think she thinks Diana Dors is a bit fast, like.'

'The lady's very photogenic, though,' said Amos.

'Oh, yes, I know,' said Maureen, thinking of Diana's glamorous image as she regarded the photographs of her bosom, which was un-heralded so far, apart from a couple of sweater shots sold by Amos to a magazine. 'Imagine that man Charlie Ellis giving himself a posh name like Morton Fraser when he's just low and common. Still, I must say he's made me look very sexy in me dressy poses.'

'With a bit of a saucy touch?' said Amos.

'I never thought about being saucy as well as sexy,' said Maureen, 'but I don't think Mum and Dad will kick up a fuss. They're both broad-minded.'

'Broad-minded is good, ain't it?' said Amos. 'Don't you worry, I'll see that no photographer ever gets you to step over the mark. You'll still be everyone's girl next door, even in outfits like Charlie supplied.'

'Oh, that's good,' said Maureen. She had achieved her ambition of becoming a pin-up glamour girl, and it wouldn't actually ruin her life if she never overtook Diana Dors. Just the front cover of a posh magazine like *Esquire* would do.

'Linda,' said Nick Harrison to his daughter over breakfast on Wednesday morning, 'you know you mentioned to me that Nigel was taking you to the cinema on Saturday evening?'

'Yes, did you tell Mum?' asked Linda.

'Not until he got out of bed this morning,' said Annabelle, looking at her husband as if he'd made a mess of the day. 'He forgot and you forgot that we're all due to attend your Uncle Boots's birthday party. He'll be sixty-one on Sunday, but of course, he and your Aunt Polly are giving the party on Saturday.'

'Oh, Lord, yes, I did forget,' said Linda.

'You and me, we're both for it,' said Nick. 'But I can't stay for a beating, I don't have the time. I'm off to the office.' He was a senior partner in a City firm of accountants.

'Don't panic,' said Annabelle, 'you're for-given. But you'll have to cancel your date with Nigel, Linda.'

'Silly me,' said Linda, 'I should have remem-bered about Uncle Boots when Nigel and I were talking about arrangements for next weekend.' She made a face. No-one in the family missed Uncle Boots's birthdays. No-one wanted to. 'Oh, I know, I'll go to Nigel's lodgings during my lunch hour today and leave a message with his landlady. I'll cancel next Saturday's date and say I'll still see him on Sunday afternoon for tea.'

'Good idea, pet,' said Nick, on his feet. 'So long now, Lady One and Lady Two.' He gave his wife a peck, his daughter a peck and then left. The necessity of reaching the station on time took priority over further breakfast-time chat.

'Yes, you must cancel your cinema date with Nigel, Linda,' said Annabelle.

Linda looked wry.

'I know that, Mum,' she said, 'so I'll definitely go round to his lodgings at lunchtime.'

'It's a shame you've got to cancel,' said Anna-belle, who was altogether in favour of Nigel as a candidate for keeping Linda happy ever after.

'It's my own fault,' said Linda, 'I should have remembered, and anyway, I expect I'll only be postponing the invite, and as it's on account of Uncle Boots's birthday, it's postponement in a good cause.'

At lunchtime, she made her way to Bessemer Road. It was a fifteen-minute walk from her copy-typist's job in an office near Camberwell Green. She found the address Nigel had given her. It was halfway down Bessemer Road, one in a row of terraced houses, and not far from his school. She knocked in expectation of bringing his landlady to the door. His landlady, she was sure, would accept the message and pass it on to him.

She waited. No-one came. She knocked again. No answer. His landlady was out, obviously. From the direction of the school she heard the noise of pupils in the playground, enjoying their lunchtime break. Well, of course, the best thing she could do now would be to go to the school and ask if someone could fetch Nigel.

She walked there and arrived at the closed but openwork iron gate. Through it she saw the young boys of this primary establishment, leaping and larking about amid a cacophony of noise. Linda smiled, remembering her own lively days as a young, scatterbrained pupil. Schoolkids always let themselves go at break times. She noted a boy, one of the few not making a name for themselves at jumping and hollering. She called to him and he came to the gate with a grin on his face. It didn't go away as he looked up at her. She thought him about ten, and belonging to the well-known fraternity of perpetually grinning boys.

'What's up, miss?' he asked.

'I wonder, could you get a message to one of your teachers?' asked Linda.

'I could, as long as it don't mean letting off a firework,' said the boy. 'You get sent home to your dad if you do, and your dad belts you.'

'It's nothing to do with fireworks,' smiled Linda, 'it's to do with asking Mr Killiner to come and talk to me. I need to speak to him.'

'Mr Killiner?' said the boy, his grin diminishing a bit.

'Yes, he's a teacher here, isn't he?' said Linda.

'Yes, but he's not in today, he's gone to his sister's funeral. She went and died last week.'

'Pardon?' said Linda.

'Yes, last week, poor woman,' said the boy. 'It upset old Killiner. Well, for a teacher, he ain't a bad bloke.'

'I don't think we can be talking about the same man,' said Linda.

'Well,' said the boy, his grin back in place, 'I

know who I'm talking about. Old Mr Killiner, our geography teacher.'

'What d'you mean by old?' asked Linda, confusion stirring.

'I dunno his real age,' said the boy, 'but he must be near on fifty.'

'That's not the Mr Killiner I know,' said Linda, and she described Nigel in detail.

'Oh, him,' said the boy, his grin broader. 'That's Walter Kilby. He's not one of our teachers, he's the caretaker. Me dad says that in America they call them janitors. Me dad reads a lot of American stories. Anyway, that's what Mr Kilby is, our caretaker, and he's in the boilerhouse just this minute, making sure the boiler's in good condition when we all come back from our summer 'olidays. Here, miss, is he the bloke you want to talk to? Has he been gamming you in that posh voice he puts on sometimes?'

Linda, trying to come to terms with what this grinning young ape was telling her, took several seconds to find words. Then she asked if this Walter Kilby called himself Nigel Killiner sometimes.

'I dunno about that,' said the boy. His grin disappeared and was replaced by a furrowed brow. It suggested youthful concern for this nice young lady. 'Here, you ain't sweet on him, are you, miss? Only he's a married man, y'know, except they say he ain't seen his wife for a year and more.' The furrowed brow gave way to a knowing look. 'He ain't been leading you up the garden, has he?'

Linda, her disbelief painful, was tight of voice as she asked the boy if he would go and fetch the caretaker. The boy suggested in turn that he should take Linda to the boilerhouse, where she could talk to the bloke on the spot, instead of at the gate. Linda, gathering herself, said yes, she'd like to do that.

The boy opened the gate.

Chapter Twenty-nine

Mr Walter Kilby, who sometimes called himself Nigel Killiner, was sitting on a packing case, munching on a lunchtime sandwich. He was dressed in blue dungarees and a cap. A shadow fell across the sunlit doorway of the boilerhouse, and someone looked in. He glanced up.

'I'm seeing you, Simpson, you little tyke,' he said in a northern accent. 'Push off, will tha?'

'Here, don't be like that,' said Simpson, the grinning boy, 'I've brought you a visitor. There you are, miss, there he is.'

'Thank you,' said the visitor.

Out stepped Simpson, and in stepped Linda. Walter Kilby's jaw dropped.

'What the . . . ?' Words failed him.

'Surprised?' said Linda, her cool expression hiding her sense of betrayal.

'What're you doing here?' asked Kilby in what Simpson had referred to as his posh voice.

'I called to find out if I could talk to a teacher by the name of Nigel Killiner,' said Linda, dreams of romance all in bits. 'But it seems I was asking for the wrong man. You're not a teacher, and you're not Nigel Killiner.'

Kilby came to his feet, looked at his sandwich and then glanced around for a dumping place. He chose the packing case and laid the sandwich on it. He was taking time to compose himself.

'Oh, well,' he said eventually, 'just a little deception. It isn't as if I don't work at the school.'

'What was the point of saying you were a teacher and using someone else's name?' asked Linda, illuminated by the light from the open door, but feeling the reverse of bright.

Kilby spread his hands.

'I ask you honestly,' he said, 'how would your parents have taken it if I'd introduced myself as a school caretaker, and with a name like Wally? The Denmark Hill area is littered with middle-class snobs and names like Nigel and Andrew.'

'Oh, really?' Linda had lost her blinkers. 'You'd know about snobs, of course. But who's worse, snobs or married men who go about acting unmarried?'

'Well, bugger the person who let that cat out of the bag,' said Kilby.

349

'Your father's not a stockbroker, of course, and your sister's not at university, I suppose,' said Linda. 'Exactly where d'you come from, a school for smart alecs?'

This smart alec shrugged, smiled a little disdainfully, recovered his wits, and then, in the broadest of Geordie accents, confirmed that his real name was Walter Kilby, that he came from Newcastle, where he'd been an office clerk, that his father was a shipyard worker, and his sister had a husband and three kids. He had moved south, and taught himself to speak like a Surrey stockbroker in the hope of landing a well-paid job with nothing very much to do. But he hadn't been able to get anything better than this work as a school caretaker, after being sacked by an advertising agency for not living up to his qualifications, which he admitted weren't his own. As for his wife, well, there was an example of marrying in haste and repenting at leisure. She lived in Chatham and he hoped she'd stay there for ever, seeing 'she were always fonder of sailors than of me.'

Linda had to listen to all this through what to her was the tangled web of his Geordie accent. At the end, she asked him what he had had in mind for her.

'Oh, some Sunday afternoons on my sofa,' he

said, reverting to his acquired refined tones. 'You'll have noticed I didn't attempt to rush you. I was taking my time. I like taking my time in that respect.'

'Well, dear me, how thoughtful of you,' said Linda, her cool sarcasm admirable considering she was fuming. 'Am I just one of a long line of girls who've been on your sofa?'

'Not a long line, believe me,' said Kilby. 'Let's say you're about the third.' He was fully recovered from the unexpected, accepting that the game was up as far as his intentions towards Linda were concerned. 'I haven't lived too many years yet.'

If his arrogance and shamelessness were breathtaking to Linda, worldly women might have found him diverting.

'How long do you think you'd have lasted with me before I found you out?' she asked.

'Long enough, I hope,' said Kilby, and Linda had a mental picture of herself being seduced on his sofa on a Sunday afternoon. It made her feel sick with herself for being taken in. Looking back, she could see now that he'd always been too good to be true. She remembered the moment in the park when some kids catcalled him. One had shouted, 'Oi, Killy.' No, she'd assumed he had. Killy for Killiner. But it had been Kilby, of course, and it had put the man out of his smooth self for a moment or two.

'Mr Kilby, I think you're wasting your talents as a caretaker,' she said. 'I think you should be on the stage. That's where all people like you can pretend to be what they're not. Goodbye.'

'Sorry and all that,' said Kilby, 'and give my regards to your parents.'

He watched her leave, then picked up his half-eaten sandwich, looked at it, shrugged and began to finish it.

Linda had an uncomfortable time recounting her tale of disillusionment to her parents that evening.

Annabelle, suffering for her daughter's very personal let-down, was furious that they'd all been taken in. Nick said that at forty-four he'd have thought himself far too old to have fallen hook, line and sinker for the kind of bait offered by a bloke he ought to have guessed was all of fishy. But his own personal feelings, he said, were nothing compared to what Linda's must be.

'I just feel sick, full stop,' said Linda. 'I'm going to spend the next few days sticking pins in myself. It's what I deserve for being a prize simpleton.'

'If you're a prize simpleton, I'm the original

village idiot,' said Nick. 'No, I'll bet the feller's fooled all kinds of people in his time.'

'Well, I hope none of us will let this ruin our lives,' said Annabelle.

'Or even our weekend,' said Nick.

'And certainly not our time at Uncle Boots's birthday party,' said Linda, and put Walter Kilby firmly out of her mind.

Nick reflected on the fact that he and Annabelle had been only too ready to accept the man as a possible suitor for Linda. Linda, modest and retiring, had never had a really close man friend. Nick very much hoped that Walter Kilby would come to a bad end, such as falling into the school boiler when it was hotting up.

He mentioned to Annabelle the next day that the best and quickest cure for Linda's smack in the eye would be the entrance into her life of a really decent bloke, say at Boots's birthday party. Annabelle pointed out that Linda was off all young men, and suspicious, in fact, of the breed as a whole.

'Hell,' said Nick, 'we don't have a daughter already set on remaining a spinster all her life, do we?'

'I wish you men wouldn't call unmarried women spinsters,' said Annabelle. 'It's a very unappealing word.'

'Believe me, I didn't invent it,' said Nick.

'I'll bet some man did,' said Annabelle, 'and I'll also bet he invented the word bachelors for unmarried men, which sounds much more pleasant than spinster.'

'Don't look at me, Annabelle,' said Nick, 'I didn't get to know a thing about unmarried women until I met you. Then I was amazed at what your lot were capable of. Talk about mesmerizing a bloke, I was hooked from the beginning. And still am.'

'Oh, very funny,' said Annabelle, but she smiled. If she liked to be the one to make the decisions, she also liked the fact that her husband wasn't argumentative about it. 'Anyway, don't try bringing home one of the young men from your office for Linda. It won't work, Nick, she won't fall for it.'

'I feel for our girl,' said Nick.

'We both do,' said Annabelle, 'and I hope the school boiler blows up when that man Kilby is stoking it.'

Which echoed Nick's idea of a suitable end for the bloke.

'No, I can't come to the dance on Saturday, after all,' said Emily into the phone, 'I'm going to a family birthday party.'

'Gee whiz,' said Brad, 'how unreal can a

family get? A birthday party with **tea and** cake, and shrimps and winkles? Man, is that sort of thing still alive?'

'Don't think I don't share your opinion,' said Emily, sounding as if she was on the way to becoming a social Bolshevik by the time she was fourteen. And that was only a month away. 'But this party's for the birthday of my uncle, who's really special. When I get married, which I'm not actually bothered about, it'll either be to someone like him or no-one at all. So I'm going to his party. Well, if I refused, my parents would drag me.'

'Parents again?' said Brad. 'Not that I'd strictly complain about yours.'

'All right, I know you fancy my mum,' said Emily.

'She's out on her own,' said Brad.

'I'll tell her you said so. Anyway, I shan't be seeing you until Saturday week, which is a fortnight before we all go on holiday to Dorset, to stay with my dad's sister. It's where my mum served in the ATS during the war, and where my dad ran a garage and taught Land Army women to drive tractors. He and Mum are talking about a walk down memory lane. Can you believe it?'

'Oh, well,' said Brad, 'I figure that most people over thirty live in the past. But it's not actually antisocial, just kinda quaint.'

'When I get to be over thirty, I'll still be myself, just as now,' said Emily. 'Anyway, that's all for the time being, so goodnight.'

'So long, baby,' said Brad, and they rang off.

Chapter Thirty

By six thirty on Saturday evening, Boots's sixty-first birthday party was in full swing, the handsome house in East Dulwich Grove packed out with friends and relatives. Even Vi's mother, old Aunt Victoria, was there. She had deserted her constant companion, her television set, to attend the party, although she had tucked herself away in a corner armchair, where Vi looked after her wants, and Boots arrived to ask after her comfort. She said she was having a very nice time, but wasn't everything getting a bit loud?

'Afraid so,' said Boots, 'and it'll probably get louder. It so happens that the party's being run as it was last year, by James and Gemma, with Gemma's record player well to the fore in a little while.'

'Oh, my goodness,' said old Aunt Victoria.

'I feel the same,' said Boots.

A little later, buffet food was being consumed,

and James was watching Cindy Stevens making herself interesting to the seventeen-year-old son of nearby neighbours. James knew he himself had been temporarily relegated to the also-rans, along with cousin Giles. Cindy was always searching for the absolutely perfect boyfriend, so James minded relegation not at all. He was pretty sure that as far as an absolutely perfect boyfriend was concerned, he'd never make the grade with any girl. A feller could be thankful for that. Well, think of having to live up to that kind of a label. He wondered what had happened to Cathy Davidson, who'd been living with her mother in Paris for a couple of years now. She was probably going great with a French boy.

James turned his attention to cousin Linda. He'd never known her so vivacious. In a small group of people helping themselves to food, she was the life and soul, which was a bit unusual. Linda was normally a nice quiet girl. Not actually a wallflower, simply not pushy. But she seemed full of gusto this evening.

'Hello,' said a voice in his ear. He turned. Cousin Emily was beside him, her plate of food now history. 'When's the music going to start?'

'When Gemma's ready,' said James, relieving her of her empty plate and putting it on the buffet table.

'We're not going to have to wait, are we?' said

Emily, looking young and appealing in a party dress of white with blue polka dots, but sounding a bit disgruntled.

'I think it'll be any minute now,' said James.

'Well, I hope so,' said Emily, 'I could be doing more exciting things, you know.'

'You can go and do them, if you want,' said James. 'Dad won't mind. I mean, you've put in an appearance and he'll settle for that.'

'Oh, your dad's great,' said Emily. The highlight of the party so far had been the few minutes she spent talking to Uncle Boots, who'd paid her compliments and been as droll as ever. 'I suppose you know Cindy Stevens has found a new boyfriend? She's over there with him.'

'Yes, it's Malcolm Jeffries from across the road,' said James. 'I introduced them.'

'Serve you right, then,' said Emily. 'Crikey, look at cousin Linda enjoying herself.'

Linda was laughing her head off over some joke that had just been told. Nick glanced at her from across the room. He knew, as Annabelle knew, that their daughter's high spirits were a facade hiding her unhappy feeling that a smooth talker had made a fool of her.

At that moment, Linda gaily interposed herself between Cindy and the boy from across the road.

'Here, d'you mind?' said Cindy.

'Oh, Cindy,' said Linda, bent on a rescue act, 'would you take a glass of wine to your mother? She's over there, by the fireplace.'

'Well, I just don't know what's wrong with her legs,' said Cindy, but she adored her German stepmother, Anneliese, and detaching herself from her new interest, she took a glass of wine to her.

'What's this?' asked Anneliese, in company with her husband, Harry Stevens, and their close friend Boots.

'Linda told me to bring you a glass,' said Cindy.

'Well, thank you, darling, how very nice of you and Linda too,' said Anneliese, at which point up came Giles to request five minutes of social chat with Cindy while she was still wondering if she'd been hoodwinked or not.

Linda, having saved Cindy's new interest from being overwhelmed, wished him good luck and moved to talk animatedly with cousin David and his wife Kate, up from their dairy farm in Kent. Annabelle glanced, wanting to keep an eye on her over-vivacious daughter.

Suddenly, the first amplified strains of music flooded the residence. In the adjacent lounge, Gemma had the volume control of her record player turned to maximum as a galvanizing introduction to one of Bill Haley's ever-popular numbers, and as a guarantee that the music wasn't lost on the people elsewhere in the house.

'Have the Martians landed?' asked David, and Linda explained through the waves of sound that her Uncle Boots's birthday parties had been run by Gemma and James for the last three years.

In the dining room, Chinese Lady had arrived beside Boots to let him know she wasn't altogether in favour of this arrangement. 'Gemma is a dear girl,' she said, 'and no-one could say she isn't, but I just don't know why you let her play her records so loud.'

'Gemma says it's to give everyone in the house the benefit of being able to hear and to dance to the beat,' said Boots. Some young people were already swinging.

'Yes, but I don't understand what she's playing,' said Chinese Lady. 'Don't you and Polly have some nice records like "The Blue Danube" and "When Irish Eyes Are Smiling"? Gemma could put them on her gramophone.'

'All our old wax records are stored in a cabinet,' said Boots, 'and if Polly or I let them see the light of day, the twins would probably leave home. Fashions change, old lady.'

'I can't hear a word you're saying,' complained Chinese Lady. Young people were rocking and rolling. Emily was going it with

James, and looking as if her evening had its fun factor.

At the Brixton dance hall, Brad was swinging the evening away with Alice Fairbanks, a close schoolfriend of the absent Emily.

'Imagine letting some old birthday party get in the way,' grumbled Alice, fourteen, and as pert as Emily herself. She was known to some relatives as a spoonfed brat.

'Come again, baby?' said Brad, whose preference was for Emily.

'I wasn't talking to you,' said Alice, 'and watch your elbows, will you?'

'No problem,' said Brad, tucking them in a bit. 'What did you mean, get in the way? Get in the way of what?'

'You'd like to know, I bet,' said Alice. 'Why d'you wear such loud waistcoats?'

'I like them, that's why,' said Brad, as the band came to a temporary halt. 'Come on, cookie, give. Let's hear you spout.'

'Well, don't tell anyone else,' whispered Alice. The whisper was essential, for ears were everywhere, along with the bodies they belonged to. 'Me and Em were going to Brighton from this evening till tomorrow night.'

'Hey, give me a break, baby, I can't swallow that,' said Brad.

'Well, what a shame,' murmured Alice, 'but it's a fact. Em was to tell her parents she was staying with me, and I was to tell my own parents I was staying with her.'

'Oh, yeah?' said Brad. 'And where were you going to put up in Brighton, the Majestic Hotel?'

'No, with a cousin of mine,' said Alice.

'So why all the plots, then?' asked Brad. He could have asked why all the lies?

'My parents don't like my cousin,' said Alice.

'Why?'

'They said she does shoplifting, but I don't believe it,' said Alice. 'Parents make up stories about people they don't like. Look, stop asking questions, will you? It's all gone wrong, anyway, with Em choosing to go to a dreary birthday party instead. Come on, you Ted, let's dance.'

Brad followed her into the rhythm of the number while thinking about Emily. What a cookie. Someone had to take hold of Em before she gave her mum and dad a heart attack. He could tell them, of course, to watch out for what their daughter might get up to with her dotty friend Alice. No, Em wouldn't like him to do that, she'd call him a lousy telltale or hit him with something like Lonnie Donegan's washboard.

He'd simply have to keep tabs on her, for her

own sake and for the peace of mind of her parents, especially her mum, a geat cookie who could knock spots off more than a few dolls, even one fresh out of Hollywood.

For all the gaudy nature of Brad's waistcoats, under them beat a sound heart.

The party was well on its way, and Boots and Polly were in the hall, saying goodnight to Tommy, Vi and Vi's mum. Tommy and Vi were taking the old lady home before the lateness of the hour and the musical vibrations became too much for her.

'Thanks for a great evening, Polly,' said Tommy, 'and I only hope, Boots, that by Monday we'll get official word that the Southend fire was started by accident.'

'Well, word should come through sometime in the near future,' said Boots, and Tommy nodded. Vi's mum mumbled something.

'Happy birthday for tomorrow, Boots,' said Vi, and then she and Tommy disappeared into the night with her mother. Boots closed the door.

Polly said, 'Your old Aunt Victoria may look fragile, but it's my belief she and your mother will last for ever. They both belong to a lasting generation.'

'So do you,' said Boots, at which point Linda

came into the hall, intent on getting Boots to swing with her. She was still keeping up an air of vivacity.

'Uncle Boots,' she said amid the noisy revelry, 'would you like to come and rock with me?'

'Come again, poppet?' said Boots, and Linda repeated her offer, but in louder tones, with Polly smiling knowingly. She was always well aware that Boots fascinated young ladies, inside or outside the family. Boots, having now heard Linda's invitation to dance, said, 'At my age?'

Someone knocked on the front door at that moment, but such was the sudden increase in the volume of sound that even Boots, Polly and Linda didn't hear it. So the knock came again, loud enough this time to be heard.

'A late arrival?' suggested Polly.

'I'll see who it is,' said Linda. She walked to the door, and opened it. A young man in a check shirt and blue jeans gazed at her. He looked a little awkward about his presence on the doorstep.

'Sorry and all that,' he said, 'but me and my parents have just moved in next door, and they'd like to know what all the noise is about.'

'Oh, sorry,' said Linda, 'but it's a bit of a loud birthday party. Are you and your parents asking for us to tone it down?'

'We'll do our best,' said Polly.

'I'm not asking for that,' said the young man, taking note of Linda looking a knockout in her party dress. 'I thought, in fact, that—' He coughed and tried again. 'I actually thought of asking if I could join in as a new neighbour. It'll be a nice change from moving furniture about, which I've been doing most of the day.'

Linda, being once bitten twice shy, made a quite calculated study of the young man. He coughed again and ruffled his hair in a fit of embarrassment.

'I see,' she said.

'No, it's all right, forget it,' he said, 'it was a bit of a cheek, anyway.'

'What's your name?' asked Linda.

'Alec Gibson.'

Linda turned her head and glanced at Boots. He smiled and nodded. So she opened the door wider and addressed the young man in welcoming fashion.

'Come in, Alec Gibson,' she said, 'come in and meet the Adams family. You can't miss them, they're all over the place.'

It was six weeks later when Rachel, needing a word with Sammy, entered his office.

'Sammy,' she said, 'I should tell you something I don't wish to. I must.'

'Go ahead,' said Sammy, looking up at her

from his capacious old desk. 'I'll do me best to grin and bear it.'

'It seems,' said Rachel, 'that a couple of months ago our canteen chef and her husband celebrated their first wedding anniversary in style.'

'So?' said Sammy.

'High on champagne, they forgot themselves,' said Rachel, 'and it means Mrs Tindall isn't going to be with us for at least two years, after all. Sammy, she's giving notice.'

'Eh?' said Sammy.

'If you know what I mean,' said Rachel.

Which Sammy did, and which, on top of other happenings, convinced him that this definitely hadn't been one of his better years.

Still, there was always tomorrow.

THE END